THE OPPOSITE OF LOVE

SARAH LYNN SCHEERGER

ALBERT WHITMAN & COMPANY
CHICAGO, ILLINOIS

FOR MY HUSBAND, ROB, WITH LOVE

Library of Congress Cataloging-in-Publication Data

Scheerger, Sarah Lynn
The opposite of love / by Sarah Lynn Scheerger.
pages cm
Summary: Fifteen-year-old Rose and seventeen-year-old Chase find a common bond
in their troubled relationships with their parents, but as Chase's family life improves,
Rose's becomes worse, pulling the couple apart.
[1. Family problems—Fiction. 2. Dating (Social customs)—Fiction.
3. Conduct of life—Fiction. 4. F Adoption—Fiction. 5. Pregnancy—Fiction.] I. Title.
PZ7.L995252 Opp 2014
[Fic]—dc23

Text copyright © 2014 by Sarah Lynn Scheerger
Published in 2014 by Albert Whitman & Company
ISBN 978-0-8075-6132-4

Printed in China.
10 9 8 7 6 5 4 3 2 1 BP 18 17 16 15 14

The design is by Jenna Stempel
Cover image © Eternity in an Instant/Digital Vision/Getty Images

For more information about Albert Whitman & Company,
visit our web site at www.albertwhitman.com.

NOW

1
CHASE

CHASE'S CELL PHONE VIBRATES ON his dresser. It sounds like a swarm of mosquitoes. He sits up straight in bed, slapping his hand down on the phone. *Hard.* The text message glows in the dark, and he squints while his eyes adjust.

Check your email ASAP. Then call me.—D.S.

Whatever Daniel Stein wants to tell him in the middle of the night had better be important. Bordering on earth shattering.

He groans. He considers ignoring it, but curiosity and goddamn loyalty get the best of him.

He drags himself out of bed, across his room, and down to the apartment's tiny kitchen/dining room/living room to flip on the computer. The computer warms up, humming to itself. Everything in his mother's apartment seems so much smaller than it was when he left nearly eight months ago. Still, it feels good to be home. Home for Christmas. In some ways it seems like he's never been gone, and in others it feels like a lifetime.

The cell phone vibrates again, muffled between his fingers. The cell is an early Christmas present from his dad, Walter. His first cell phone ever. Chase flips it open. Another text. Hurry, bro. Urgent.

Chase types in the user name and password for his email account. Three new messages. But when he opens his inbox, only one message jumps out at him. Untitled, but from his old girlfriend, Rose. He hasn't heard a word from her since he left. Maybe now that he's back in town, she'll want to reconnect. His heart catches.

He clicks on the message, opening it. Addressed to Daniel, Becca, and himself. Short and sweet.

> I'm writing to say good-bye. Becca, you can have anything you want from my room. Chase, I saved you a bunch of sketches. Thanks for being my friends. Please don't hate me for doing this. Love, Rose.

His mouth dries. What does that mean? *What the hell does that mean?* He stares at Rose's artwork, tacked to his wall, especially his favorite—that black-and-white chalk drawing of two hands connecting. It looks like her hand is reaching for him, as though he can hold on to her or save her or something.

Chase dials Daniel's number before he can sort out his thoughts. Daniel picks it up after half a ring. "Did you see it?"

"What the hell does it mean?"

"She's gonna kill herself! That's what it means. She's giving away her things. She's saying good-bye. Becca's freaking out over here." "Freaking out" sounds about right for Daniel's sister.

Chase tries to breathe. "I know it sounds like that. But I don't think Rose is the killing-yourself kind of girl."

"We gotta call 911," Becca's voice breaks through on the phone, like she just grabbed it from her brother's hands.

"I'm going over there," Chase decides. "Maybe I can talk her out of it."

"Shit, Chase, it might be too late." Daniel's voice pops back on.

"Or we might be wrong. Maybe she's running away. If we call the cops, we'll give her up. We both know her parents have kept her a prisoner in that house. Maybe she's finally had enough."

"I don't know…" Daniel breaks off. Chase can't remember another time he's ever heard Daniel speechless.

"Here, look. She sent the email ten minutes ago. There's time for me to get over there."

"Unless she has a gun."

"She doesn't have a gun." Chase sounds more confident than he feels. "I'll keep my cell phone on me. And I'll run."

BEFORE

2

CHASE

CRASHING AT DANIEL STEIN'S HOUSE had undeniable perks. The biggest perk was the sister factor. Younger sisters have hot friends, especially when they're only a year behind you in school and they just got their braces off. The second biggest perk, and the one that most often led him to stay over, was avoiding his own mom and the brewing of World War III on the home front.

Chase didn't bother to knock, just let himself right in like always. He found Daniel lounging in the living room, his earbuds tucked into his ears. Chase flicked a dangling blue-and-silver foil menorah and looked pointedly at Daniel. "Chanukah decorations?"

"It's been November for a whole freaking week, bro," Daniel said, taking the earbuds out. "Besides, you know my mom." He gestured to an overflowing box of Halloween skeletons and bats, decorations that had been up three days ago.

"I know your mom." Chase flopped onto the taupe suede couch—the kind of couch you could sink into. Everything about the Stein house felt like home. Well, not like *his* home. But the way he always imagined home *should* feel. "Is she cooking tonight?"

"Are you inviting yourself over *again*?"

"There a problem with that?" Chase grinned.

"Not as long as there's enough food for me." Daniel patted his belly. For such a compact guy, he sure could put away a lot of latkes and roast. "Besides, you're not the only one. Becca's got a friend staying over too."

"Seriously?" Chase had been hoping that.

"Yeah, that Rose girl. The one who looks like an exotic porn star."

Chase knew who she was right way. "She's hot," he agreed. Suddenly, he wished he'd taken the time to pull on a clean T-shirt or comb his hair. He leaned over to catch a look at himself in the long, oval hallway mirror. His brown hair hung all messy and half covering his eyes, like it always did, even when he *had* combed it.

Daniel grinned. "I thought that'd cheer you up."

"Cheer me up? I'm a goddamn pillar of sunshine. What're you talking about? I don't need cheering up!"

Daniel ignored this, leaping up and tackling Chase on the couch. He rubbed his knuckles in Chase's hair. "What, your mom bring home some guy again?"

"Don't want to talk about it." Chase grabbed on and held both of Daniel's wrists in one of his hands, keeping him an arm's distance away. Chase nearly doubled Daniel's size, so Daniel twisted and squirmed, trying to wrench a hand free.

How the hell did Daniel know, anyway? Was it written on his forehead in red ink? Chase didn't want to tell Daniel that he and his mom, Candy, had gotten into it again. Just a yelling match. But bad enough that his little sister, Daisy, had hid under her bed to cry. Chase found her there all red faced and puffy, her stuffed rabbit damp with tears. Daisy hadn't done that since their dad left three years ago.

Chase loosened his hold and Daniel scrambled away, back to a safe distance on the couch. "Your dad's not back, is he?"

"I don't want to talk about it," Chase repeated. For all Daniel's self-piercings and pen-doodled tattoos, he was a good kid with one of those normal cookie-cutter lives. Not like Chase.

"Okay, okay." Daniel grinned. "Go visit the girls. That'll cheer you up."

Chase ran his fingers through his curls and took a deep breath. "Right on, bro. I like the way you think. I'm gonna wander over there like I'm looking for you. Sound believable?" Chase didn't wait for an answer, just turned and headed that way.

Rose Parsimmon and Becca Stein sat so close to each other on the worn plaid couch that they were almost sitting on each other's laps. Only one thing was sexier than a hot girl in shorts. Two hot girls in shorts. Thank god he lived in Southern California, where shorts could be worn ten months out of the year.

Rose held a pencil between two fingers and appeared to be sketching something on a piece of white paper. Chase took a deep breath and walked over to the edge of the coffee table directly in front of the couch. He went to sit down, hoping the table wouldn't crumble under his weight. Rose leaned her pencil to the side, using the edge for shading.

Becca lifted her eyes from *Cosmo*, giving Chase a long, hard look. "*Excuse us.*" Becca Stein and sarcasm were old friends.

Chase ignored her, studying Rose. She picked up her pencil for a moment and straightened, examining her drawing from a distance. Chase edged close enough that his knees nearly brushed hers. She was tanned, the color of a gingerbread cookie. Her skin seemed soft and clean.

Finally, Rose looked up. Bored brown eyes. He wanted to back out of the room immediately, but he held his ground. "Hey," he greeted the girls, trying to sound casual.

"Hey," Rose answered quietly. Politely. No indication that she would like to rest her gingerbread brown legs on his.

"Don't you have better things to do than sit here and drool over my friends?" Becca asked, chewing on the tie of her sweatshirt. That girl always had something in her mouth. A pen or pencil with the end gnawed off, a piece of gum, or when she could sneak it, a cigarette.

"You hungry?" Chase joked back. "Your mom doesn't feed you enough?"

Becca took the sweatshirt tie out of her mouth. "For your information, I'm trying to quit smoking. Daniel's been on my case, but mostly because my parents would flip if they found out." Becca pushed the sleeve up her arm, past the elbow. "They think I'm a good kid, you know. I can't ruin it for them."

Rose laughed through her nose. "Funny, isn't it?" She nudged Becca with her foot. "Your parents think you're an angel, so you pretend to be one. My parents think I'm a little shit, so I do my best to pretend they're right. Wouldn't want to disappoint them."

"Oh, so you're a little shit, huh?" Chase saw his opening and grabbed it.

"A shit and a half." Rose met his gaze head on. "They would've returned me ages ago if they didn't think it would make them look bad."

"I don't get it." Chase tried not to stare at her eyes. They were larger than average and the color of mud puddles—but not in a bad way. "You can't return your kid. What're you gonna do? Shove her back in?"

"They wish." Becca moved Rose's sketch aside, then lay her head in Rose's lap. Rose played with Becca's hair, sectioning off three strands of hair and preparing to braid. "Rose is adopted, you dork."

"Oh, come on, *Chase*," Rose said. His heart skipped a beat when she said his name. "You can't tell me you think I look anything like my parents."

Chase pictured Mr. and Mrs. Parsimmon. He'd seen them bringing Rose to and from school for years. At *first* he had noticed them because they didn't match Rose at all. And then he'd noticed them because their daughter was hotter than hot. The Parsimmons were old for parents— like more than halfway to grandparenthood, with skin as white as dough.

"Yep. I'm Satan's love child," Rose said nonchalantly, reaching into her pocket and pulling out a piece of sugar-free peppermint gum. "It is what it is. The trick is to have as much fun with it as possible."

"Yeah, but your fun always winds up with someone being grounded," Becca jumped in, complaining. "Although as long as it's not me, I don't really care." Becca reached her hand out for the gum, and Rose ripped the piece in half. "You are a true friend," Becca told her solemnly. "And you're an amazing artist." Becca pulled the sketch up from the coffee table and turned it so Chase could see.

It took him a second to realize what he was looking at. Two large eyes took up most of the space on the white page, but there were fingers too, near the edges of the eyes. It almost looked like someone had been hiding her eyes with her hands and had just peeked out from behind them. And then, as he looked closer, he saw a figure within the pupil of the eyes. A child's silhouette. All alone.

"You made that?" Chase asked, knowing he sounded stupid, since obviously she had. "That's, like, *art*."

Rose smiled then, a full smile, all the way up to her eyes, and her whole face changed. He felt suddenly too large for his body. His tongue was heavy too, with nothing intelligent to say. Luckily, Rose spoke for him. "Just one of the many things my parents don't seem to understand about me. Pop quiz," she said. "What's the opposite of love?"

"Hate."

"Wrong," Rose informed him. "The opposite of love is not giving a damn."

"Oh, come on." Chase challenged, his words still awkward. "I'm sure your parents care about you." *How could they not?*

Rose snorted. "They *think* they care. They care about molding me into something I'm not. They just don't care what *I* want. Or how I feel." She paused for a moment, her eyes far away. "Not that they even know what I want."

Chase couldn't help but ask, "What do you want?"

The question hung in the air unanswered for long enough to make him squirm. But then the faraway look melted from her eyes, and she turned to him, playful. "I'd tell you, but then I'd have to kill you."

Chase laughed, eyeing her petite frame. "I'd like to see you try."

Her eyes sparkled. "I bet you would. But I don't know you well enough. Not yet."

3
ROSE

ROSE TURNED HER SPOON UPSIDE down in her mouth, letting a bite of ice cream melt onto her tongue. And people-watched. Or rather, Stein-watched. The Steins were perfect candidates for one of those cheesy Disney Channel shows about an almost perfect but definitely quirky family.

All six of them—plus that Chase kid who couldn't stop staring at her—sat around an oval dinner table long after everyone finished eating. Mostly laughing with the Stein twins—who she had secretly nicknamed Tweedle Dee and Tweedle Dum because they still dressed alike and had identical little-kid pot bellies—as they spouted off stupid jokes. There was something about little kids giggling and sniggering that became contagious.

Rose scooted back her chair. "I'm doing the dishes," she announced.

"I think I'm supposed to argue with you," Mrs. Stein said, absentmindedly rubbing the green streak of paint under her chin, undoubtedly from the synagogue day-care she ran. "Say that you're our guest and all that. But I can't tell you how nice it will feel to keep my feet up." She stacked her plate on top of her husband's.

Becca snorted. "Maybe you could hire Rose to organize." Mrs. Stein's house always looked like a tornado had just spun through it.

"That's what we've got *you* for, Becca-loo!" Mr. Stein pointed out, all cheerful.

Becca groaned.

Rose balanced six plates and headed toward the kitchen. Halfway there, she swung around to face everyone. "You guys joke more than any family I know."

"Only when we have company," Mrs. Stein said with a smile. "When we're on our own, we're terribly boring. It's insufferable."

Chase stood up to help Rose carry the dinner glasses.

"I got this," Rose told Chase.

"Don't you want help carrying this over?" Chase looked like an oversized teddy bear—like Baloo from *The Jungle Book*. He seemed like the kind of guy you'd want to hold you till you fell asleep. Like the kind of guy who'd let you sleep there, even if his arms were getting numb and he really had to pee.

"No thanks. I got it." Rose knew what kind of help Chase might give. And she didn't need that right now. Just some alone time to think.

She stood at the kitchen sink with her arms in soapy water up to the elbow, scrubbing dishes like Cinderella, dipping her hands in and out of the warm soapy sink, and listening to the white noise of the running water. She let her thoughts slide by aimlessly until she heard two abrupt slams of car doors, one right after the other.

She knew right away that it was the cops. Cop car doors had different slams than doors to station wagons or Hondas. Even their slams meant business. And then the doorbell, two short, hard rings. Rose edged over to the door that led from the kitchen to the dining room and peeked in.

The cops were there for her. No doubt about it. From her position,

Rose could see the rest of the dining room and the front entranceway. Becca stood behind the front door, almost barricading her body from the cops—as if they had noses like hounds and could sniff out the package of cigarettes she'd hidden under her mattress. Like that was enough to haul her off to Juvie.

"I'm sorry to bother your family during dinner," a bushy-haired cop began. "We've got a report of a missing teenager. Do you know the whereabouts of Rose Parsimmon?"

Mrs. Stein twisted her fingers in her skirt. "Can I ask why? What has she done? What do you want her for?" Rose liked the defensiveness in her voice. The ownership, even.

The second cop had a hard jawline. "Chronic runaway. This time she took off with her mother's credit card. Charges have been filed."

Mr. Stein stepped forward and spoke softly, then he and the cops stepped outside. As soon as the front door squeaked closed, Mrs. Stein swiveled around to face Rose's head, still poking out of the kitchen. At first she said nothing, just studied Rose's eyes.

"What is this about, Rose?" Rose sunk back into the kitchen, like she could hide. Then, as if trying to coax a cat down from a tree, Mrs. Stein held out her hand. "Come out here, Rose."

Trapped, Rose shuffled out to the entryway. Mrs. Stein held out both hands. "Look, Rose, we know you have problems at home, and we want you to feel like you can come to us with anything. But this…this puts us in a bad position."

Rose thought of a million things to say, but she couldn't move her tongue. It felt like it had been injected with novocaine. She looked over at Becca for help, but her friend avoided her gaze by examining imaginary dirt under her fingernails. The only one looking directly at her was that kid Chase. He watched her with something like compassion in his eyes. Like he understood.

Before she knew it, Mr. Stein had led Bushy-Haired Cop back into the house and right over to Rose. "Look here. I have to take you with me." The cop cleared his throat. "Am I going to have to cuff you? And make a scene? I'm sure you don't want to cause any more embarrassment to this nice family."

Rose pulled her sleeves all the way down past her fingertips. "Whatever." She tried to look tough. "Here—you gonna search me first?" She robotically turned her pockets inside out and stepped up for a pat-down. Then she headed for the front door. No one said anything.

Rose lay halfway down in the backseat of the black-and-white.

"We gonna book her?"

"I say we just take her back to the house. Let the parents deal with her."

Bushy-Haired Cop twisted around in his seat. "Why don't you give us the credit card? We can return it to your mother and—"

"She's *not* my mother," Rose snapped.

Hard-Jaw Cop studied her in the rearview mirror. He waited and let the car idle. "Miss Parsimmon, I've been around a long time. Either there's something going on at home, or you're nothing more than a delinquent with a pretty face."

Rose turned her head toward the car seat, smelling the stink of the people who'd sat there before her. She didn't want the cop to read her eyes.

"They're not hurting you, are they?"

No comment.

"Because if they're hurting you, tell us. We can help you."

Rose slowly turned her head back toward the cops. She felt like she hadn't slept in days. "They're not molesting me, if that's what you mean." She laid her arm over her eyes. "They don't beat me either." *But there're a lot of ways to hurt someone. And no, you can't help me. No one can.*

Rose's last memory of her own mother slammed her in the face. Mama had been sitting in a cop car then, just like Rose was now.

Rose could still see the cop stuffing Mama into the back of a police car. Rose scrambling in after her, heart pounding. Holding on to her mom's neck like she was an anchor and her mother a ship. "Mama!" Her mom's long, silky hair spilling around Rose like a shield.

Mama wrapping her arms around Rose, whispering into her ear, "I love you, Rose. No matter what. I love you."

Those were the last words Rose ever heard her say.

Because before she knew it, some cop was peeling Rose's fingers and arms from her mother's neck, pulling her away from her mother, and then holding her in his arms—a big girl like she was—already five, being held like a baby. But Rose didn't fight it, just buried her head in the cop's shoulder and cried.

After a brief stay in a foster care shelter, the social worker had driven her to the Parsimmons' house. *Long term foster placement*, she explained. *Nice people. It'll give your mom some time to figure things out.*

Except for a few visits to check in over store-bought cookies and milk, the social worker just left her there. Rose concentrated on biting the chocolate chips out while the social worker's words floated past her ears. *Probation. Have not been able to make contact since her release. Off our radar. Upcoming court date.*

Rose decided that if she couldn't talk to her mom, well, then she wouldn't talk to *anyone*. And she didn't. Not for a whole year. Actually, Mrs. Parsimmon seemed to like Rose's silence at first.

"My little princess," she'd whisper, as though Rose might break if she spoke too loudly. "Just like a porcelain doll. So perfect."

Mrs. Parsimmon brushed Rose's long hair over and over, until it felt like silk. Rose could still remember the soft pull of the brush against her hair, the rhythmic strokes, and how it felt good...but she couldn't help but feel *bad* that it felt good. She couldn't help but think about her real mother.

Rose remained silent until the moment in that big cement building the social worker called "Court", when she first heard the man in the black robes refer to her as Rose *Parsimmon*. That wasn't her last name! At first she thought it was a mistake. But suddenly she knew. *She knew.* And the heaviness of knowing made her feel like she'd sink right through the floor all the way to the molten center of the earth. *She belonged to them now.*

Even now, with it just a memory, Rose felt the nothingness flood her senses. Because that had been when she'd tried to stop caring. When she tried to adopt "the opposite of love" as her mantra. When she tried to stop giving a damn that no one ever tried to help her call her mom. But the thing that hurt the most was that no one ever asked her if she *wanted* to be adopted. Because apparently, her opinion didn't count for shit.

4
ROSE

THE COP CAR SEAT COLD against her back, Rose tucked her chin into her knees. "What happens if I refuse to go back home?" she asked the cops.

"How old are you?"

"Fifteen and a half."

"Oh, you got a ways yet." Hard-Jaw Cop sighed. "You're stuck with your parents until you're eighteen. Unless you get emancipated. But that's kind of a process, from what I hear. You have to have your parents' approval, first of all. Then you have to be able to prove you can live independently, pay your own bills, and provide your own medical insurance...which basically means you have to have a full-time job."

"Oh." Rose chewed on the inside of her lip.

All too soon, the car pulled up to the curb in front of her house. Through the side window, Rose could see Mrs. Parsimmon sitting on the front steps, dabbing at her cheeks with a tissue. Rose figured if she'd saved all Mrs. Parsimmon's tears over the years, she'd be able to fill a pool and do the backstroke.

Mrs. Parsimmon eyed them from her seat. Suddenly she burst up as if someone had dangled a winning lotto ticket in front of her. And barreled down the steps in her flowered bathrobe.

Rose pulled her knees closer to her chest, burying her head against them. She could sort of pretend she was somewhere else that way. That worked for a moment. Until Mrs. Parsimmon got close enough to the car that Rose could hear her through the glass window—muted, though, almost like she was underwater. Bushy-Haired Cop sighed and pushed open his door. Suddenly, the volume hit Rose full force.

"Rose! I was so worried about you! Thank the lord you're alive!" Mrs. Parsimmon wailed. She should have been a school "yard duty." The woman had lungs.

Rose pressed her bony knees into her forehead until it hurt. She didn't move to get out of the car. She had learned years ago that *silence* was her friend. And her best weapon. When Rose first came to the Parsimmons' household and didn't speak for a whole year, the shrink called her a "selective mute"—meaning that she *could* talk but she *didn't* talk.

Not talking was power, really. Because besides torture, what could anyone do to *make* her talk? After a while, people didn't even expect her to talk. Like Ariel, whose voice was stolen in *The Little Mermaid*, Rose got by with gestures.

The car door opened. Hursula's strong hands wrapped all the way around Rose's skinny arm until her fingers touched. "Get. Out."

Rose allowed herself to be pulled away from the safety of the musty car. She imagined herself as one of those skinny blow-up man-kites they use to sell secondhand cars. Light enough to be blown about, too weak to resist...ready to be torn apart and whipped to oblivion in a storm.

Good old Bushy-Haired Cop stepped up toward Hursula. "Ma'am." He put his hand on her shoulder. "You're very upset. Why don't I walk you back up to the house, so my partner can have a few more words with your daughter?"

She nodded, and Bushy-Haired Cop led her by the arm, like he was escorting her on a date or something.

The police walkie-talkie blared something, and Hard-Jaw Cop turned to where Rose stood on the sidewalk. "Sorry, Miss Parsimmon, but we've got to jam." He pressed his business card into her hand. "Here's a word of advice. Give her back the credit card. Whatever's going on between the two of you—trust me—it's not worth it. You're too pretty to go to Juvenile Hall. They'd eat you alive."

Bushy-Haired Cop trotted back to the car. "Let's roll. We got bigger fish to fry."

Rose watched as the cop car pulled away from the curb. She couldn't help but feel sort of cheated. She *had* run away, after all. And committed theft. Property destruction too, since she'd cut the credit card into eighteen pieces.

Rose walked slowly toward the house, wondering if she could just sleep on the porch for the night. How cold would Southern California get in early November? As if to answer, the wind brushed past her, making her skin ripple into goose bumps. She could feel the hair stand up on her legs. Little stubbly prickles. Too bad she was by herself. She needed someone who'd wrap his arms around her and share body warmth. That overgrown teddy bear of a boy from Becca's would do.

Rose heard the slap of Mrs. P.'s house slippers as she stomped through the kitchen and across the living room. Crap. "I don't understand, Rose." Her voice started out flat, but when she spoke again, it sounded like she was pleading. "We try to give you the perfect life here with us."

It took everything in Rose's power to keep her face blank. Because she couldn't believe Mrs. P. considered this the "perfect life." No contact with her real mom? No visitation? No communication? *Please.*

"Surprise, surprise. The silent treatment." Mrs. P. shrugged sadly, her eyes glistening and looking almost pretty for a moment, although Rose would have never told her that. "The old standby." She waited, her eyes drying up. "Your father's gone to lie down already. You're gonna give that man a heart attack. This stress is killing him, you know."

When Mrs. Parsimmon was upset, she reminded Rose of the love child of *Peter Pan*'s Captain Hook and *The Little Mermaid*'s Ursula, the Sea Witch, mostly because she was heavy and angry and got way too close to Rose's face when she was talking.

Rose visualized Hursula's words bouncing off her skin—like she wore full-body steel armor. As for Mr. P, she'd bet anything that he'd spent the evening watching infomercials, instead of lying down in complete stress-case mode.

Hursula went on, "From now on, you are not to step foot off this porch without permission. You are not to go anywhere unsupervised. I will personally walk you to the door of your first period class, and I will walk you home."

Rose's stomach lurched at the thought.

"Maybe we'll finally get through to you. And that's not all—you have a month to get a job. You will bring your check directly to me. You will pay me back what you stole."

Rose would've liked to point out to Mrs. P. that she hadn't charged anything on the card. She'd just cut it into eighteen pieces to make a statement. All Mrs. P. had to do was report it missing and order a new one. But she kept her lips shut tight on principle. Sometimes *not* talking took more energy than talking.

Hursula raised her voice and spoke slowly, the way people do when someone is hard of hearing. "Are you coming in to go to bed?"

No freaking comment.

"Well, freeze your butt off if you like. I can't help it if you're too stubborn to come in and sleep in your own bed." Hursula disappeared for a moment. Then she came back, throwing a couple of thick quilts at Rose, which knocked her in the head.

"Take the quilts," Hursula ordered. "I know you. You'll be calling CPS to report me for child abuse—'she made me sleep on the porch with no blanket.'" She pulled her robe tighter around her. "Or you'll run to that Stein woman. Like it or not, my friend, she's not your mother. *I* am." Hursula turned on her heel and slammed the screen door behind her.

Rose blinked back tears. It was gonna be a helluva long night. Rose wrapped the quilts fully around her body, like she was a human enchilada, and ducked her head in too, burrito-style.

She thought, for a second time, how nice it would be to have that teddy-bear boy right next to her. For warmth. For company. And to royally piss her parents off.

$$\ggg\!\!\longrightarrow \longleftarrow\!\!\lll$$

Rose woke with a neck so stiff she actually couldn't turn it. She'd given up on the porch swing midway through the night and had instead propped herself up underneath the living room window. Every muscle in her body ached.

The screen door squeaked open and closed. Rose remained motionless, pretending to still be asleep. Heavy footsteps thudded up to her. Boots—work boots. Mr. P. wore them every day, even though he'd retired from the construction business last year. The footsteps stopped in front of her enchilada-quilt huddle. She could almost feel the porch give under his weight. Mr. P. was built solid—like a big, old sack of sand.

The man woke up at 5:00 a.m. every day. *That* was not normal. Every single morning for as long as she could remember, he'd walked to the Daily Drip. The walk was supposed to be good for his heart, anyway.

Nearly a minute passed as Mr. P. stood over Rose. She pictured him standing there, his hands stroking his salt-and-pepper beard, his skin weathered like the ancient cloth tarp he used to cover his car, and the pores on his nose big enough to bury treasure.

Finally, the work boots thudded past her, down the creaky step and toward the sidewalk. She could hear his feet pad away down the street, until she no longer heard them at all. Only then did she dare to move. *Holy crap.* Her entire left side contracted and stiffened as she adjusted her position.

Rose gingerly climbed back onto the porch swing. She folded in her legs and wrapped the quilt around herself again. When she closed her eyes, she felt rather than saw the sun edge up into the sky. It cut the chill in half almost immediately. The quilts insulated her with her own body heat, and the sun gradually baked her face.

"Comfy?" A sudden voice jolted her.

"What?" She squinted, her eyes unaccustomed to the light. A dark shape loomed above.

"So did you pull it off? Were you disappointing enough?" That boy from the Steins'. Daniel's friend. Chase. Standing on her porch, blocking her sun.

Rose fought off the cloudiness of sleep. "What the hell are you doing here?" She wrapped the quilt tighter around herself, even though she was fully clothed underneath.

"Just passing by." He crouched next to her, looking rugged. "I couldn't sleep, so I took a walk."

"Past *my porch* at the crack of *dawn?*" How did he even know where she lived? Although on second thought, she wasn't exactly discreet.

"Um." Chase's cheeks turned bright red. *Oh my god, he's shy.* "I guess I was worried about you."

"I can take care of myself."

"I know you can." He cleared his throat. "You just looked sort of upset when you left."

"Yeah. Getting arrested tends to do that." Rose said, saucier than she'd intended.

Chase didn't seem to have an answer for that one, just nodded. "Seriously, though," he finally said. "You shouldn't sleep outside. Didn't you hear about those pit bulls escaping? It's not safe."

"Ah, shucks, I didn't know you cared." Rose felt herself softening. She couldn't help but smile as she studied his face. The outside corners of his eyes turned down in a way that made him look gentle.

"Maybe I do." Chase sat down on the swing next to her.

"So you think that by sitting with me, you're gonna somehow protect me from killer pit bulls?"

"Either that, or we'll both be dog meat." Maybe it was the rising sun behind him, but Chase's skin kind of glowed.

"Just don't let Mrs. P. catch you here. I'm grounded." Rose moved the blanket to make a bigger place for him. "Can't be seen hanging with the opposite sex."

"Don't worry." Chase grinned. "I can run fast." He settled himself next to her. "You gonna share that blanket, or what?"

She shared.

She must've fallen back asleep that way, sharing a blanket with a strange boy. Because the next thing she knew, Mrs. P. was shaking her awake, and Chase was nowhere to be seen.

She wondered for a moment whether she'd dreamed the whole thing. But as she folded up the blanket, she caught a whiff of Chase's rugged smell, and she couldn't help but smile.

5

CHASE

THE LUNCHTIME CAFETERIA LINE STRETCHED all the way past the choir room. Chase stood in the line for less than a minute, being jostled by the movement of the students. He gave up and wandered instead past Rose and Becca's tree trunk. He tried not to look over at her. No need to be so obvious.

"Hey you, Chance!" Rose startled him out of his thoughts, throwing an orange at his back, right between his shoulder blades.

It took every ounce of restraint to keep from running up like a panting dog. Instead, he slowly turned. "Chance? My name's Chase."

"Oh." Rose bit her lip like she was trying to hide a smile. "My bad."

You faker. You knew my name. Chase tried to think of something intelligent to say. They'd barely made eye contact since that morning on her porch a week ago. He hadn't wanted to get Rose into any more trouble than she was already in, so he'd left her sleeping there as soon as he heard the sounds of someone waking up inside.

"I've got a favor to ask. One Disappointment to another." Rose beckoned him closer. She patted the patch of grass next to her. Then she leaned over and whispered in his ear. The puffs of her breath sent chills through his body. "I am *dying* for a smoke. But the parent police are breathing down my neck. You've got to get me a pack."

As much as Chase wanted her lips closer to his skin, he pulled away. Considered her for a moment. "What makes you think that I can hook you up? I don't smoke. Besides, they card everywhere."

"Oh, come on, Chase. I can't ask Becca to get them from her cousin 'cause she's trying to quit." Rose said, looking over at Becca. Becca stuck a grape Blow Pop in her mouth and smiled around it.

"What's in it for me?" Chase said, proud of his comeback.

"Are we negotiating, then?" Rose sighed. "All right. I'll kiss Becca for thirty seconds and you can watch."

Chase lost his breath. *Was she serious?*

Becca pulled the grape Blow Pop out of her mouth. "I taste like grape," she said thoughtfully. "Can't say that I blame you for wanting an excuse to nab a smooch, Rose. *I'd* want to kiss me if I could."

"Tempting." Chase felt embarrassment rushing in like a wave at high tide. He fought it off. "But look. I'm taking a real risk. Not only do I have to find a way to get cigarettes, I have to find a way to get them to *you*."

Becca talked around the Blow Pop, making her speech a little warbled. "He's got a point," she said. "Your parents are watching you like a hawk every second you're out of school. And if Chase brings you cigarettes here and gets caught, he could get suspended."

Rose kicked Becca's foot. "Thanks, Becca. Way to give him ammunition."

"There's only one thing I want." Chase waited a moment for Rose to make a sexual innuendo, but she didn't. "I want to take you on a date."

Total silence for a full minute. Chase found himself staring at the ground, scuffing it with his shoe. "Look, Chase," Rose's voice sounded softer than he'd heard it before. "I can't go on a date. My parents won't let me breathe or pee without asking. There's no way they'd let me go out."

Chase looked up. "A lunch date, then. You eat lunch at school with me every day for the next week." He grinned, and even Becca looked at him with something that resembled admiration. "And in return"—he paused for effect—"I will bring you a pack of Camels."

"Make it Marlboro Lights, and it's a deal."

Monday: Lunch with Rose Parsimmon felt like a verbal Ultimate Fighting match. Before Chase even sat down next to her on the first day, it was—"So where's my smokes?"

Him: "Is that all I'm good for?"

Her: "Pretty much. This is a flat negotiation, nothing more."

Him, putting his hand on his chest: "Oh, that hurts. I feel so used."

Her: "And you aren't getting any either."

Him: "Well, you're a sorry first date, aren't you?"

Rose laughed, then leaned back against the oak tree and tore a bag of Doritos open with her teeth. "I just want to blacken my lungs and get a little buzz." She gathered her long hair in her hands like she was pulling it back into a ponytail, then let it go. The hairs rushed back and found their places all over again like soldiers in formation. "So where'd you wind up getting the cigarettes?"

"I can't reveal my source." He looked around for a moment, then at the large oak tree behind her, and tried to figure out how close he could sit without pissing her off. Luckily the grass still glistened with moisture from the weekend's rain, so he planted himself on the only remaining dry spot under the tree. Close enough to feel the skin of her bare legs on his own.

First her skin felt cool to the touch, and then it warmed him, warmed his whole body like a toaster oven. He closed his eyes for a moment and thanked the lord for the weekend's rain, that it was still warm enough for shorts, and that Becca had detention this period, so they had a few moments alone.

"Seriously?" she asked, not pulling away.

"Seriously," Chase countered. "You'd never go out with me again if I told you where to get them on your own."

Rose picked up Chase's hand playfully. Her fingers brushed against his left wrist. The wrist bore a small dark circle. "I know what this is," Rose whispered. She pushed up her sleeve to reveal a row of the same dark circles.

The summer before he turned thirteen, and two months before his dad, Walter, left for good, Chase had talked a neighbor into buying him a pack of Camels, which he hid in the far left corner of his closet underneath a pile of dirty laundry. He'd sat, barefoot and shirtless, his right leg hanging out the unscreened window, and smoked nearly the entire pack in one sitting. One right after another, over and over until he thought he might puke. And then he *had puked*. And after he'd brushed his teeth, he lit another and another.

He could hear them fighting, his parents. Crashing. Screaming. Threatening. Crying. Don't cry, Chase willed his mother. *Hasn't she learned that yet?* Chase had considered calling the cops, but thought better of it. The neighbors had done it before, and it never really helped. Sure, it ended things for the moment, but he'd pay. His mother would pay.

So instead of calling the cops, instead of stepping in and shoving Walter out of the way, instead of creating a distraction, Chase pressed his last cigarette into his wrist. Hard. He bit down on his lip and pressed harder. Until the pain was so loud that he couldn't hear the fighting any longer.

Remembering this, Chase balled up his fists. They were

each the size of grapefruits. Looking at them balled up like that reminded him of Walter. Chase had always thought you could tell a lot about a person by their hands. Maybe because Walter's bulging fists had come flying at him so many different times from so many different directions.

Chase turned his attention back to Rose. Her fingernails were cut short and uneven. Her fingers were bare. Rose's hands looked like she didn't care. No—scratch that. Like she wanted it to *look* like she didn't care. Because Chase was pretty sure that she did.

He touched the dark circle on his wrist. "I don't smoke. Not anymore, anyway." He thought instantly back to his mother, Candy, always trying to quit cigarettes and chocolate and swearing. Chase tried to remember when he started calling his parents by their first names. Maybe when Candy started passing him off as her little brother. Everyone said she looked way too young to have a kid. So she just pretended she didn't. "I'm trying to reform myself, I guess," Chase added.

Rose made a funny noise—kind of like she was choking, but when Chase looked closer, he saw that she was laughing. Damn. He'd thought he might have a chance to perform mouth-to-mouth. "*Reform* yourself? You're talking like you're some kind of sorry-ass delinquent."

"Well, maybe I am." *Little does she know. She hasn't seen me get into it with Candy. She hasn't seen Daisy cower under the bed.*

"Oh, come on." Rose shook her head, her hair falling into her face. "Just because you don't do your homework and you got in a couple of fights after school, that doesn't make you a delinquent."

The warning bell rang, signaling the beginning of the six-minute passing period before fifth. "Well, *you* seem to have the art of delinquency down, Rose. Maybe you should give me lessons. You *are* stuck having lunch with me for four more days."

"Don't remind me." Rose groaned, but almost playfully.

"Speaking of which," Chase began, standing back up, "tomorrow we eat somewhere else. It's a surprise."

Rose bit her lip like she was trying not to smile. "I'm hard to surprise," she warned him.

"Have confidence, Rose," Chase said, walking backward toward his locker. "I'm better at this than you think."

6
ROSE

TUESDAY:"I CAN'T BELIEVE I'M LETTING you kidnap me for a lunch date," Rose whispered the following afternoon, stumbling in the darkness. Chase pressed his hand across her eyes, and she could smell a faint muskiness that might have been cologne or laundry detergent. His hands were so big that one of them could completely cover both of her eyes, leaving her no chance of peeking.

Sounds of students faded away as Chase helped her step up slightly into a room. Her feet tapped against the floor as she entered, making her think it might be the linoleum floor of a classroom. The air chilled her skin and sent goose bumps rippling down her arms.

"Cold?" Chase asked. He wrapped his free arm around her, warming her. The other hand loosened its hold, and Rose strained to see through the fingers.

A few more steps, then, "Voilà!" Chase lifted his arms from her, and for a second she stumbled, trying to get her bearings.

A classroom. With a stove and a sink and a fridge. "Welcome to Foods and Nutrition II." Chase held his arm out like he owned the place.

A tiny table sat in the middle of the floor, covered with a red-and-white-checkered tablecloth that looked suspiciously like one she'd seen at the Steins' a few weeks before. "I'm the T.A. for this class fourth period," he explained, looking uncertain for a moment as he waited for her reaction. "Mrs. Crawford loves me."

Rose just stared at the room, at the table, and at what looked like two paper bowls of spaghetti. "You made me pasta?" She didn't move to sit down.

"Better than Doritos, right? Becca gave me the lowdown. Spaghetti is supposed to be one of your all-time favorite foods."

Rose considered telling him that Becca was a liar and she hated pasta, but when her mouth opened, nothing of the sort came out. "Only angel hair."

"My sources speak the truth, then." Chase pulled her by the elbow toward the heaping bowls of angel-hair pasta, swirled in a red sauce that smelled of garlic, basil, and sweet onions.

She allowed herself to be led, but still didn't sit. "You're not seducing me, I hope you know. This is purely me filling my end of the deal, remember?" It felt strange, having someone do something so nice for her without wanting something in return. *Unless maybe he did.* Maybe he'd read what other guys had written on the bathroom walls and maybe he figured he could—

"Stop worrying," Chase told her gently, cutting off her thoughts. "Just sit. And eat."

So she did. She twirled the long strands around the prongs of the fork and managed to bring a bite to her lips without dropping any on her lap. Cheesy as it was, Rose couldn't help picturing the scene from *Lady and the Tramp*, when both dogs slurped the same piece of spaghetti and wound up mouth to mouth.

"Tell me if you like the sauce, so I know whether to take credit for it." Chase ran his fingers through his hair, leaving it messier than before.

"I like it, you dork." Rose tried to sound sarcastic, but she couldn't help smiling at him. He looked so vulnerable, sitting there red-cheeked and nervous.

He smiled back. "It's Ragu. I would've had candles too, but it turns out they're against school regulations. Fire code and all, you know."

"Oh, so now you're a rule follower," Rose teased. "See? You *do* make a sorry-ass delinquent."

"I thought you were going to take me under your wing and show me the art of true delinquency." Chase took a great big bite of pasta, and sauce dripped onto his chin.

Rose leaned over to wipe it off with her index finger. She held it up for him to admire, then licked it off. She sighed happily, "I *do* have my work cut out for me, don't I?"

7
CHASE

WEDNESDAY: CHASE COULDN'T HELP BUT think it was a good sign that Rose had made him muffins for their third lunchtime date. They'd been mostly edible, and Chase had managed to eat three. Honestly, he'd have eaten a mountain of them if it would've made Rose happy.

Still, his stomach felt a little queasy tonight. Chase wasn't sure if it was from the muffins or from watching his mom get ready for a date. That always turned his stomach. Chase watched Candy apply her eyeliner so carefully that you'd think she was doing brain surgery on herself. She spread it on thick. Something twisted in the pit of his gut. Chase gripped the door frame with both hands, bracing his weight. "Going out again tonight?" This was the third night in a row.

Candy's eyes flicked from her own face to his in the mirror. "Yeah." She leaned in and pulled her upper eyelid out flat as she painted it.

Candy'd been sporting a new boyfriend, a real winner like always. Night manager at Sam's Subs. The kind of guy who wore his shirts open so you could see little sprouts of chest hair. And fake-gold necklaces. Thick accent, although he didn't talk long enough for Chase to figure out from where. Stoned 90 percent of the time. The man reeked of bud, like it was leaking out his pores through his sweat.

Chase tapped the door frame with his palm to get her attention. "Daisy has a spelling test tomorrow."

"Shit. You're right." Candy put down her mascara wand and swiveled around to look at Chase directly. "Can you quiz her tonight?"

"I might be busy," Chase lied. That was crap, of course. He had nothing to do. It wasn't like he ever even opened his own homework. And it wasn't like he could see Rose outside of school or anything.

"That's crap." Candy pointed out. "Quiz her on her spelling words. Only watch how she writes the letters too. She still flips her *r*'s and *d*'s. God knows why. She'll have to start riding that short bus if she doesn't get it together soon."

Chase ducked his head under his own arm to make sure Daisy still sat out of earshot, her school notebook spread out on the kitchen table along with some pretzels and crayons. "Don't say shit like that," Chase told her, his words sounding sharp even to his own ears.

"She can't hear me."

"Maybe not, but I can." Chase straightened up. "Don't say shit like that."

Candy said nothing for another ten minutes, until she stepped out from the bathroom as a finished product. Chase lay across the couch, his feet stacked up on the armrest, and the buds of his iPod firmly planted in his ears. She'd dressed in a miniskirt and a tight top cut low to accentuate her boobs.

She was not a big person, but for the size of her overall frame, her boobs were big. Plus she wore those push-up underwire things and that made them look even bigger. Chase would've loved to not know the details of the kinds of bras she wore, but he sorted the laundry and it was hard to not notice these things.

"Come on, Mom. Seriously?" Chase carefully pulled the earbuds out one at a time. "No offense, but you look a little desperate." Rose could pull off an outfit like that and look hotter than a firecracker, but looking at Candy made Chase cringe.

Candy met his eyes with a heavy stare. "Nice, Chase, nice. I can always count on you for a solid vote of approval."

"I just say it like it is." Chase's voice picked up steam. He couldn't help but notice the way Daisy set down her crayons and stopped chewing her bite of pretzel.

"No—you just like to put me down." Candy's voice matched his own, only her edge sounded shrill. "You and your dad both."

And the counterattack. Right on schedule. Chase couldn't help himself. "Why're you bringing my dad into this?" He stood up, a full head and a half taller than Candy, and at least twice as heavy.

She did not back away, although all it would've taken was a flick of his finger to knock her right off those three-inch heels she wore and onto her ass.

"We both know he was a piece of shit. You trying to say I'm a piece of shit too?" Chase didn't even realize he'd been yelling, until he saw Daisy frozen, half standing, totally motionless except for the tears rolling down her cheeks.

Chase stopped. He reached out his hand toward her. "It's okay, Daze."

But Daisy spun on her heel, knocking over her chair, and hightailed it to her room.

Candy stepped back from him. "Whatever, Chase. What-the-fuck-ever. I'm out of here. Don't wait up."

"Wasn't planning on it," Chase whispered, deflated.

He found Daisy behind her winter sweaters in her bedroom closet. He could hear her sniffling from outside the closet door. His throat tightened up. Shit, he wasn't going to cry too, was he? It wasn't his fault his stupid little sister got all weirded out by a little yelling. He hadn't done anything out of line. Had he?

Funny thing was, he'd been the one to show Daisy all the best hiding places. The closet and under the bed were favorites. Chase slid the closet door open and stepped inside. "I'd go for the snowman sweater myself," he tried to joke.

She said nothing.

"What's up, Daisy-Dukes?"

She didn't answer him, just wiped her face on an off-white sweater. He couldn't help but notice that she smelled like pretzels. "I don't like that."

"What?"

"I don't like that voice. That's your angry voice. It makes my stomach hurt."

Chase considered this. "You know I'm not like Dad, right, Daze?"

She sniffled.

"You know I wouldn't hurt you. Don't you?"

Daisy nodded but didn't look at him. And all of a sudden he remembered standing in this very closet as a little boy, no more than four, thinking the legs of his overalls totally covered him up, thinking Walter would never find him there. He remembered Walter shoving the closet door to the side so hard it came off its hinges. Chase remembered squeezing his own eyes shut. If he couldn't see Walter, then Walter couldn't see him, right?

He'd run to hide when Walter yelped. A pain yelp. Because he'd stepped barefoot on the Thomas train Chase had forgotten to put away. He remembered Walter, still rubbing the sole of his foot, yanking him out of the closet by the elbow. *What you hiding in here for, boy? You afraid of me? You afraid of your own dad?* He remembered how he'd looked anywhere but at Walter's eyes, hoping for a way to escape. Not that different from the way Daisy looked right now.

Chase kneeled and touched her hand. "I would never hurt you. I would never, ever, ever hurt you. I promise." It mattered so much that she believed him.

She looked up. "Princess pinky swear?"

He tried not to laugh, relieved. "I princess pinky swear times a million. I will never hurt you. Okay?"

"Okay." Daisy whispered. She bit her lip and then added, "Are we all going to hell?"

"What?" Chase lifted her chin to face him. "Where did that come from?"

"Because you and Mommy fight all the time. And we don't go to church." Daisy's eyes seemed wide and dark as plums. "This girl at school says anyone who doesn't confess their sins will go to hell. But we never go to church anymore. Not even on Easter."

"Don't you think going to hell has more to do with the kind of person you are than whether you sit in a sweaty church every Sunday?" Chase asked.

"I guess so." Daisy didn't sound convinced.

"Listen, Daisy-Dukes. I'm definitely not the person who has all the answers about religion and sin and all that." Chase stood up and held out his hand. "But somehow I doubt this girl from school has all the answers either. So how about you decide for yourself if you want to go to church, and if you do, I'll take you. Okay?"

"Okay," Daisy whispered for a second time, accepting Chase's hand and climbing out of the closet.

They studied for the spelling test over a dinner of Top Ramen and Mountain Dew. Then Chase indulged Daisy by enduring her favorite teenybopper television shows for an entire hour. He tried to keep his mind from wandering back to Rose, but failed. Did she actually like Chase, or was she just repaying a debt? As much as he wanted to believe the muffins were a sign, maybe they were just muffins.

A thought grabbed on to his mind. He wouldn't know unless he made a move, would he?

8
ROSE

THURSDAY'S LUNCH WITH CHASE: THE temperature dipped to the low seventies, and it seemed as though the trees all lost their leaves overnight. Rose settled herself into her favorite spot in the grass, close enough to Chase that her bare legs rubbed against his. She'd shaved (and moisturized) that morning on purpose.

"If I hadn't given you my word, I'd be *so* done with you for lunch." Rose turned to Chase. "Only one day left."

"Oh, *come on*. I'm almost as cute as Becca." Chase said, then bit into an apple, chewing like he was deep in thought.

"You wish." She knew the second she'd said it that she'd jumped in too quick. "You're no match for Becca." Rose watched his face for a minute, trying to decide if he knew she was kidding. She wanted to touch his arm, but she didn't. "Besides, you don't taste like grape."

"Nope." Chase sunk his teeth into the apple slowly and ripped off a big chunk. He pushed the bite to the left side of his mouth, in his cheek, like a lopsided chipmunk. Then Chase just looked at Rose for a moment, studying her like he was trying to decide what to do next, before he pulled her in close to him. "I taste like apple," he pronounced.

And then he kissed her. A real kiss. Long and deep. The kind that sent goose bumps racing down her arms and legs. She could taste the apple wedged in his cheek. Sweet with a slightly tangy kick.

It felt so good that Rose got lost in it for a moment, but then she pushed him away. "Back off! Do you want to ruin it?"

Chase seemed confused. "What are you talking about?"

"I thought you weren't gonna make a move!" Rose stood up, shaky. She could still taste apple when she brought her fingers to her lips. She wasn't sure whether she wanted to lean in for another kiss or give him a good kick in the balls.

"What do you mean? You're the one sending me mating signals like you're in heat!"

"Go to hell," Rose said, though this time without as much conviction. "And never mind besides."

"Never mind what?"

"Never mind getting a job with me."

"*What* are you talking about?"

Rose looked up at the overcast sky, like she was explaining the obvious. "I was *gonna* ask you to apply with me—to get a job together so we could hang out without the parent police breathing down our necks. But never mind."

"You are a piece of work, Rose Parsimmon." Chase ripped into the apple again. He talked around his bite. "But I like you anyway."

Rose felt a sudden, unexplainable urge to giggle. "Why do you take such big bites? You look like a cow." She did sort of want to kiss him again, but thankfully, she did not.

"And you know what?" Chase said casually. "The next move is yours to make. If you want it. Because you are *way* too complicated for me to figure out." He studied her for a moment. "I'll tell you what. You're in charge of lunch tomorrow."

Rose just grinned. "I think I can handle that. The question is, can you?"

Friday: Rose crept past a cluster of sophomores in navy-blue cheerleading skirts (cut way higher than dress code was supposed to allow) and up to Chase's mess of a locker.

She poked her head around the open metal door. "*Pssst!*"

"Shit." Chase looked away from the books, balled-up pieces of paper, and scrunched lunch bags he'd been shoving in there. "What're you trying to do, give me a heart attack? It's not lunch yet. It's only second period."

"Locker patrol," Rose announced, straightening her posture and faking a military voice. "Checking for any, uh, contraband that would be better served in other hands."

"The only contraband I had was for you. Otherwise I'm a law-abiding citizen." Chase wedged another book inside. He wore a short-sleeved T-shirt that made the circumference of his arms look huge. Not fat huge, just so totally solid. That boy needed to go out for football. Or wrestling. Or bodybuilding.

"Time for your first lesson." Rose curled her fingers around the locker door and tapped her short fingernails on the dingy metal.

"Lesson in what, exactly?" Chase grinned, showing all his teeth. "This might be fun."

"You *wish*. Not that kind of fun. Get your mind out of the gutter." Rose swatted at him, and he ducked. "Lesson in delinquency. We're cutting class. I'm in charge for lunch, remember? I'm taking you out."

The hesitation scrawled across his forehead immediately. "Uh..."

He made this way too easy. Rose decided to have fun with it.

"Come, on, Chase. I know you want to." She edged up close to him and wound her leg around his, linking her ankle with his and causing her entire thigh to rest on his jeans.

He laughed under his breath, like he felt uncomfortable but was trying to hide it. "I want to." He shifted his weight under her leg, but just barely. "I just don't want to deal with the automated call home, reporting my absence."

"Holy shit, you've got a lot to learn." Rose snapped her gum, blowing a bubble toward his face for emphasis. It popped too early and sagged down, deflated. She unwound her leg from his and stepped back. "I don't need the parent police breathing down my neck any more than you do. *Think*. What's today?"

"Friday."

"Think harder."

"Uh, November the seventeenth?"

"It's the eighteenth, Einstein." As much as she tried to hold it down, she could feel her own smile break through. This was fun. "But no. Think *harder*."

"Uh. Your birthday?"

Something caught in her throat, and it wasn't the bubblegum. Because he was getting closer. It *was* someone's birthday, just not hers. One of the cheerleaders turned halfway to peek at her from under a silky fan of totally blond hair. Then Blondie whispered something to the pixie-like cheerleader on her right.

"Harder, Chase, harder!" Rose moaned with theatrics, just loud enough to cause the circle of girls to turn and snicker. She winked at him. "And yes, I *did* just say that. Gotta give the cheer squad more ammunition for those bathroom walls. They need new material. God knows they're not capable of thinking of anything creative themselves."

Chase fumbled.

"Come on, Chase." Rose stepped close again, so she could whisper. She tugged on his broad shoulder and pulled his earlobe down to her level. He smelled good, kind of a mix of hair gel and fabric softener. "It's the rally. Today's the rally between fourth and fifth period. And what happens at rallies?" Rose released his shoulder, and he straightened.

As the meaning of her words hit home, Chase's eyes lit up like Fourth of July sparklers. "Nobody takes attendance."

"Right on! And lunch period's after. That means we can slip out for a whole hour and a half." Rose patted his chest with two hands, satisfied. The boy was rock solid. "Your mission, should you choose to accept it: meet me outside the girls' locker room after fourth period lets out. We have an errand to run, and then I'll buy you lunch."

"You're persuasive. How could I say no?" His eyes crinkled up in the corners, in that way that made him seem so gentle. His kindness frightened her for a split second, although who the hell knew why.

But there was also something about him that pulled her in. That made her want to be honest with him. To let him really *know* her. She couldn't put her finger on what it was about him. He was cute, sure, in a teddy-bear-on-steroids sort of way. But lots of guys were cute. She guessed it was this—he seemed like the kind of guy who might really "get" her. And if that happened, it'd either be the best thing in the world for her, or the worst.

Rose called back over her shoulder to him, "And they say peer pressure is dead." Then she walked away, feeling the heat of eyes against her back. Not sure, of course, whether those eyes were his or whether they came from the group of gossip girls in short-short skirts with calves made of steel.

9
CHASE

"GIVE ME A BOOST," ROSE ordered, standing knee-deep in the overgrown outer yard past the baseball field.

"Couldn't we just go through the student parking lot?" Chase asked. The campus supervisors were all about seventy-five years old, and they spent more time working things out in the bathroom than they did standing their posts.

"Adventure, Chase. Have you never heard of adventure?" Rose whirled toward him, and her eyes shone like a wild animal's. "God, you got a shitload to learn here. Give me a boost." Chase kneeled in the grass by the far field so that Rose could step on his knee and scale the fence.

"Not that way." She turned and held his hands in her own. "You're impossible. I hereby give you formal permission to touch my butt."

And now it was Chase's turn to feel like a wild animal. His heart skittered about in his chest. He placed his palms on each of Rose's butt cheeks. They felt firm under his hands. He'd never touched a girl's butt before, and it sent goose bumps tickling across his skin. He boosted her up, and she swung a leg over the top of the fence. Chase followed shortly after, self-conscious about how the fence curved under his polar-bear bulk.

Once off campus, something changed. Chase couldn't have defined the change, but he felt it. Silence weighed down the air. Not the peaceful, wilderness kind of quiet that he felt sometimes walking alone. But a heavy silence. Like something was bothering Rose. Like this wasn't just a pleasure trip.

She walked with a purpose and at a quick pace along the dirt road behind the school, and then onto the tree-shaded sidewalk. Chase followed. "So, uh, Rose? We've been walking for ten minutes, and you haven't said a word."

Rose stopped cold, turning to face him. She met his eyes with her own, but the wild animal had melted away.

"So much for meditative quiet." Rose sighed an exasperated sigh. "I'm not talking because I'm busy working myself into a royal funk."

"On purpose?" Chase digested this. "Why?"

Rose faced forward again and kept walking. "Do you seriously want to get in the way of my royal funkdom?" She pushed ahead toward a shopping complex with eight to ten stores. "I'm warning you, it could be hazardous to your health."

"So is smoking. And running away from home."

Rose half smiled at that. "Point taken." She smoothed her hair back away from her face, but the strands slipped right back. "Nah. I just gotta get my mom a present. It's her birthday."

"Today? The seventeenth?" Chase shoved his hands in his pockets. Girls were so totally confusing. Or maybe *Rose* was just so totally confusing. In a royal funk because she needed to buy her mom a gift?

"It's the eighteenth!" Rose fake-shoved him. "And yes, I think so."

"What do you mean, you think so?" Chase countered.

"I mean I can't remember exactly. I just know we used to

celebrate her birthday about a week before Thanksgiving. You know how it is when you're a little kid. Time sort of mushes together, and I don't think I have it totally right. A few years ago, I settled on November eighteenth."

"Oh, you're talking about your, uh, your..." Chase said.

"My bio mom. My *only* mom." Rose stepped in front of him just then, blocking his path. He hadn't been expecting that, and he bumped into her. "Clumsy, much?" she sassed in a teasing way. "If I didn't know better, I'd think you were trying to cop a feel."

"Me thinks the funk is evaporating."

"Me thinks you're right. Me glad I brought you." Rose grabbed on to his arm and dragged him into a boutique store, the kind of place that sold overpriced chocolates in cute little shapes, T-shirts with sappy sayings, and mini novelty books with sappy-ass titles like "Friends Forever."

Rose ran her fingertips along the counter. In front of her stood a row of carved figurines made entirely out of wood. The figures had no faces, but not in a creepy way. Whoever had carved them had flecked off enough curves from their faces to give them a human look. Maybe even a gentle look. Rose picked up a slender figurine of a woman holding a small child. She brushed her finger across the woman's blank face. "This one," she whispered.

Chase mutely trailed Rose's steps as she slipped in and out of aisles. Along with the faceless figurine, she selected a plastic bag filled with dark chocolate almonds and an oven mitt decorated with a rooster. She placed two crisp twenty dollar bills next to the cash register.

"Want to become a valued member?" the perky cashier asked, folding her hands in front of her cheery green apron. Chase wondered how many times a day she asked that question.

"Nah. I'm good." Rose tapped her fingernails on the counter as the cashier wrapped the items in tissue paper. Then she folded up the leftover cash—fourteen dollars and twenty-seven cents—and shoved it in her pocket.

The sunlight accosted them as they stepped outside. Chase glanced at his watch. Nearly thirty minutes until they were supposed to be seated in fifth-period class. "You buy your mom a present every year?"

"Yep. Started when I was about ten." Rose shuffled everything around in her paper bag, like she was trying to make order of it all. "Before that, I hadn't figured out how to get my hands on cash."

Chase had a sinking feeling that he knew exactly how she did get cash, but he decided not to ask. He knew Rose was still looking for a job. "And then you send it to her?"

The funk settled back onto Rose's shoulders and seeped into her eyes. "Would if I could. Don't know where she's at," she said. "Nah. I just save them up. Got a box under my bed. When I find her, I'll give her the whole bunch. And she'll know I've been thinking of her all these years. That I never forgot."

"Makes sense," Chase said softly, moving into the center of the sidewalk so that he wouldn't step on Homeless Hillary, one of the two noticeably homeless people in Simi Valley. No one knew if her name was really Hillary, but that's what everyone called her. She'd been around since he was a kid.

Rose yanked the chocolate almonds out of the bag. "Happy Birthday, Myrtle!" She whispered, placing the bag of chocolates into the woman's sleepy lap.

"Wait—" Chase froze. Confusion. "That's—that's not your mom, is it?"

Rose just crossed her arms and stared at Chase. "Oh yeah, real strong family resemblance."

"I didn't think so. But it's her birthday too?"

"No, you idiot. I don't know her birthday, just like I don't know her name. But she's got a birthday one day a year. I'm either early or late."

"You give her a gift every year?"

"Yeah. She's probably *someone's* mom. Just not mine. Hopefully someone out there is giving my mom a gift on her birthday too."

"That's so..." Chase searched for the right word. It just seemed so out of character for Rose, harsh as that sounded. But maybe she had more layers than he knew.

"So what?"

"So...*nice*."

She laughed, and it seemed a pure laugh. Not sarcastic or sad or anything else. "Yeah. I *can* be nice. Once in a blue moon. Then I give myself permission to be a bitch the rest of the year." She pulled the rooster oven mitt out too. "Guess who this is for?"

"Our other resident homeless person?"

"Nah. It's an oven mitt, you moron. You kind of got to have a home to have an oven."

Chase felt his cheeks redden. "Who's it for, then?"

"Mrs. P." Rose looked away from Chase for a moment. Then she slid her eyes up to his. There was no hint of joking. "For putting up with me. I'll save it for Christmas." And then the sparkle in her eyes returned. "Or Kwanzaa. I almost got her one that says 'Happy Holidays,' because she hates those non-Christmassy holiday-neutral sayings. She thinks they're offensive."

Chase laughed. "You are hilarious, Rose Parsimmon. And full of surprises." He wrapped his arm around her small frame.

She leaned into him, resting her head against his chest. "That's me. One big surprise."

And since it seemed like her guard was down, he asked what he really wanted to know. "You got plans to find your mom?"

"That's highly confidential." She lifted her head, then twirled out from under his arm, a full three-sixty, so that she faced him head on.

He grinned.

"Just know this. I'm not sitting around all day throwing a pity party. I've got ideas. Three years till I'm eighteen and I can go where I want." She linked her fingers through his and started walking back toward school. "I've been coming here to buy my mom a present every year for the last five years. This is the first time I brought anyone with me."

"Yeah?"

"Yeah. Not even Becca."

They walked in silence for a long time. Chase listened to the scuffing of their shoes against the pavement. And the swoosh of passing cars. Once they left the sidewalk and looped onto the dirt path behind the school, he could hear their breaths. Chase's stomach growled.

Rose stopped in her tracks. "Shit. I forgot to buy you lunch."

"That's okay," Chase waved it away, hoping she couldn't hear the churning in his gut. "There are only a couple periods left."

"No." Rose dumped her backpack on the dirt and dug through it. "Wallah." She produced a Snickers Bar. "It's got peanuts. So that's protein."

Chase grinned. "Practically a balanced meal. Want to share?" Chase ripped it open and took a bite, then held out the bar to her.

Rose ignored Chase's outstretched hand. "Nah. I'll just have a taste." She stood on her tippy-toes, slipped her cool hands behind Chase's neck, and kissed him.

Chase nearly laughed. There he was, kissing the hottest girl in school, with food in his mouth for the second day in a row. This kiss felt different, though. Yesterday he'd been nervous, so it had a tentative, gentle feel. This time the kiss felt almost aggressive. Long and deep, like she was trying to swallow him whole. When she finally pulled away, he had no idea how much time had passed.

"Thanks for the taste," Rose whispered, unwrapping herself from him and wiping the chocolate from her lips. Chase self-consciously did the same.

He tried to say, "You're welcome," but looking back he wasn't sure if he'd even moved his mouth.

"Shit." Rose strapped on her backpack and grabbed his hand. "Let's hurry. I don't want to taint your perfect record with a tardy." They ran together, breathless, until they came to the school fence. "Here, give me a boost." She placed both hands on the chain links. "And yes, you may touch my butt."

Chase didn't complain.

10
CHASE

ALL CHASE COULD THINK ABOUT on the walk home from school was Rose.

Rose's eyes, deep and brown.

Her long hair, somehow forever silky.

Buying those chocolate almonds for Homeless Hillary.

The way she kissed. Like she was hungry for him.

Thoughts of Rose completely hijacked his mind. Maybe that was why he didn't notice Candy's mood until dinnertime.

Candy banged the pot onto the stove, splattering hot Campbell's Tomato Soup. Pinpricks of scalding soup landed on Chase's skin, piercing it. *Ouch*. He stepped back. "Tell me, Daisy," Candy said, in her complaining I-know-best-and-you-don't voice, "Do you think I enjoy getting personal phone calls from your principal?"

Daisy pulled her scraped knees to her chest and wrapped her arms around them, ducking her head like she was trying to fold herself up and disappear right into the kitchen chair. Poor kid. He hadn't even known she'd been in trouble.

"They definitely weren't calling me to say you've made the goddamn honor roll!" Candy swiveled her head over to Daisy, her eyes laced with pointed judgment. "And for stealing? It's embarrassing. *You're* embarrassing."

Daisy sat motionless—like the rest of the family was a swarm of bees and she didn't want to get stung. Chase's pulse quickened.

"Do you know what people will say?" Candy's lip-lined mouth looked like she had taken a sip of spoiled milk. "I know what people already think of me around here. And now...my daughter, the *thief.*"

That last word caught his heart. Chase closed his eyes. He didn't need to listen to this. Daisy could tune out Candy almost like pressing the mute button on the tube. But not Chase. He had no mute button. His face felt hot.

Candy continued, "And what are you gonna tell me? That you borrowed her watch? That she gave it to you? That you found it?"

Daisy made a sound Chase couldn't describe, as though she wanted to defend herself but couldn't find the right words.

Candy dropped a loaf of bread on the table. It knocked against Daisy's juice, tipping it over. Rivers of grape juice raced past a fork and streamed over the corner, soaking into Daisy's faded denim shorts. She scooted back in her chair. The dark purple liquid pooled on the edge of the table and drizzled onto the linoleum. Immediately it seemed to spread out toward the thin beige carpet that covered the living room half of the dining-living-kitchen room combo. "Shit," Candy cursed. Daisy held on to her wet shorts like she'd peed in them and was trying to cover it up.

"Help me, will you?" Candy said to Chase. "Grab a towel or something. The landlord will have a fit if we stain his carpet."

Daisy stared at her grape-juice-stained hands as if an answer was written there. "I just...I..." She started.

Chase shot her a look and thought to himself, You don't owe her an explanation. Me maybe, but not her.

"It was just sitting there," Daisy whispered. "By the handball court. I didn't think it—"

"Shit, Daisy." Candy wiped the table with a dish towel, catching the drips at the edge. "That's the problem with you. You never think. I don't know what it takes to get it through your goddamn thick head."

Chase gritted his teeth and tried to breathe. *Stay calm. Don't get into it. It's not worth it.*

Candy kneeled to mop up the purple puddle by her feet. Then she gathered the soaked towel up in her arms. "I know you're not the sharpest tool in the shed, but come *on*."

In less than a second, Chase saw Daisy's eyes register the meaning of the words and fill with emotion. Not hurt. Not anger. Shame. As if she was thinking, agreeing, "I am stupid." She wilted, her shoulders drooping forward, and Chase saw her distance herself a mile without taking a step. Her eyes just retreated inward, and her face went dead.

Chase balled his fists. Somewhere deep inside himself churned a guttural roar, and he turned on his heel to get away from it. "*Shut up!*" He threw the words toward Candy, but pointed his eyes away from her and toward his escape route. Anger burst through his veins so hotly that he could hardly see. The furniture colors blurred together as he searched for the door. *Out. Out. Get out of here. Stay calm.*

But as he shoved through the door, he slammed his right fist into the wall. It broke through the stucco as easily as if it were Styrofoam. He turned back, only to catch the expressions on Candy's and Daisy's faces. They looked at him like he'd turned into the Incredible Hulk right in front of their eyes. He'd seen those expressions before. But only when they were looking at Walter.

Chase ran away from those faces, barreling down the stairs two at a time, his chest so full of blistering air that he thought his heart would implode. He tore down the street, his eyes open but blind. He listened to the heavy sound of his sneakers scuffing against the sidewalk. Somehow the rhythm of it soothed him, and it gradually allowed his thoughts to slow. *Breathe*. Chase's skin glistened with sweat, and his thick legs vibrated from the pace. *Breathe*. Chase slowed his run to a walk.

An hour later, the knuckles on his right hand began to throb.

11
ROSE

TAKING CHASE ALONG TODAY HAD been a bit of a risk. The more she opened up, the more she'd be hurt if he wound up being an ass. But unless her radar was totally whacked, Chase didn't seem like that kind of guy.

After school, Rose beelined for her room, closing her door completely behind her with a soft click. She lay on her puke-worthy pink carpet, reaching far under her dust ruffle for the shoe box she'd hidden. Both the Parsimmons had bad knees, so they'd never be able look under there.

With her head half under the bed, Rose laid out the mementos from the last five years. Today's faceless figurine, a rock so shiny and smooth that it felt like silk in her hands, a pair of seashell earrings, a twisted French vanilla candle, and a little ceramic placard with the following words painted on in swirling black cursive: "Mothers hold their children's hands for a short while, but their hearts forever.—Author Unknown."

Mrs. P. had a hidden box too. Only Mrs. P.'s box didn't contain gifts, and Rose didn't have bad knees, nor any fear of climbing. Mrs. P. had hidden her box on the top shelf of her walk-in closet, behind her rows of shoes. Rose discovered this hiding place when she was eleven and Mrs. P. started leaving her alone for chunks of time while she went to the market. Rose took extra care to make sure she placed everything back exactly where it went, and Mrs. P. had never been the wiser.

That whole year when she was eleven, Rose snatched every unsupervised opportunity to explore a new part of the house. Most of what she found was boring—a sewing box, a wedding album from years ago, and ancient handmade quilts. But in her search she also found Mrs. P.'s hidden box and a file of paperwork on herself. The paperwork all seemed to be legal documents and, for Rose at age eleven, nearly undecipherable. But the meaning of the box became clear instantaneously.

Rose remembered sitting cross-legged on the carpet when she opened the box for the first time. She sifted through the contents, a strange churning feeling in her gut. A photo of Rose at age five, her face dirty and tear-streaked, and missing a tooth. A plastic ring, bubblegum pink, that Rose remembered getting from one of those twenty-five-cent toy dispensers in the drugstore. A business card for a smoke shop with clearly printed letters on the back side. She remembered her mother placing it in her pocket.

Emergency—911 Maria—895-4932
Fire station on the Blvd.
I love you, Rose.
—Mama

Rose learned to read by four and a half, and whenever Mama had to leave her alone for a job, she put the card in her pocket. In case of emergency. Rose learned how to dial the phone in room they rented, and grandma-like Maria lived one floor up. Rose didn't remember ever feeling frightened. A couple years ago, Rose had tried to track Maria down by dialing her number, but all she got was that automated voice saying the line was no longer in service.

There were also newspaper clippings, all crinkled along the edges. Rose unfolded them carefully, fearful that she'd tear them. The headings puzzled her. "Prostitution Still a Problem on Hollywood Boulevard—Outreach Programs in Development." "Adoption Returns: An Alarming Number of Adopted Children Are Returned to the System." "Reactive Attachment Disorder Common among Adopted Children." "The Modern Chumash: How They Are Faring Both On and Off Reservations." "Treatment of Choice for Maladjusted Adoptees: A Combination of Cognitive Behavioral Therapy and Psychiatric Medication." All the articles were dated back six years, back around when Rose was formally placed with the Parsimmons.

It took Rose a full year and a half longer to figure out her mom had been a prostitute. It bothered her a lot, at first. Then she sort of got used to the idea. Everyone had called her mom Jewels. Whether that was her street name or her real name, Rose didn't know. She just remembered thinking it was the prettiest name in the world. And Jewels had found a way to survive on the streets. To make enough money that she and Rose could rent a room. And eat. It all worked just fine until Jewels got caught.

Rose ran her finger over the swirling black words on the ceramic placard. Someday she'd track her mom down. Give her the gifts. Tell her she understood. If Rose had calculated correctly, she figured Jewels would be about thirty-two years old. If she hadn't gotten herself out of that lifestyle by now, Rose would help her.

The only sticking point was this—Rose didn't know Jewels' full name. Or her own, for that matter. The records had been sealed, and none of the file documents referred to Rose as anything but Rose Parsimmon. It was as if her original last name had been erased from this earth. As if it never existed.

12
CHASE

CHASE TRIED TO KEEP HIS eyes focused on those stupid Saturday morning cartoons Daisy dragged him out of bed to watch. Images of Rose climbing the school fence, kissing him, and wrapping her arms around his neck merged with those of Candy and Daisy staring at him like he was a monster.

Chase glanced to his left for the hundredth time this morning and saw the jagged hole he'd left deep in the wall. His eyes felt dry and scratchy, maybe because of all the crying he'd done under his covers last night. And his brain seemed muddled. Knowing what he wanted to do was one thing, but actually doing it was another.

"Let's see a movie." Candy held a cup of steaming coffee with both hands. She'd slept in a big T-shirt and boxers, and still had her hair pulled back in her just-woke-up ponytail. Chase heard Candy's words floating past, but he didn't bother looking up.

Daisy bounced off the couch. "A movie?" Her voice squeaked. "At the theaters?"

"You would think I just offered to buy you Disneyland." Candy said, chuckling. "Yes, you little spaz. At the theaters. They've got some good discount movies playing. And I've taken the day off."

"Yes! Can I bring a friend?"

Candy tapped her fingernails on her coffee cup. "I thought we'd just make today a family day."

"Cool!" Daisy turned and leaped onto Chase. "Can you come with us?" When he'd come home last night, Daisy had kept her distance. Like he might combust if she wasn't careful. But that didn't last. Any remaining hesitation had long since melted away.

Candy had been slower to warm up. But she'd made his favorite breakfast this morning—sausages and pancakes. For some reason, this got under Chase's skin. Pretending things were okay when they weren't. Big surprise.

So when Chase came back to Candy's statement with a retort, "You mean the 'budmeister' isn't tagging along?" his sarcasm seemed thick, even to his own ears. Even if he was talking about Candy's loser boyfriend.

Candy rolled her eyes. "Did you hear me say *family* day? Clearly we need to work on getting along better as a family." Her mouth stretched thin. "Are you coming or not?"

"Nah." Chase turned his eyes back to the screen. Like he really wanted to hang out with his mom and his baby sister all day. He had important things to do. Like taking a nap, watching TV, making it to the next level on a video game, or fantasizing about hotter-than-hot Rose Parsimmons. Trying to figure out "what" they were exactly. Was it all still a bargain for her? Lunch for a week in exchange for a pack of cigarettes? Or was it something more? Chase tried to reassure himself. She wouldn't have kissed him like *that*, if she didn't feel something.

"Please, Chase! Please?" Daisy gave him the puppy dog eyes and wrapped her arms around him. "Please?" She smelled all fruity and sugary, probably from the Froot Loops she'd scarfed down for breakfast.

"Nah. I got things to do," he told Daisy, tousling her hair and trying to swallow around the tightness in his throat.

Candy pressed her lips together hard, like she'd expected this.

Chase had a thousand things he wanted to say, but he folded his arms and turned back to *SpongeBob*. He said nothing.

It took until the next morning for Chase to finally work up the balls to talk to Candy. He walked up to her room first thing in the morning and peeked around the corner. Still in bed. Hair like a bird's nest. Mascara and eyeliner caked on from the night before, only streaked across her face. Used tissues scattered around the bed like holiday decorations. So she'd been crying.

Chase watched her sleep for a while, not sure what to do. Then he felt like some kind of a pervert, watching his mother sleep. So he woke her up. Her eyes were instantly awake—immediately sharp—as if she'd only been resting, not sleeping. No anger in those eyes. Just this sadness, heavy and thick, showing she knew why he'd come.

"I'm sorry," Chase mumbled, looking at his feet. "For what I did."

"I know." she'd murmured. "I'm sorry too. For the way I went after Daisy. That girl needs a wake-up call sometimes, but I know I don't always go about it in the best way. Parenting doesn't come with a handbook, you know."

Chase nodded.

"You reminded me of him." Candy smoothed her hair, then sighed. "Of your father."

Ouch. She might as well have socked him in the gut. Chase took a sharp breath in. He stood for a moment, and then he sank down next to her. "I reminded myself too."

Candy looked at him, her eyes full of something he didn't know. "You *acted* like him, but you aren't like him. I know you, Chase. You aren't your father."

"But…"

"But you saw what he did to me, what he did to you. For all those years. Maybe you thought that was normal. Maybe you thought that was okay."

"No!" Chase pushed the word out of his mouth like it had a bad taste. "I *never* thought it was okay!"

"Look, Chase." Candy sat herself up in bed so her eyes were level to his. "I let that be a part of your life for too long, and I am *so* sorry."

Chase looked at his hands.

"Here's the thing, Chase. When he drank, your dad was an angry man. Felt like the world wronged him, you know, and all that. If he so much as bumped into a wall, it was the wall's fault for being in his way." Candy put her hand on Chase's shoulder. "You are not that way. Sure you get royally pissed off, but it's different from the way your dad did. So my take—for what it's worth—is that you gotta find a way to get some serenity in your life."

"Serenity?"

"Like peace. Peacefulness." Candy swung her legs over the side of the bed.

This irritated Chase for a minute, although he wasn't sure why. "And how the hell am I supposed to do that? Smoke bud like your boyfriend?"

"Real mature, Chase. Thanks. He happens to have a medical condition, just so you know. Anything he smokes is prescribed."

"Just like ten percent of the seniors at my school. A medical condition, my ass." Chase tried not to laugh. "You really pick the winners, don't you?"

Candy stared at him, unblinking. Just as he figured he'd blown it, she sighed and crossed her arms, but then a chuckle escaped. "I dumped him last night. You were right. A royal loser." Soon her tough front melted, and they were both laughing.

13
ROSE

BECCA CORNERED ROSE AT SCHOOL on Monday morning. "Tell me you love me!" she ordered, looking like she was trying not to smile.

"You know I do." Rose crossed her arms. "But what do you want?"

"I found you the perfect job." Becca danced around in a circle.

"Illustrating for Disney?" Rose joked.

"Get real. My mom's day care is opening a new class. They need to fill three afternoon positions. You and I can each take one."

"Day care?" Rose's voice went up three octaves. "You know I'm allergic to children. They make me itch." Lie. She liked little kids, but they didn't go with her image.

"Oh, come on, it's easy. You can sit and talk about Disney movies all day long. It'll be perfect for you."

"Hmmm." Rose considered, her thoughts tripping ahead of her. Three positions. "Only if you get Chase hired for the third spot."

Becca laughed so hard she nearly choked on her own tongue. "Are you serious? If he sits down in the wrong place, he'll squash one of the little buggers."

"That's the deal." Rose winked. "Take it or leave it."

"You owe me," Becca warned.

"I always do."

Rose found Chase at his locker, and he said "yes" before she even finished explaining. But now, on the first day of work, little kids hung on Chase like a tree trunk, begging for rides, books, and games. He looked petrified, like there were spiders crawling on him rather than kids.

Rose kicked Chase's foot. "Relax. This isn't rocket science. Let's just pull out a bucket of blocks. That should occupy the little monsters."

Chase raised his eyebrow at Rose. She raised her eyebrow right back. Passing messages with their eyes wasn't quite the same as a date, but it was something. Rose could feel tension emanating from their two bodies like a magnetic force. Not a bad tension. Just a pull—a desire—that made her skin long to connect with his, even just to hold his hand.

Within an hour, Rose sported yellow paint streaked in her hair like bad highlights. Becca's whole mouth had turned a lovely color of blue after a four-year-old dared her to sample the play dough. Chase seemed to be warming up. He followed a mess of munchkins around, acting like a dragon. He tugged Rose's hair as he dragon-stomped past.

And suddenly, the pull was too much. Rose elbowed Becca. "Chase and I'll get the snack ready."

Becca glanced at the clock and rolled her eyes. "I'm not sure it really takes two people to pour apple juice into Dixie cups, but whatever." She kneeled next to a little girl with braids and helped her pin the paint apron over her clothes. "I'm going to time you, though. You're both on the clock."

Rose grabbed Chase by the hand. "Remember, I'm your best friend in the world," she said as she pulled Chase into the kitchen.

Becca snorted. "You're assuming best-friend status means I wouldn't rat you out."

Rose just winked and tugged Chase along with her. His hand felt heavy in hers. She eyed him as they sliced oranges and broke graham crackers into fourths. Rose shifted her position so that she stood directly next to him. She leaned in to him and laced her arm through his. "Here. I'll help you." She arranged the crackers on plates, all with her arm linked. Then she stood on her tippy-toes and pressed her lips onto his cheek. She felt just the faintest prickle of stubble, like maybe he'd started shaving already.

He stiffened.

"What's your deal?" Rose unlinked herself and moved back away from him. She'd always been so careful not to care when she flirted with a guy. To make it purely physical and purely fun, something she could toss away at a moment's notice. But something about Chase was different, and that scared her.

"It's only our first day," Chase whispered. "I don't want to get fired just yet."

"Oh, so that means we should wait until the second day to make out on the kitchen counter?" Rose grinned mischievously. "Get real, you dork. I just kissed your cheek. A little harmless flirtation never hurt anyone. Just makes work more fun."

Chase twisted and faced her. "Look, Rose, this isn't a game to me." He cleared his throat. "I really like you."

Rose's heart skipped a beat, a warning sign. "I like you too." She averted her eyes and focused on setting all the Dixie cups onto a tray. "Just trying to spice things up."

"Well, if that's your goal, you're doing a good job." Chase picked up the second tray. "But I'm not sure I can handle all that, uh, spicing and at the same time stay focused on the sixteen preschoolers in the next room. Can we save it for after work?"

"There *is* no after work for me, Chase." Rose tried not to sound whiny. "This is it. I'm grounded."

"Not forever."

"You don't know the Parsmissions." Rose carried her tray carefully toward the door. She pushed through it but let it slam closed behind her, right in Chase's face. She sighed. Maybe Chase didn't get her after all.

14
CHASE

FOR THE NEXT WEEK, ROSE seemed to sink within herself. Chase hoped he hadn't completely blown his chances with her. She seemed like the kind of girl who wouldn't get burned twice. And he hadn't *meant* to burn her. God, he was an idiot. He had the hottest girl in the tenth grade hitting on him, and what did he do? Told her "not now"? Was he clinically insane? He wished he could go back in time and redo that moment. Somehow it came out wrong. Or she took it wrong.

Chase tried to play it cool and focus on not seeming desperate. Girls didn't like desperate. Girls liked confident. Aloof. Or so he thought. Because except for a few meaningless make-out sessions in dark hallways at random parties, he hadn't had a whole lot of experience in the girl department. Maybe if he was more experienced, he'd know how to handle a girl like Rose. But things at work were hopping, and the learning curve was steep, so that helped him occupy his mind. Plus, just being near Rose made his pulse quicken.

"Can I sign out my kids?" A tight-lipped woman tapped her foot and crossed her arms. The kids scrambled up and over to their mother, the little one tripping over an untied shoelace. "Clumsy!" She smacked the kid on the butt, hard enough to look like it stung, but he didn't flinch. Chase handed her the clipboard silently, biting his lip to keep from saying something rude.

The last mother slipped in. "Sorry I'm late. I got caught up." The woman grinned so wide her mouth looked horse-like, showing a row of clear braces. Those things were supposed to be invisible, but they weren't. Just kind of yellow, but not in a gross way. "I know Rebecca, of course."

Becca straightened up. "Chase and Rose, this is Mrs. Rosenberg." Chase and Rose nodded blankly. "She's Matthew's mother and our assistant rabbi at Beth Shalom."

A little boy scrambled to his feet, dropping his Matchbox car with a clatter. He squealed, "Mommy!" He moved like a penguin as he toddled toward her.

"I hope he wasn't too much trouble for you," Mrs. Rosenberg said almost to herself, not like she really expected an answer. "Come here, little man." She pulled the boy into her arms and kissed his head. She looked back up at them, her eyes still shining. "Thanks again, guys." She flashed that wide smile again and headed out the door, whispering to Matthew about dinner and bath time.

Chase pulled his backpack strap over his shoulder. "She seems cool," he said after Mrs. Rosenberg had moved out of earshot. "I'd like to come with you sometime," he said absentmindedly, packing up his things.

"Who're you talking to?" Rose asked.

"Becca. I'd like to come to temple services some time. Just to check it out."

Becca opened her mouth in mock surprise. "You gonna convert?"

Chase shoved his hands in his pockets. "From what? Don't you have to have a religion in order to convert to something else?"

"I thought you were Baptist or born again or something," Becca said, wandering around the room, returning stray toys to their places.

"When I was little, we went to church. A few different ones, actually, depending on my dad's mood. Now I'm kind of on strike."

"What for?" Rose jumped into the conversation. *At least she was starting conversations again.* She grabbed a sponge from the sink and started wiping down the tables.

"I guess it's the same reason Daniel's all gung ho about Buddhism."

"The meditation?" Becca asked from under the play-dough table.

"No—just something different from what you know." Chase shifted his weight. "Maybe I'm religion shopping. Your rabbi just seems so... chill. Kind of Zen-like too. She probably does yoga and eats granola and hand-squeezed orange juice for breakfast."

"Oh, is that what you look for in a rabbi?" Rose bit her lip like she was trying not to laugh. Okay, now she was finding him funny again. Maybe there was hope.

"No. I don't know—maybe she seems in touch, or centered or some crap like that." Chase stretched his backpack straps in front of him, his eyes on Rose.

"God help us. Daniel's rubbing off on you, and I can only handle one Zen freak in my life at a time." Becca wiped her hands on her jeans, surveying the room. "I think we're pretty much done, guys. You can take off, if you want."

Rose glanced at the clock. "Five minutes early? Five whole minutes of freedom until Mrs. P. arrives to put me under lock and key?" She mock-twirled like a dancer. "Question is, just what can I do to fill up five whole minutes?" She paused and eyed Chase.

"Well, we *are* off work. Technically." Chase hoped he wasn't noticeably salivating.

Rose flipped her hair over her shoulder. "What *exactly* did you have in mind?" He could tell by her grin that she was going to make him work for it.

"Let's just say, five minutes is a perfect amount of time."

Becca pressed her hands to her ears. "You guys do realize I'm still here, right? *Please!*"

Chase opened the door to the coat closet and swung his arm to invite Rose in, acting like she was stepping into a limousine, rather than a coat closet. "Yeah, I guess a little privacy is in order."

Five minutes later, he could tell with certainty that he had *not* blown it with Rose Parsimmon.

15
ROSE

ROSE HAD FIGURED OUT A survival trick a long time ago. Finding secret projects gave her something to look forward to. Not projects in the traditional sense. Projects Rose-style. Like planning and exacting a devious plan (and watching the Parsimmons' reactions). Collecting secret gifts for her mother. Sneaking through the Parsimmons' files to try to learn more about her biological mother. Seducing a boy. It'd started out that way with Chase, sure. And looking forward to stolen moments helped her get through the days. But it was turning into much more.

And that made her nervous.

At first she'd tried her best to make it flirty and fun with Chase, and to stay away from anything meaningful, but apparently he was not that kind of guy. He'd looked so cute, standing there a couple weeks ago being philosophical about religion. Since then, she and Chase had made it a point to be super-efficient when they cleaned up at the end of the day, in the hopes that there might be a little extra, uh, *free time*.

Like today. Rose swept the entryway of the day care while she waited for the last few kids to be picked up. Becca disinfected the tiny toys. And Chase wiped down the tables. Rose gave him a playful kick in the butt as she passed him. Definitely a squeeze-worthy butt.

Suddenly her eyes spotted something and she froze. She stared outside the open classroom door. As carefully as if she were walking on a plate of thin glass, she tiptoed outside.

"What the...?"

"She's gone loco," Becca teased loudly. "Crazy in the head."

Rose hunched over the ground and held out her palm, face up. A rough pink tongue lapped at it thirstily. Two large almond-shaped eyes stared up at her. Then the kitten nuzzled her knees. Rose scooped it up into her arms. "Look what I found," she whispered, breathless.

Becca followed her out, straddling the door frame. "It's a stray."

"No shit, Einstein." Rose's retort came slowly, without its normal sting. Instead her voice was filled with wonder. "She's tiny. And all alone."

"She might belong to someone." Chase peeked over Becca's shoulder.

"There's no tag, and she's out wandering by herself. She'll need a warm place to sleep." Rose stood up and leaned against the stucco outside wall, feeling the rough stubble press against her back. "So...I say she's mine now."

"Well, put her somewhere—we've still got to finish cleaning, and we have a few more kids here," Becca urged, still standing in the doorway.

"Can I wear your sweatshirt, Chase?" Rose scarcely took her eyes off the cat, as if she might vanish into midair like some magician's idea of a cruel joke. Chase tossed the Nike sweatshirt at her, and with it came a wave of his smell. She slipped it over her head, and for a moment, the rugged sweetness engulfed her. It was almost as if his arms were wrapped around her. Rose tucked the bottom of the sweatshirt into her jeans, making a little pocket. She pulled the neck of the sweatshirt out so that she could gently place the kitten inside. "There. You gotta love a baggy sweatshirt. You can hide almost anything. Remember, Becca?"

Becca groaned. "Don't remind me. And don't tell Chase. You'll corrupt him."

"Hey, is there room in there for me?" Chase asked, pulling out the neck of the sweatshirt to peek in. A soft purring sound drifted up. "So you're gonna keep the cat? Will your parents care?"

"They won't know. I'll wear your sweatshirt home. I'll tell them it's Becca's."

Becca scrunched up her nose. "I don't get it. Why don't you just ask them if you can keep the cat? You know Mrs. P. is a sucker for cats."

Rose wrapped her arms around her middle protectively. "No way. If they know, it's one more thing they can take away from me from the next time I commit some mortal sin." Rose peeked down at the kitten, all curled up. "No," she said into her sweatshirt, her voice all muffled. "This kitten is my secret."

Chase stepped away. "Well, what are you gonna call her?"

"I have the name picked out. Brace yourself for its beauty." Rose waited. "Nala."

"Nala?" Becca asked, starting to laugh. "Like from *The Lion King*?" She shook her head. "Shit, Rose. You're a Disney addict. You need serious help."

Rose glanced at the clock, and then stuck her head out the front door. "I do need help. The warden is coming, and I've got to sneak Nala home without her making a noise."

Rose stayed another five minutes while the last few kids were picked up, and then she left, Nala snuggled next to her. As she walked out the front door, she couldn't help but smile. Because now she had a new project. Just in time to help her survive winter break.

16
ROSE

IN ROSE'S WHOLE LIFE IT had never snowed in Simi Valley, but for the entire two weeks of winter break she felt as if someone had draped a cloak of snowy gloom over her. Probably because with no school and the day care being closed, she was home pretty much all the time. Nala, instant messaging, and a few Walmart trips were her only reprieves from listening to Mrs. P. explain the benefits of purchasing a live Christmas tree versus a plastic tree, the constant home improvement infomercials they had running, and the advice of Dr. Phil blaring from the television screen.

Rose didn't have a computer in her room, so to instant message, she hid Nala in her closet with a fluffy blanket bed and set herself up at the computer in the Parsimmons' office, armed with a glass of water and red licorice. She pulled up two sites, so if Mr. or Mrs. P. happened to walk past, she could simply click on the second site. That way they wouldn't see she was chatting with a b-o-y.

Chase: I got a present for you.

Rose: Really?

Rose couldn't help but feel that bubbly, little kid excitement.

Chase: Yeah. I've missed you. I'm going through Rose withdrawal. When can I see you?

Rose: I can sneak out.

Chase: Nah. I don't want you to get in trouble. Can't I just come over?

Rose: That would be the trouble. No way. I'm grounded, remember?

Chase: I can hide it for you on the front porch.

Rose: Okay. Leave it in the planter tonight. Late. After ten, at least.

And now a new project. Rose didn't have anything prepared to give Chase. But she could draw him something. She padded back to her bedroom, past Mrs. P. stringing popcorn onto dental floss with a sewing needle and glued to a show about conspiracy theories. Rose eased the door shut so that the click was barely perceptible. And pulled out her art supplies. The one set of gifts from the Parsimmons that she truly treasured. She'd given them hints that year, cutting out the ad for the art kit and laying it on the kitchen table.

Nala nudged through a crack in her closet and wrapped herself around Rose's legs. The pencils took on a life of their own in her hands. She sketched an image of Chase, with six day-care kids climbing on his back. She hoped he'd like it. Rose folded in halves, then fourths, and then eighths, until she felt confident that it was small enough to be hidden. She wrote Chase's name on the front in sprawling cursive and then tucked the sketch into the planter.

Rose waited up. Long after the television switched off in the Parsimmons' bedroom, she crept out into the hall and sat in the armchair by the window, her face pressed against the cool glass. And waited.

She must've fallen asleep there, because when she woke, the sun had already begun its slow creep into the sky, and when she craned her neck, she glimpsed a small red box with a bow. Rose glanced at the clock, hoping she still had some time before Mr. P. got up and made his trek to the Daily Drip. She slipped out the front door, retrieved the box, and hid it in the sleeve of her sweatshirt. Then padded her way back to her room.

She only opened it once she had closed her door safely behind her.

A necklace. Dainty. Gold chain. And a curved golden heart in the center. She'd seen it before, at that boutique store in town.

So totally not her style.

But strangely enough, it didn't matter. She latched it around her neck and fell back asleep in bed with the heart pressed to her lips and Nala warming her toes.

17
CHASE

THE FIRST WEEK BACK AFTER winter break, someone dumped a baby. Just like you'd dump a ripped T-shirt or a used condom. Thrown away like trash, right there in the girls' locker room after school. Wrapped him all up in a towel and just left him to be discovered by a janitor. Alive.

Gossip and shock swarmed around the school. So did cops.

"It had to be a student, right?" Becca put a pen cap in her mouth, sitting cross-legged in front of the big oak tree at lunch. Rose squatted next to her, wrapping her arms around herself and leaning against Chase. Work at the day care had been busy this week, making lunch the best time to connect. And now that Daniel had started joining him at Rose's and Becca's tree trunk, the whole gang sat together. Chase ignored Daniel's moans and groans about being seen with his little sister.

"Who else could it be?" Rose seemed wired. Like she'd just downed two Monsters. She stood. "Becca, can you stop chewing that pen cap? Damn, you're so orally fixated." Becca stuck out her tongue. "Aren't you glad I'm taking Intro to Psych this term?"

"I don't get it." Chase complained, his voice sounding strange.

Even. Controlled. Steady. The opposite of how he really felt inside. "In Freshman Health they practically cram a menu of options down our throats. Everyone's all obsessed with that safe-haven law—like this girl could've just dropped the baby off at the hospital, no questions asked. They couldn't even tell her parents."

"Yeah, but come on. Wouldn't your parents know anyway?" Becca asked.

"Ninety percent of parents are clueless," Rose pointed out.

"Or maybe *your* parents are ninety percent clueless." Becca stuck the pen cap back in her mouth like a toothpick.

Rose grinned. "That might be more like it. They're clueless about the cat, that's for sure. Nala's all set up with a little makeshift bed on my shoe shelf in my closet. She could totally jump down, but she doesn't *know* she can jump down, so she just plays up there all day while I'm at school. I've got a mini litter box set up, and I can dump it easy enough. Maybe their eyesight and hearing are going, but the parents don't have a freaking clue."

"Couldn't they search your room or something?" Chase asked. Rose smelled nice, like girly shampoo and fabric softener. All he wanted to do was grab her hand and pull her somewhere they could be alone. It'd been torture staying away from her all winter break.

"They flunked Parenting 101, okay? I'm about ten steps ahead of them." Rose ran her hand through Chase's tousled hair, and it caught in the unruliness. As she worked her fingers through his curls, she brought Chase's head toward her and he could see right down her shirt. Chase's heartbeat tripled its normal speed.

Rose acted all natural, like she hadn't just given him a peep-show tease. "This whole thing is unbelievable. I feel sorry for the girl, whoever she is."

"Yeah, but if you're stupid enough to get yourself pregnant, you gotta figure out something." Becca brought the pen cap out of her mouth for a moment, like it was a cigarette, but she caught herself. "I mean what do you do when life gives you lemons? You make lemonade, right?"

Chase shook his head to clear visions of Rose's black bra from it. And what he knew lay beneath the bra. God, he was horny. He had to get himself under control. "I've always hated that expression."

"You don't make freaking lemonade," Rose argued. "If any fool gave me lemons, I'd tell him to pucker up and I'd shove those lemons right up his ass."

"Why does that not surprise me?" Becca smiled and sighed loudly.

"How do you make that okay in your own head?" Chase asked. "Dumping a baby?"

"You can make a lot of things okay in your head. You can make anything okay." Rose stared at her hands.

"Or...you cannot." Chase touched Rose's chin with his fingertips, raising it slowly until her eyes met his own. "You just can try to be a better person instead."

"Thanks, Chase, for the inspirational sermon." Rose held her gaze there, unblinking, the corners of her eyes crinkling. "But where's the fun in that?"

And in that moment, an idea struck Chase. He pocketed it away. He'd need it later.

"Mom?" Chase hung back by the door frame, watching Candy use a hair dryer to blow out her hair with a round prickly brush. "Did you go to church before you met Walter?"

She paused and looked at him funny through her reflection in the mirror. "Not really. Just Easter and Christmas, that's about it. Why?"

"I don't know." Chase wrapped his fingers around the door frame, trying to think of how he could say what he wanted to say. He struggled for a minute and then just threw it out there the best he could. "If you weren't all that religious, well…" Chase fumbled his words. "I guess I'm wondering why I'm here."

"Why we live in Simi Valley? What do you mean?" Candy shut off the hair dryer.

"No. Why I'm alive. Why I exist." Chase noticed how much taller he was than his mother. She stared at him blankly, like he was speaking a foreign language. He sighed. "It's no secret that I wasn't exactly planned. You were sixteen. Did you ever think about other options?"

"What?" She put down the hair dryer and left the round brush dangling from her head. "What do you mean?"

"Come on, Mom. I'm nearly an adult. Shit," he said, groaning. "Just give it to me straight."

Candy brought her hands back up to the round brush and slowly released her hair. "Sure." She sighed, deflated. "Sure, I thought about other options."

"Oh."

"Come on, Chase. I panicked." Candy turned away from the mirror to face him directly. "I knew even back then that Walter sure as hell wasn't gonna be no Prince Charming. He'd already slapped me around a couple of times. And there was a free clinic the next town over…so I thought…well, I thought…" She broke off.

"Oh."

"But then I couldn't. *I couldn't.* I started to fall in love with you, and I couldn't. You probably weren't more than the size of a popcorn kernel, but I loved you. I loved who I imagined you to be." Candy's eyes misted over. "And then the first time I felt you move inside me…shit. Then I could think of nothing else."

"Oh."

"Sure, when you actually showed up, you were a hell of a lot more work than I thought you'd be. I felt in over my head, like I was drowning even a couple of times, and I sure as shit know I messed up a lot of things. But I always loved you. And whether you know it or not, you taught me a lot about life and about myself. I'm grateful for that."

"Oh." Chase chewed on something in his mind. Something he didn't want to ask. Because he didn't want to know the answer. *I bet Walter was pushing for an abortion, because then he would have been off the hook. He probably didn't even care that it was a sin. Because beating your wife and your kids has to be a sin, and he seemed to find plenty of time for that.* Instead he just nodded. "I guess I already knew that."

Candy reached out for his hand. Her touch irritated him, but he didn't pull away. Her acrylic nails glowed tangerine. "You doing some soul-searching, bud?"

"Maybe." Chase shrugged, not really sure where his thoughts were taking him, and not sure he wanted to go there, anyway.

"Well, here're my two cents on soul searching if you want to hear it, because I've done my fair share." Candy paused like she was waiting for him to answer, but he didn't, so she went ahead. "A little soul-searching can make you a better man, but too much of it can drive you completely crazy."

18

CHASE

ROSE SAT IN THE MIDDLE of the day-care classroom, her hair braided thickly today, making her look more like an Indian princess than ever. She wore a white scarf and a form-fitting turtleneck, snug enough to make her boobs look big. Chase couldn't help but stare. He tried to pull himself away, but it felt like his feet were glued to the floor.

If anything made Chase believe in a higher power, it was beauty. Natural beauty, like the rolling Santa Susana mountains that surrounded Simi Valley, where the Hollywood types went to film movies and episodes of television shows. And the beauty of a smoking-hot girl. If he wanted this relationship to progress any further—and he sure as hell did—he had to put his big idea into action. That meant he had to work up the courage to talk to Mrs. P. If he could win her over, convince her he was good for Rose, maybe he could take Rose on a real date.

Rose's cheeks were flushed as she sat there on the floor, building and rebuilding a Lego tower that Matthew knocked down over and over. "More!" Matthew laughed, clapping his hands.

Becca scrubbed the art table down and threw Chase an "oh please" look, so Chase forced himself to move around the room, cleaning up, or at least trying to look as though he was cleaning up rather than just salivating over Rose. Nearly all the kids had been picked up, after all.

Mrs. Rosenberg brushed past Chase's shoulder as she made her way over to Matthew. "I guess you got some good playing in today." She touched the clump of glue stuck in his hair. Then, "Rose, do you mind if I ask you a question?"

"Nope." Rose shook her head, one of her braids hanging over her shoulder. Chase wet a sponge in the sink.

"Rebecca told me you're an only child and that you were adopted, and I've been curious about your experience." Chase saw Rose stiffen visibly, and Mrs. Rosenberg put out her hand. "I'll tell you why. My husband and I are planning to adopt a second child. We don't want Matthew to grow up without a sibling. And so my question for you is, 'Would you have wanted your parents to adopt a second child?'" Mrs. Rosenberg said, wetting her finger in her mouth and trying to wipe a smudge off Matthew's face.

Chase wiped the snack table down, pretending he wasn't listening. "Oh, you don't want to adopt," Rose warned Mrs. Rosenberg.

"Why not?"

"It won't be the same." Rose lowered her voice. "You won't be able to love an adopted kid as much as you love Matthew. Because he or she won't be your blood."

"Well, you're wrong about that. Matthew is adopted, and I can't imagine loving him more." Mrs. Rosenberg flashed a toothy smile.

"No shi—I mean, seriously?"

"Yes. And I want him to have a brother or a sister."

Chase stacked the baby chairs. He watched Rose wrap her fingers around a braid and pull it a little, as if that would help her understand. "You just—you look like you belong with him, like you match or something."

"Well, I do. I waited for him for a long time. And God put us together. Now I've just got to get him working on finding Matthew a sibling." Mrs. Rosenberg smiled, then she exited the classroom door, holding Matthew, his arms wrapped tightly around her neck. She lifted her hand to wave good-bye.

Rose waited until the door clicked shut, and then she snapped at Becca, her voice low. "Why are you spreading my business?"

Becca spoke softly, her voice matching Rose's. "Sorry, Rose. But not everyone thinks the way you think, you know. Maybe it's not so bad to get another person's perspective. Most people who adopt love their kids."

"Not *my* parents," Rose countered reflexively, watching them leave.

"You're one of my best friends, Rose, and I love you…but that's a load of crap."

Rose's head jerked up. Her eyes sparked hot enough to start a fire. "And who the hell asked you? You don't know what happens in my house."

Becca folded her arms in front of her chest. "I'm your friend, Rose. That gives me the right to tell it to you like it is." Chase seriously considered slowly backing out of the room with his hands up, but he didn't want to look like a wuss. "Your parents are controlling, simple-minded hicks. But that doesn't mean they don't care about you. Why would they adopt you if they didn't want you? Why would they keep you if they didn't want you? Have you ever thought about that?"

Rose stood up stiffly, her arms stuck to her sides and her fists clenched. Chase dumped a bunch of plastic dishes into the playhouse kitchen. "You don't know anything. You don't know what they've done to me."

Chase's heartbeat doubled. *What had they done to her?*

Becca's cheeks flushed, and she stepped closer. "Do you ever think maybe your parents *wanted* to connect with you? Like way back, when you first got adopted?" She took in a deep breath, like a swimmer doing laps. "Maybe *you* pushed *them* away. Maybe *you* were the one that didn't want *them*—maybe *you* were the one who didn't love *them*, instead of the other way around. Your parents drive you crazy—and they drive me crazy too—but they wouldn't make it their life's mission to 'save you' or 'fix you' if they didn't care."

Whatever they'd done, it must have been bad.

Chase watched Rose's face grow stony and distant. Her eyes glazed over and she physically shrank inward, like a turtle retreating into its shell. Today was most definitely not a good day to introduce himself to Rose's mom. He'd have to wait for the right time.

"Who ever said I wanted to be saved?" Rose whispered.

NOW

19
CHASE

RUN! **CHASE BARRELS TOWARD ROSE'S** house, wearing what he'd worn to bed—his flannel pajama bottoms and a mismatched sweatshirt. *Faster!* He barely feels the burn in his calves, quads, and chest, even though his legs have never pumped so hard. The streets of Simi Valley blur past. Cracked sidewalk lined with trees, and blocks and blocks of tract housing all melt together as if he's riding a motorcycle, maybe because of his speed or maybe because he's crying. He wipes his arm over his eyes, pumping faster.

His thoughts zip past, one after another, misfiring, ricocheting around his brain. Chase nearly skids to a stop in front of the Parsimmons' porch. Once there, though, sweaty and panting like a dog, Chase panics.

What's he gonna do now? It's the middle of the freaking night, somewhere between Christmas Eve and Christmas morning. Last thing he needs is Mr. Parsimmon coming after him with a shotgun or something. Shotgun. Maybe Rose *does* have access to a gun. Crap.

Chase edges around the back of the house, looking for Rose's window. He cups his hands around his eyes and presses them to the glass. Blackness. Double crap. He raps his knuckles against the glass softly. *Come on. Open the window.* No answer. Too bad he can't don a Santa suit and slide down the chimney.

He balls his fists and presses them against his temples. *Shit. Time for a judgment call.* If Rose isn't dead, now she'll hate him more than she already did. He makes his way back to the porch, gritting his teeth, and rings her doorbell. The *ding-dong* echoes through the house, loud. Loud enough to wake the neighbors. Then other sounds. Shifting, creaking, padding of feet, clicking of the screen door.

Mrs. Parsimmon peeks out, her hair standing up at all ends. Her eyes widen. She hesitates, looking around and taking in his whole appearance. Chase touches his hair. He must have a windblown, curly bed head of his own, and his eyes must be bloodshot from the crying. "You look a mess, young man." She holds the screen door in front of her like a shield. Like she isn't sure if he'll attack her. "It's the middle of the night. Does your mother know where you are?"

"Rose," he blurts out at first, like an idiot. "I've come about Rose. I think she's going to hurt herself. Maybe she already has."

Shock registers in Mrs. Parsimmon's eyes. It lasts a good sixty seconds, while she ushers him into the house. She flings open Rose's bedroom door. The shock hardens, then crystallizes. Because the room's empty. Bed made, neat and smooth. Closet closed. Walls bare, but with tiny holes, as if she'd tacked things up with pushpins and then pulled them all out. Desk straightened. A pile of sketches stacked in the corner. Mrs. Parsimmon takes a deep, jagged breath in, like she's stepped in a pool of freezing water.

Chase stares at the room, trying to interpret this sick gut feeling, this intuition that floods his senses. The room doesn't have Rose's energy at all. It feels barren. Empty. *Dead.* No trace of her personality.

He remembers the way Rose looked when he'd last seen her mother escorting her to school. Zombie-like, as if she'd retreated into herself. Man, is that how she's been for the last eight months? Like a shell?

He turns to Mrs. Parsimmon. "When was the last time you saw her?"

Mrs. Parsimmon's upper lip trembles—not in an about-to-cry way, but rather like she's about to combust. A fine line of sweat gathers along that upper lip. "Why do you care?" she accuses Chase sadly, but she doesn't wait for an answer. "I have been trying to get that child on the right path for the last eleven years." She flings open the door to the closet. Half empty. "But she blocks me at every turn." She sighs, long and deep. "Sometimes it feels so personal, like she's just looking for ways to hurt me. And what's this? Running off on Christmas? That's a royal slap in the face if I ever saw one."

Chase tries to keep her focused. "Where do you think she'd have gone?"

"That child hasn't spoken a word to me since we pulled her out of school."

"That was like eight months ago." He hears panic in his own voice.

"Not a word. I have never seen anyone so stubborn."

"She hasn't spoken for *eight months*?" In a weird *Twilight Zone*–like role reversal, Chase is the parent, and Mrs. Parsimmon the child. She even looks like a child, sitting there slumped on the bed all forlorn, as if she's being punished. "Are you *serious*?"

The sarcasm jolts Mrs. Parsimmon out of herself. "Don't you dare judge me! It's not like I didn't try to get her help! She spits any *help* back in my face!" she cries. Chase just stares back at her with even eyes. "You have no idea what I've gone through with that girl. What she's put us through. I know she makes us out to be jail wardens, but we have done our best. We've given her everything she could have ever wanted."

Maybe she wanted more than things. Maybe she wanted to feel loved. Maybe I made her feel loved. But if so, why did she push me away?

Suddenly Mrs. Parsimmon seems to see the sketches on the desk for the first time. She reaches for them, holding them in trembling hands. Chase leans in to get a good look. The one on the top had been sketched entirely in pencil, but it is soft and detailed. Chase feels like he could almost step into the picture.

It appears to be a family portrait of some kind. A delicate-looking elementary-aged Rose sits in the middle of a strawberry patch, covered in strawberry juice or mud, or both—difficult to tell since there is no color. She holds in her hands an enormous basket of strawberries, almost bigger than her own head, and she appears to be giving it, offering it to younger, thinner versions of the Parsimmons.

What strikes Chase the most about the picture—besides how freakishly good it is—are the facial expressions. He sees in the Parsimmons' eyes something that looks like hope, and maybe affection, even. And on Rose's face, there's a joy, a pure joy he doesn't think he's ever seen before, like she's been caught up in the moment and just allowed herself to feel good.

"She looks so happy," he whispers, thinking he's never seen her draw anything like this. It seems out of character, almost, and he wonders why she did it. Until he turns to look at Mrs. Parsimmon's crumbling face, and then he knows. *This is a gift.*

Tears stream down Mrs. P.'s cheeks, and she adds, whispering too, "Here's the craziness of it all. Ninety-nine percent of the misery in her life is misery she's created for herself. Why does she only see what she's lost and not what she's gained?" Her voice solidifies, gathers strength, and now she's no longer whispering. "Let's face it—if we hadn't adopted her, she'd have wound up turning tricks on Hollywood Boulevard just like her mother."

Chase's blood starts to sizzle. He needs to get out of there, get moving, before he says something he shouldn't. "Look, I've got to find her before she does something stupid. If she comes back here or if you think of where she might be, call me." Chase gives Mrs. Parsimmon his cell number.

He leaves her sitting there on the bed, holding the picture in her hands and crying. Chase runs down the porch steps, not sure which direction to go. He looks around and up, seeing the mountains that hug the edge of the valley. On a whim he decides to jog past the nearest bus stop and, if she isn't there, to hit the train station. He dials Daniel's number as he runs. "What happened?" Becca picks up right away, breathless. She must have been holding the phone.

"She's gone. The room is all clean and empty. No note."

"I should've gone over there months ago, Chase. I knew she wasn't okay. I just didn't want to deal with her parents." Becca's voice breaks.

Chase doesn't say anything for a while. "I could have too. I let her push me away because I didn't want to deal with it."

"Oh, come on, you two," Daniel's voice butts in. "Get a grip. Rose is a tough girl. You both tried to connect and she didn't let you. So stop blaming yourselves and let's focus. At least you didn't find her hanging from a noose, right?"

"Thanks, Daniel. I really needed that mental image." Chase stops running and leans over, his cell-phone-free hand on his knee. "And what are you doing anyway, listening over Becca's shoulder?"

"It was that or putting you on speakerphone. What's wrong with your voice? You're all out of breath."

"No shit. I'm running."

"Running where?"

"I'm going to hit the bus stops and train station. I still think she just took off. She wouldn't hurt herself. She would think killing herself was chicken shit." Chase isn't sure if he's trying to convince them or himself. Every time he closes his eyes to blink, he sees that image of Rose in the strawberry patch and wonders if that was the last time she'd really felt happy. The thought scares him.

"I hope you're right." Becca's voice again. "We'll come meet you.

We can use Daniel's truck. It'll be faster than you running all over town." Chase agrees. His legs are already feeling rubbery from the combination of running at high speed and the cold night air. He gives them directions and hangs up.

Once his lungs no longer feel like they're on fire, Chase begins running again, this time at a more reasonable speed. Picking the bus stop is a crap shoot, but Chase figures Rose won't be expecting anyone to be on to her so quickly. She probably sent her good-bye email moments before she left the house, thinking her friends wouldn't get the message until morning.

So in all likelihood, she would have picked the bus stop closest to her house. But are the buses even running in the middle of the night on Christmas morning? And what are the chances of him finding her in time?

BEFORE

20
ROSE

"OUR FIVE MINUTES IN THE coat closet are nice and all, but I'm ready for something more," Rose whispered in Chase's ear, while Becca finished up a mini story-time with a circle of kids.

"My thoughts exactly," Chase whispered back. "I have an idea."

"Me too. Come over tonight. I'll sneak you through my window." Rose looked at his tousled hair and his "Procrastinate Now" T-shirt that matched his eyes perfectly, and wanted nothing more than to have him waltz in like Prince Charming and rescue her from her life.

"Are you insane?"

"A little." Rose sighed. "Look, Chase. I *like* you. More and more every day."

Chase studied her, his eyes soft.

"If you come late enough, they'll be asleep." Rose tried not to sound like she was pleading. "And if they catch me—I'm pretty much grounded from the world already. What else can they take from me?"

Chase scanned the room. "Come help me set up the art easel." He led her outside, past the water table and tricycles. He busied himself unscrewing paint caps and clipping up oversized pieces of butcher paper. Finally, he brought his eyes to hers. "I like you too, Rose. I like you enough that I don't want to screw this up."

"I won't let you. Just let me be in charge."

Chase gave her a funny look. "I know your biggest goal in life is to be a rebel. To pay your parents back for whatever they've done to you— but I don't want a part of it. I want your parents to like me. Plus even if we were sitting in your room doing homework, I'd be scared shitless that they'd catch me there."

Rose started to interrupt.

"Just listen for a sec." He put his hand on her shoulder. "I *really* like you. I want to get to know you better, if you'll let me."

"That's what I'm talking about. I want you to *know* me better." She dipped her voice seductively and looped her arm around his neck. "Come over tonight." Rose wasn't used to anyone turning her down.

"I'm not talking about sex. I'm talking about really getting to know who you are."

"I don't let anybody know me that way."

"That's what I thought." Chase moved back and straightened the sand table. "But there's a first for everything. Remember when you took me to buy that gift for your mom? You'd never taken anyone with you before." He waited while Rose nodded. "That went okay, right?" She nodded again. "So I've been thinking—maybe I could walk home with you and your mom today. Introduce myself."

"You must be suicidal." Rose got a strange feeling in her chest and throat, a tightening almost.

"No—just really into you," Chase said under his breath.

That afternoon, Rose hung back as they walked home, leaving Chase and Mrs. P. to walk on ahead. Rose put on her headphones but turned the music low enough to be background noise. She wanted to be able to hear what they were saying.

"So where's your little hat?" Mrs. P. asked in a tone that sounded almost friendly.

"My what?"

"Your Yamaha."

Chase put his hand to his head as if he'd forgotten what was up there. "Oh, you mean 'yarmulke.' I'm not Jewish."

Rose watched as Mrs. P. leaned away from Chase so that she could get a better look at him, far sighted as she was. It was fun to watch her struggle to change and rearrange her thoughts before they settled into concrete. Kind of like a game show. And for three hundred, can Hursula change an opinion? "Well, then what're you doing working at a Jewish day care?" She stage-voice whispered, "You gay?"

Rose smiled in spite of herself. She hung her head low so that her hair covered her face. Chase didn't answer at first. Then, "No. No, I'm not." Chase's voice sounded tight. "I just like little kids." *Thank god he knew enough not to say he liked me.*

Mrs. P. sucked her breath in loudly. "You *like* little kids? What exactly do you mean by that?" she asked in her you-might-be-a-pedophile-and-I'm-a-TV-show-cop kind of way.

Chase made a choking noise.

Serves you right, Rose thought, for walking and talking with the enemy.

"Nothing, ma'am," he said. "I just like working with kids."

"Well, then." Mrs. P. brushed her hands together as if they were covered with chalk. "You from around here?"

"Born and raised. You might know my mother. She works at Salon Joli."

Mrs. P. wrapped her button-down sweater tighter around herself. "I prefer Fantastic Sam's myself. They do a perfectly good job for half the price."

Chase stared straight ahead. Rose watched his back stiffen. "So, uh, I think I had some of your coffee cake at the Boys and Girls Club Halloween dance in middle school," Chase managed finally, turning his upper body slightly back as if he wanted to check in with Rose, but he never made eye contact.

"Bundt cake. Everyone thinks it's from a bakery, because I dust that powdered sugar over it just so." Rose could see Mrs. P.'s whole body react, like a plant growing toward sunlight. *Damn, Chase is good.* "You've either got quite a memory, or that cake was better than I thought. I haven't baked anything for the Boys and Girls Club in a couple years."

"Yeah, I stopped going in the seventh grade. I thought I was too cool, I guess." Chase chuckled, but in a self-conscious kind of way. "I saw Rose there sometimes."

If asking about her baking was like a beam of sunlight, mentioning Rose's name brought on a thick, gray thundercloud overhead. Mrs. P. turned back to eye Rose, scuffing her feet along the ground, hair covering her eyes, earphones on. "Unfortunately, Rose was *excused* from the Boys and Girls Club."

"Oh." Chase slowed at the stoplight, leaning over to press the Walk button. At first Rose wondered what he was thinking, but then he said, "Rose is pretty good with those kids at the day care."

"She probably is. She's got a young heart, that's for sure." Mrs. P. held up a warning finger to Chase."And that, by the way, is part of the reason she's not allowed to date." She narrowed her eyes and raised her voice. "Got it?"

Chase nodded, his shoulders slumping. When they reached Rose's house, Chase turned to her and gave her an awkwardly curt wave with a "see you at school tomorrow." He shook Mrs. P.'s hand. Then he headed off, with "discouraged" written all over his hunched shoulders.

"See?" Rose wanted to scream. "See what I put up with?" Rose could've told Chase an hour ago that talking to Mrs. P. was a freaking waste of time. So why did her chest feel so heavy?

Then inspiration hit. She'd just have to take this into her own hands. Stop waiting for his approval. She'd been sneaking out since the age of eleven. She had the technique down. She'd go to *him*.

The Purim carnival at Temple Beth Shalom seemed like a Cinderella's-ball-meets-Halloween party. Little girls ran around in princess costumes. The boys dressed as kings. And every time someone said the word "Haman"—who Rose learned was the bad guy from the Bible story of Purim, people twirled noisemakers made of metal or banged their fists. The sweet smells from triangle pastries with jelly-filled centers reminded Rose of misshapen jelly donuts. The synagogue had roped off the parking lot, and set up tents and booths throughout.

Rose stood watching. The Parsimmons let her out of the house to "help" with the carnival, 100 percent clueless about her real purpose. Nala nestled in her sweatshirt, keeping her warm.

Chase stepped up to her elbow in his comfortable-looking dark green sweater. He waited next to her for a moment before either of them spoke. "Some holiday."

"Agreed. Religion is not my thing," Rose said. Chase placed his hands on her shoulders and spun her to face him. "I think I just question everything too much. I'm not even sure I believe in God."

Chase's eyes studied her. She'd always thought they were brown, but up this close she could see tiny flecks of green. Maybe the green of his sweater made them stand out. "Really." A comment, not a question. "That's sad."

She'd never thought of it as sad. "What kind of God would keep a child separated from her mother?"

"Depends on the mother. Maybe a kind God."

"What if the mother was good? Just poor. And young. Couldn't afford to buy her child much," Rose said.

"Could this mother feed her child?" Chase's eyes stayed focused on her own, as if he was watching her reaction.

"Mostly. Not real healthy crap, but food. Day-old donuts. Bread. Crackers."

"I don't know, Rose." Chase laced his fingers through hers and led her away from the carnival toward the street. Rose could've sworn his fingers were charged with electricity. It raced through her body. "I mean, a lot of shitty things happen in life. That doesn't mean there's no God."

"Well, he's not doing a very good job if shitty things are happening all over the place, is he?" Rose turned again to those eyes, the green flecks jumping out at her. She wanted to dive into his eyes.

"Maybe he's not that involved. Maybe we're like ants to him. Maybe he doesn't try to manage each of our lives. Maybe he just tries to keep things running smoothly. Like maybe he only looks at the big picture, not individual people."

Chase took big steps. He didn't seem to be *trying* to walk quickly, but Rose had to take two small steps for every one of his big steps, so she felt like she was hurrying. "Or maybe he's trying to teach us something." Pause. "Like if a parent was abusive or something. Doesn't seem like there's any good in that. But maybe he wants those kids to learn something."

"Sounds like a load of crap, if you ask me. I have no interest in a God who lets me hurt so I can learn something. I'd rather be ignorant." Rose noticed Chase's pace had slowed. "So where are you taking me?" she asked.

"Don't look at me." Chase laughed. "I'm not taking you anywhere. You're in charge, remember?"

Rose lifted her face to the sun. She breathed in, thinking. This was her chance to make things happen. On her timeline. "Take me to your house."

"Really?" Chase's voice jumped an octave, and he dropped her hand. "Are you sure?"

"Don't get your hopes up, Chase. You're not getting any." Rose stared him down. "I just don't want to be out. My parents have spies everywhere. Nosy do-gooders from PTA or the neighborhood watch. They'd like nothing more than to report to my parents how Satan is corrupting my body and soul."

"Well, we can't have that. No do-gooders. And no more corruption for you either." Chase touched her cheek softly.

Rose smiled. "The good news is that I don't believe in Satan either. I am in charge of my own corruption. Come to think of it…I better get back to work corrupting *you*."

"So corrupt me," he said, before grabbing her hand again and leading her down the sidewalk. Out of the corner of her eye, Rose thought she saw him smile.

21
CHASE

CHASE HASTILY PULLED THE SHEETS and comforter up on his bed, smoothing out the wrinkles the way Candy had taught him. He collected a few pairs of jeans and some boxer shorts in his arms, then deposited them in the hamper.

"Don't mind my house," he apologized.

First of all—it wasn't a house. It was a two-bedroom rented apartment with mismatched pieces of furniture from random garage sales. The kitchen table stood on three solid legs and one that had cracked and had been duct-taped back together. The television only got four channels without static, so Daisy'd been sitting about ten inches away from the screen, trying to watch some rerun of *The Simpsons*.

"My, uh, dad hasn't paid child support since he left…so we haven't been able to really fix up the place," Chase explained, fingering his navy blue bedspread.

"You think I care about shit like that?" Rose asked incredulously. She picked up a magazine and paged through it. "You should see my house. We have a whole living room we're not allowed to use. And you can't even wipe your hands on the towels in the guest bathroom because then she'll have to wash them again. And she doesn't want to wash them all the time because then they'll fade. So I can't even take a piss in the bathroom closest to my bedroom."

Chase smiled.

"Don't laugh. It sucks. If there is a hell, I'll bet it's filled with kitchens you can't eat in and bathrooms you can't pee in." Rose set down the magazine and eyed his bed. "And beds you can't sleep in." With that, she stuck her hand in her back pocket and pulled out a folded piece of black construction paper. It had been folded over and over until it was the size of a playing card. "So I made you something."

"You did?" Chase asked, surprised but trying not to show it.

"It's nothing." She handed it over, waited two seconds, shifted her weight, then grabbed it back out of his hand. "Here." She unfolded it for him, smoothing it out flat with her hands. "You probably won't get it."

He stared at the paper, completely black except for what looked like chalk outlines of hands. Two hands, one reaching for the other, like right before they linked fingers. "I get it," he answered a little too quickly, hoping she didn't ask him what it meant. "You drew this?" She nodded slightly. "You're really good."

"It's us." Rose shoved the picture at him, looking down at her fingernails. "It's me giving you my hand." She looked so small suddenly, Chase thought. "It's symbolic."

"Symbolic, huh?" Chase half grinned."Are you giving yourself to me?"

Rose looked at him squarely, and for a second Chase thought she was angry. Then she laughed. "Get your mind out of the gutter. How many times do I have to tell you we're not having sex today?"

Not *today?* Chase's heart leaped at her choice of words. Because that meant the door might be open another day. He forced himself to stay focused, though, and came up with a good comeback. "What can I say? I have a Y chromosome."

"Yeah. I suppose I can't blame you." She shoved his shoulder playfully. "Besides, symbolism is up for interpretation, right?" Rose leaped into the center of his bed, bouncing like on a trampoline. "So, your sister's cute."

"Yeah, *I* like her. Sometimes I think she's the only real family I've got." Chase smoothed the picture, then set it on top of the pile of crap on his desk.

"What about your mom? And where is she, by the way?"

"Candy's at work, like always. She's never here."

"Is your mom's name really Candy?" Rose covered her mouth with her hand.

"Born and raised. It's not even a nickname. It's the actual name on her birth certificate." Chase shrugged. "Candy's fine, I guess. I know she loves us. We always have enough to eat and clothes to wear. But she's never been a storybook mom. She doesn't do much to help us with our homework or sit down and ask us about our day. She's more like a big sister than a mom. She was our age when she had me."

"Crazy." Rose drew her knees up to her chest. "And he beat her, huh?"

"What?" Chase's head snapped up.

"Your dad, he knocked her around." Rose tucked her chin behind her knees. "You were talking about yourself before. You know—that bullshit about God not trying to manage everything…child of abusive parents learning something. It sounded to me like you were talking about yourself."

"What are you, a shrink?"

"I probably could be, for all the hours I've spent on the couch. I always just sat and stared at the walls for the full fifty minutes. But to watch them write that check every week—painfully, I might add—that was priceless. Money thrown away." Rose straightened up a little. "You don't have to tell me, you know."

"What does it matter?" Chase sank down next to her on the bed, mostly so he wouldn't have to make eye contact. He'd never told anyone about that. Daniel just *knew*. He'd seen the bruises and the shame that made them raw.

"It doesn't really matter, I guess. Just trying to figure you out." She twisted her body so they were eye to eye again. "Did you know people share personal things about themselves all the time without realizing it? I know more about you than you think."

"Oh yeah?" Chase shook off his cloud and tried to make his tone light.

"Yeah." She leaned in closer to him. "I bet I know your zone."

"My zone?"

"Your erogenous zone." She kneeled on the bed and brought her body close to his. He could feel her breasts press into his shoulder as she touched her mouth to his ear. "Your ears," she whispered. The hotness of her breath sent a lightning bolt through him. She kissed his earlobe gently, and then it was like she was French kissing his ear and he could only tolerate it for a moment. Too intense. He pulled away.

"I was right, wasn't I?"

It took Chase a moment to find his voice. "I have goose bumps in places I've never noticed before. Does that answer your question?" He leaned back against the pillow. He could feel his heart pulsing and pumping blood through every organ in his body. "Give me a sec. I'm still recovering."

"I knew it!" She flopped back down on the bed triumphantly. The bed bounced a little. Chase brought his hand to her smooth arm. "It's a skill, I tell you."

"I won't argue. That *is* a skill. My ear is still tingling."

"I wasn't talking about my tongue. I was talking about being able to read people." Rose pulled him toward her by his shirt. Before he knew it, he found himself actually lying on top of her. He figured he nearly doubled her weight, and he worried about squishing her. "Now you try," she whispered. "Tell me about me."

"You're beautiful," he breathed, smelling the sweetness of her. She smelled like scented hand lotion, girly shampoo, and winterfresh gum. He could hardly smell the cigarettes.

She rolled her eyes and sighed. Like beautiful was nothing.

He touched his nose to hers for a moment, then pulled far enough back to be able to see her whole face without going cross-eyed. "I guess I'd say that you were talking about yourself before too. About the child separated from her mother."

Rose didn't answer, just used her weight, what there was of it, to roll him over and put herself on top. "That's better."

"So, uh, what happened with your real mom?"

She waited a moment, then spoke softly. "Don't know, really. Other than she got arrested." Rose stopped and studied him, like she was trying to decide whether to tell him something. "For turning tricks." Pause. "Does it surprise you that my mom was a whore?"

Chase didn't know how to answer that. It didn't surprise him really, but that might be kind of insulting. "I never thought about it."

"Well *I'm* not," she told him firmly, sitting up, her legs still wrapped around him. "I'm not a whore. I never give it up unless *I* want to."

"I know you're not a whore," Chase whispered. He wanted to reach out and touch her hair again, but she seemed so fragile for a moment, and he didn't want to break her.

"Oh, come *on*," she snapped. "When I came over here today you thought you were gonna get some." She paused. "And I'm sure my name is all over the boy's bathroom in Sharpie."

It was, but Chase didn't want to say so. "That doesn't make you a whore."

"Don't you want to know how many partners I've had?" she challenged, but in a for-curiosity's-sake way.

He did, kind of, but he wasn't about to ask.

"I've had sex more times than I can count. It's overrated." She stood up from the bed, pushing her hair back from her face, flushed. "But I'm an emotional virgin. I've never done it with someone I loved."

He thought for a minute, then admitted, "Same here." He'd never done it before period, but this didn't seem like a bad lie.

"So that's why I'm keeping my clothes on today."

"Why?" he asked, confused and maybe a bit relieved.

"Because I don't trust you enough to love you. It's too dangerous."

Love me? Chase thought. But her face seemed far away, like she'd put on an invisible mask for protection. She edged toward the door. "Shit...I'm not sure I remember what love feels like." She stuck her hand behind her to open the door to Chase's room. "All I know is that this feels real. And I don't want to screw it up." Then a delayed second later she grinned. "No pun intended."

22

ROSE

WHEN CHASE AND ROSE SLAMMED in through the front door earlier that afternoon, Daisy had been sitting all close to the tube, her dirt brown hair sprouting out in every direction.

"No hello?" Chase had teased his sister, tousling Daisy's hair, messing it further, and she ducked her head under his arm. "Hey, Daisy, this is my friend Rose."

Daisy eyed Rose warily.

With no forethought, Rose brought Nala out from behind her back. Her claws scratched against Rose's skin. "Want to see something cool?" she whispered conspiratorially. *When in doubt, bribe.*

Daisy nodded, slowly at first and then eagerly. Nala sniffed Daisy's hands, then carefully stepped from Rose to Daisy. Nala placed her front paws on Daisy's shirt, her claws catching the material. Daisy giggled and nuzzled her nose against Nala's fur.

"Can I hold the kitten while you guys hang out?" Daisy asked breathlessly.

Rose ran her hand over Nala's back, feeling her arch to the touch. Her black fingernails slid through the white fur as easily as if they were on skis. She looked over at Chase, then back again to Daisy. She heard herself say, "Sure." And then, "Actually, I could use someone dependable to cat sit from time to time."

Daisy's face looked incredulous, like Rose had just offered to pay her to eat a bowl of French vanilla ice cream. "Cat sit?" Rose nodded. "Yes! Yes! Yes!" She bounced on the faded couch cushions.

Chase knocked Daisy on the head softly with the base of his hand. "You're supposed to negotiate a fee first, silly."

"Are you kidding? I'll pay *her* to let me watch the cat!"

Chase held up his hand. "As Daisy's representative, I'll negotiate her fee." He leaned over to whisper in Daisy's ear. She nodded, her smile stretching from one ear to the other. Then he stood up again. "My client requests payment in jelly beans."

"Jelly beans, huh?" Rose bit her lower lip, trying to hold in her smile. "Any particular kind of jelly beans?"

"One moment, please. I will consult with my client." He cupped his hand around his ear and leaned back down toward Daisy. "Jelly Bellies are preferred," he announced. "But please remove all buttered popcorn flavor as my client and I agree they are disgusting." Daisy tugged on his arm and brought her lips up to his ear. He smiled. "Oh yes. Watermelon, coconut, and bubblegum flavors are house favorites. Extras will be looked upon kindly."

Daisy's smile stretched clear across her face.

After a good half hour in Chase's room, Rose pushed through Chase's door—her clothes still intact—and came back into the living room/family room/kitchen combo. She found Daisy dozing on the couch, Nala curled up on her chest. Nala opened one lazy eye to look at Rose, then closed it sleepily. That was when she told Chase that Daisy could cat sit every night, just while she continued to "get to know him" better.

Chase half smiled, like he was imagining that, but then he shook his head skeptically. She noticed that the top of her head came to his chest. "How in the world is that gonna work? There is no way your parents will let you off your leash to come over here. Are you kidding?"

"They don't have to know," Rose said, turning away quickly.

"I could come over to your place. Your mom likes me." Chase smiled extra wide in an I-know-I'm-adorable kind of way.

"No!" Rose practically shouted. She lowered her voice. "If I sneak out late and pad my bed, they won't catch me." Rose sighed and said seriously, "So no coming to my house. *Ever.* That's a rule. They can't know about *us.* I will come to yours, and the wardens won't find out."

Chase slung his right arm over her shoulder like a seat belt. He turned her around so that they were eye to eye. "There is nothing I'd like more than to see you every night," he began. "But watching you self-destruct is not exactly a turn-on."

Rose stood for a moment, not sure whether to argue or slap him. He was so darn cute when he was being protective. She kissed him instead. Pressed her lips firmly into his. "I have other ways to turn you on. Besides, self-destruction is not on my agenda. Spending time with you is." She shook her head. "Don't worry about anything. Just come along for the ride."

"I don't know—"

"The Parsimmons go to bed at eight. I'm supposed to be in bed by then too. Which is ridiculous, of course. Only people over sixty or under ten go to bed that damn early," Rose complained, trying to get him to understand. "They come in to make sure I haven't stolen the family fortune or smuggled a boy into my bed, but after they fall asleep—they are out for the count. After that, I could have a rock concert in my room and they wouldn't wake up."

"What if they hear you open your window?"

"They won't. Last year they bought these air-purifier machines they saw on an infomercial. They basically just blow air around the room. But they make mega noise. I can totally sneak out without them hearing."

Chase did not look convinced, so Rose went on, "Look, Chase, it isn't up to you. The only part that's up to you is whether you let me in your front door. And Daisy might beat you to it on that one. So that means the only thing that's up to you is whether you let me in your room."

"Somehow, I don't see myself turning you down."

"Yeah, that's what I thought." Rose moved onto her tiptoes. She kissed him again, this time longer. Her lips tingled and her head vibrated. She wished she could carry that feeling back home with her, but like the buzz from cheap beer, she knew it would wear off by then anyway.

23
ROSE

ROSE MEASURED HER DAYS IN Chase time. Passing periods—maybe she'd get a glimpse or a quickie peck. Lunchtime—sprawling under the tree, her head in his lap, sharing food and joking around. Work—chasing kiddos, but always with the subtle awareness of his eyes on her and the possibility of five minutes in the coat closet after the kids were picked up and the area disinfected.

It fed her. It sustained her through the rest of the day. And then at night. After the Parsimmons' were long asleep, the thrill of padding her bed, removing the screen from her window, and sneaking over there.

Even though she rarely arrived before nine thirty, that little ragamuffin Daisy was always up. The kid had no bedtime. Or structure at all, it looked like. Daisy was the polar opposite of Rose in just about every way possible, But when Rose looked at her, she remembered herself. The innocent "self" that existed years ago. The eager—hopeful—believing self that had withered away and disappeared. She'd like to blame the Parsimmons for squashing that part of her, but who knew? Maybe it was just life.

$$\gg\!\!\!\longrightarrow \longleftarrow\!\!\!\ll$$

During Rose's entire first year with the Parsimmons, Mrs. P. had dressed her in pink, frilly dresses that seemed like they belonged in an old-fashioned picture book rather than on a real girl. The frills itched something awful, but Rose didn't fidget. The itching distracted her and made it easier to stay ice-cube numb.

Numbness worked for her. She didn't have to speak. Didn't have to think. Didn't have to feel pangs of homesickness for her mother. Mrs. P. held her hand and paraded her up and down grocery aisles, while people commented. "What a lovely little girl." "How sweet. Doesn't she look just like a porcelain doll?"

Mrs. P. ate up the compliments like chocolates. She even bought Rose her own porcelain doll that stood on a little stand. Rose touched the doll's delicate little nose and her delicate little fingers, and knew she was indeed a porcelain doll. She'd shatter just as quickly.

"Hi, precious, what's your name?" This coming from the checker with hot pink fingernails longer than Rose's toes. They looked like claws.

Rose stared at the fingernails.

"Oh, she doesn't talk," Mrs. P. explained, wrapping a protective arm around Rose. Then in hushed tones, "She's adopted, you know. We're just not sure what kind of traumatic experiences she's had."

Of course this was before Rose knew the word "adopted." And long before she knew the phrase "traumatic experiences." She just kept staring at the fingernails. If they weren't so pink, they'd seem like they belonged on a wicked witch's hands, not connected to a woman with platinum blond hair and cheeks streaked with blush.

"Poor thing," the woman whispered, and that time Rose knew they were talking about her, and she agreed. She was a poor thing. The police had taken her mother away and forgotten to bring her back. Maybe her mom couldn't find her. Maybe the Parsimmons had forgotten to leave their address.

"Yes." Mrs. P. clucked her tongue. "Just sits there all day, quiet as a mouse. The only thing she seems to enjoy is watching Disney." Rose watched Disney movies over and over—except for *Bambi* and *The Lion King*—she couldn't handle the scenes where they lost their parents.

Mrs. P. held her hand back out to the car, and Rose followed mutely. Hoping, wishing, promising to be good forever if only her mother would come back. *Maybe Mama will come for me today.*

Of course everything changed when Rose figured out that they'd given her a new last name. That she belonged to them. When she started talking. Because talking only seemed to complicate matters. Nothing she said was ever what Mrs. P. wanted her to say. Suddenly it was as if the porcelain doll that she'd been had fallen to the floor and shattered, and inside was something horrible and ugly, like the Sea Witches' evil eels in *The Little Mermaid*. And once she started talking again, she didn't want to stop, even though her words dug her deeper and deeper into a hole.

As much as Rose hated the Parsimmons for keeping her from her mother, she didn't want *them* to hate *her*. So she tried to make it better again. She tiptoed into Mrs. P.'s bathroom and found red lipstick in the top drawer. She painted her lips like a true porcelain doll, and she combed her hair over and over again until it shined. She ran out to show Mrs. P., her feet padding on the soft carpet. She smiled, ready to accept the compliments that were sure to come, and to wait to be paraded up and down grocery aisles.

"Rose Parsimmons!" The sharpness in Mrs. P.'s voice knocked the smile right off Rose's face. "Just what did you get into?" Mrs. P. pressed her own lips together so tightly that they almost disappeared. She pulled a tissue from her pocket and wiped off the lipstick until Rose's lips burned. Mrs. P. locked up her lipstick after that.

A few days later, Rose climbed on Mr. P.'s lap while he watched football with the guys from work. She sat stiff and worried about their loud voices, the way they yelled at the screen, and wondered if they were like the men her mother used to bring home. She smiled her porcelain-doll smile, ready for compliments, but Mr. P. didn't seem to notice. So then she leaned forward and said something she'd heard before. Something she'd heard her mama say to the men, something that made them smile, something that got their attention. Well, it got his attention all right.

Mr. P. yelped, like she'd bitten him or set fire to his hair or something, and he stood up so fast that she fell right off his lap. Thud! Her tailbone ached. She stayed there on the floor, looking up at Mr. P. and his work buddies, and wondering what she'd done wrong.

After that, the Parsimmons took to locking their bedroom door at night. When Rose saw monsters in her closet, she pulled her blankets down the hall and curled up in the hallway right outside the Parsimmons' bedroom, because she knew they wouldn't let her crawl in bed with them.

Shortly after that, the Parsimmons started watching Dr. Phil on the tube, searching for answers to their "problem" child. Clipping articles from random magazines and printing out boatloads of info from Internet sites, all proposing to have miracle cures for the "acting-out adopted child." They dragged her to doctors—shrinks and psychiatrists—trying experimental techniques like wrapping her in a mat and making her pretend like she was being reborn. They put her on a cocktail of medications. They took her to a new doctor and made him examine her—down there. Just the thought of it made Rose feel like she might puke. And then she decided.

Screw porcelain dolls.

Rose had never told anyone her memories from childhood, but during those evenings at Chase's apartment, lying in his bed, she found bits and pieces slipping out. At first she tried to hold them in, telling herself that Chase didn't care to hear her sob story, telling herself it was dangerous to share too much. But as she relaxed around Chase, she loosened the hold on her tongue. And the memories slid out.

He mostly just listened.

But that was okay.

Rose managed to dodge Candy until a windy evening in late March.

When Rose arrived, Daisy grabbed her hand and dragged her to the couch. She looked about six in her ratty princess pajamas—the sleeves not reaching past her elbows and the bottoms barely hitting her knees. "Look, I made Nala a little bed over here for when she visits." She'd fashioned a soft sleeping area out of a FedEx box with what looked like an old sweatshirt padding the bottom.

"Nice work, Daisy," Rose said, handing her the cat.

A petite woman with big hair and a thigh-length skirt poked her head out of a bedroom and asked, "Who ya talking to, Daze?"

Rose's heart fluttered. Chase's mom?

The woman caught Rose's eye and stepped forward. "Oh, hey there. You Chase's new friend?"

Rose nodded, wondering how much Candy knew about her. Word spread fast in Simi Valley, especially after Rose got caught TPing her own house, and she never quite knew how people would respond to her. Not that she cared.

Daisy reached her sticky hand for Rose's and led her over to Candy. "Her name is Rose, Mom, and she's paying me in jelly beans to cat sit."

When Candy laughed, her eyes crinkled around the edges, and for a moment, she looked like a teenager. "Right on!" She sidled up to Daisy and held out her hand. "I get a commission, right?"

Daisy looked confused.

"That means, I get some jelly beans too, baby."

Daisy smiled at first, then grew serious. "Only the gross flavors. You can have black licorice and popcorn."

Rose reached into her sweatshirt pocket and pulled out a box of multicolored candies. This was the first time she'd been able to bring the jelly beans as promised. Every week the Parsimmons took her paycheck and held it hostage, so she'd had to wait until she could slip a five out of Mr. P.'s wallet.

"I ate most of the buttered popcorn on the way here. You're right. They *are* gross." Rose said, handing the opened box to Daisy, whose eyes widened. "Although it was dark enough outside that I accidentally ate a bunch of piña coladas too. You might want to consider that for your list of favorites. Not quite as good as watermelon, but better than bubblegum in my book."

Rose thought about reaching out to shake Candy's hand, but she didn't. Too corny. Instead she just turned to her and said, "Hi. I'm Rose."

"Hey," Candy said, all nonchalant. "Make yourself at home." She moved past Daisy and flopped onto the couch, stacking her feet on the coffee table. "I think Chase was in the shower, but he should be done by now. *Hey, Chase!*" she hollered, loud enough to shatter windows. "Your girlfriend's here!"

Rose cringed. Chase ducked into the room, his face all sheepish and his shaggy curls still wet from the shower.

"You gonna watch the tube with me and Daisy, or do your own thing?" Candy asked.

"Uh." Chase shifted his weight. "Probably just hang out in my room and talk."

"Sure. Just talk." Candy laughed. "Don't forget, we're sitting right out here, so keep it G-rated."

Rose felt her face heat up. Chase just ignored Candy and turned his attention to Daisy, who'd scooped up a handful of Jelly Bellies and was sifting through them. "Okay, Daisy-Dukes. That's enough. The rest we'll save for tomorrow."

Daisy made a halfhearted groan, but went ahead and placed the rest of the Jelly Bellies in the kitchen cabinet next to a box of saltines.

"Way to go, *Dad*," Candy teased. "How responsible."

Chase chuckled. "Someone's got to watch out for her."

Candy stood up and fake-swatted his ass. "Hey, hey! I resent that!"

"Resent it all you want. It's the truth."

Candy fake-shoved him. "Okay you little lovebirds, go have your talk. Daisy and I have some serious *American Idol* watching to do."

Chase put his hand around Rose's waist and pulled her toward his bedroom. The funny thing was, they really did just talk. Okay, so they *mostly* just talked. Rose made Chase set the alarm by his bed for midnight just in case they fell asleep.

"Your parents really put you on Ritalin when you were six?" he asked, smoothing her hair.

"Yep," Rose said. "They meant well, they just didn't know what to make of me." Or any kids, really. It was obvious the Parsimmons had never had a kid before. They didn't understand that blueberry muffins made crumbs, milk spilled, and hands got sticky. It didn't take long before Rose stopped trying to please them. She made crumbs with every blueberry muffin. She dropped her milk on purpose, shattering the glass.

Chase looked at her as if he wanted to swallow her up with his arms. So she let him. It felt so good to be touched. Like a parched desert after a rain, she drank it up. And never wanted it to end.

24
CHASE

WHEN CHASE SPILLED THE NEWS to Daniel, he socked Chase in the arm. "You mean she shows up every night?"

"Pretty much."

Daniel sang "Booty call!" And socked him in the arm again. "Bro—do you know how many guys would die to be in your shoes? She's got to be one of the hottest girls in Simi. At least top ten."

Chase grinned. "No booty call. More like a support group with, uh, *benefits*." Sure he and Rose fooled around. She'd let him take off her shirt a couple times, and man, was that nice. It was kinda hard to keep control of himself physically when they were together. He'd never really been serious about a girl before, and sometimes his body got ahead of his mind. He struggled to rein it in. But they also mostly talked. No sex, and Chase wasn't pushing it. Not that he was nervous or anything. Just that, well, he hadn't ever done it before, and he sure didn't want to get it wrong.

Plus it had been kinda cool just getting to know Rose. He felt pretty sure she hadn't shared herself with anyone before, not in this way. Chase had tacked that picture she drew for him right on his wall, next to his posters. Rose hadn't really been "giving" herself to him, he decided. She'd been "sharing" herself with him. There was a difference.

With all that baring of the soul (and body), Chase began to feel obligated to share himself, as well. It stressed him out. Because did guys talk about that kind of stuff? He and Daniel knew each other backward and forward, but that was because they'd been buddies since elementary school. He hadn't *told* Daniel about his life; Daniel just *knew*. So with Rose, he started off easy. Told her about the good times. Fishing in the lake and basketball on TV. Learning to ride a bike.

When he got to the topic of Walter, the words stuck in his mouth, hanging back. Relax, he told himself. It's not like you're broadcasting your business to the world. You're just telling your girlfriend. Thinking of her as his girlfriend made it okay, so he went ahead and blurted it out. Told her that for years Walter cracked his first beer to help him wake up in the morning. On work days, he'd mix some vodka into the orange juice from his lunch thermos. He'd end work with a visit to happy hour and come home mean. On weekends, he stayed drunk from Friday night right through Sunday—church included. Some people were more fun when they were drunk. Walter was just plain mean.

"Scary," Rose said, gazing into his eyes. She kissed his nose. "And you were only a kid."

"I guess I was. But it's funny…I feel like I've been old forever." Chase stared at those little cottage-cheese bumps on the ceiling. "I never knew what would set him off. But as a kid, I always had this sense that Candy *should've* known. Like it was somehow her fault."

Candy should've known that he had burritos for lunch and not to pick up burritos for dinner. Candy should've known the towels in the bathroom were hung crooked. Candy should've known not to talk to the mailman. Or the guy at the checkout counter at the drugstore. "Saying that out loud sounds so stupid," Chase said. "It was just so easy to blame her."

"Maybe because *he* blamed her?" Rose suggested softly.

"Maybe." Chase remembered blaming Candy for setting Walter off. Blaming her for taking it. Blaming her for not taking it—for crying or fighting back. It'd been so easy to blame her and so hard to respect her.

"And then, he started taking off for chunks of time." Chase said. During those weeks, Candy would invite Chase and Daisy to come sleep in her bed. They'd bring in extra blankets and lie there in the dark, listening to each other breathe. His mother would whisper, as though someone else was listening, "We're the Three Musketeers. Nothing can get us down."

Chase and his sister agreed. They both knew it wouldn't last, but for the moment, it didn't matter. The warmth from his mother's bed warmed his soul like chicken noodle soup, and that warmth would last for days.

"What happened when he came back?" Rose smoothed his hair away from his forehead.

"It was worse. It was a nightmare." Chase said, his chest heavy from remembering it all. Walter would accuse Candy of cheating on him. He'd smell the sheets. He'd rant and rave, throwing her laundry across the room. It got so that Walter just checked in and out of their lives like they were some kind of seedy motel, a place to crash and trash with no cleanup obligations. After a surprise visit that ended in a black eye, Candy said, "Enough."

"And finally she got the balls to end it." Chase could still remember his mother's face when she told Walter off. Her face muscles looked like they were vibrating, filled with so many different emotions that he couldn't identify.

"Leave." Her voice vibrated too. Shaking but strong. She stood at the front door, blocking his father's re-entry. "I'm not gonna hang around here, waiting." Her voice gathered momentum, and she spoke faster now. Louder. "Waiting for you to show up here and teach me another lesson."

Chase and Daisy huddled together in his bedroom. Using the door as a shield. He peeked through the crack, his vision narrowed. All he could see was Candy's face. Chase wrapped his arm around his sister, holding her tight. He could feel her shaking.

"Was it bad?"

"Yeah." Chase's voice cracked. He remembered Walter slamming the door nearly off its hinges, and Candy jumping back to avoid getting hit. Daisy pressing her face into his side and wrapping her arms around his stomach. When Chase tried to pry her arms away, he couldn't. Strong little kid. Chase felt something wet beneath his bare feet. She'd peed in her pants. And now he'd stepped in it. It grossed him out a little, but he tried not to show it.

Daisy peeked up at him, her face streaked with tears. She didn't speak, but her face showed her embarrassment.

"It's all right." Chase loosened her hold. "I'll clean it up while you change your pants."

By the time Chase finished scrubbing the carpet, Candy had already gone to the landlord and asked him to change the locks. Chase was old enough to watch Daisy, she said, and it was about time she started dating again.

"And then he left for good?" Rose nuzzled her head in the crook of Chase's arm.

"Pretty much. He still sends cards a couple times a year—birthdays and Christmas, although they're both usually a month or two late."

"Do you think your mom wants to get married again?"

"Yeah. I think she's lonely." Sometimes he caught Candy crying at night, like she missed Walter or something. It was like missing a splinter or a blister. How could she miss someone who only brought her pain? Besides, she met more eligible bachelors at the salon than there were flavors of ice cream.

And ever since she dumped the stoner, she'd been dating Bob the Plumber. He seemed halfway decent and, like Candy said, "a keeper." Made good money too. After all, Candy reminded them, she had to pay the bills, and her $12.33-an-hour job as a receptionist and hairstylist-in-training at Salon Joli didn't cut it. Someday, Candy would move up to hairdresser and earn the big bucks. She just had to get the hang of cutting bangs. They always wound up longer on one side.

Chase had shared more than he'd intended to. Rose just lay there on her side, her hand propping up her head. Her long, fine strands of hair spilling over her shoulders and across her smooth brown skin. Her eyes wide and clear, drinking in his words like there was no one more important in the world. He reached out to touch her hair. "I can probably get you a free haircut at the salon, if you're ever interested." It felt like silk.

"Not sure." She fingered the strands around her face, then grinned. "I don't think I want her anywhere near my bangs."

"Oh, come on!" Chase rolled onto his back. "The lopsided look is in!"

"Ah, ah, ah," she warned, wagging her finger in his face. "Careful, or I'll think you're trying to get into my pants."

Chase couldn't resist. He lunged for her finger and grabbed it in his fist, pulling her closer. "Correct me if I'm wrong, but your pants have been folded on the floor for the last hour and a half."

Rose pulled her finger away, laughing, then pressed it into his bare chest. "That is for purely scientific purposes."

"What?"

"Haven't you ever noticed how it's warmer under the covers without pants?"

"No." It sounded like a load of crap to him.

"Yes. I'm conducting experiments. Measuring body heat and all that." She let her skin melt into his. "See how warm this is?"

Her skin did feel toasty warm. It was all Chase could do to manage his impulses.

She chuckled, watching his face. "And I'm studying something else too." She waited, but he didn't know. "I'm studying how long it will take you to make a move."

"A move?" Chase complained. "I thought I wasn't supposed to make a move! You wanted to be in charge, right?" For a moment, he felt legitimately frustrated, until he realized her whole body was shaking with laughter.

"All right, all right." Rose climbed on top of him and kissed him with little feather-like kisses. His forehead. His chin. His neck—that almost tickled. His chest...Chase closed his eyes. He felt her pull back. More discouraged than curious, Chase slowly opened his eyes. "I don't get it," she said slowly. "You act like you're this big disappointment or something. Your parents sound more disappointing than you do."

Chase closed his eyes again. "Can't you go back to what you were doing before?" No way did he plan on telling her about the fist he'd put through a wall.

She teased his lips with her finger. "Not sure if I'm in the mood. Come on, tell me what you've done that is so bad."

"If I tell you, you'll do that thing again?" Chase cracked one eye open to see her nod, then he closed it again. "Okay, fine. I just disrespected my mom is all. And I promised myself I won't ever do it again."

"Doesn't everyone disrespect their parents?"

Chase remembered the way his fist crunched through the wall. "It's just—she's been through so much crap with my dad. She doesn't deserve any more crap. And Daisy doesn't deserve to have all that drama up in her face. " Chase held out his arms. "That's all you get—take it or leave it. Now kiss me!" he commanded, hoping she'd go back to the neck.

She did.

25
CHASE

CHASE LEFT EARLY FOR SCHOOL the next morning. He shoved his hands deep in his pockets and thought. He'd never in his life talked to anyone the way he talked to Rose. He felt kind of guilty for making Walter sound so bad. He wasn't *all* bad. Chase had a handful of positive memories too.

A week after his fifth birthday, Walter let Chase sit up front with him while they drove down the long road to Lake Casitas. Just the two of them. Walter bought a bag of Flamin' Hot Cheetos, trail mix, and a big Cherry Slurpee for the drive. Chase kept digging his hand into that Cheetos bag until his fingers were coated in red crumbs and his mouth was on fire. He'd sucked his fingers one at a time and then brushed the rest off on his shorts.

Before they'd left, Candy had tossed out to Walter, "Keep it dry today, Walt, okay? You got precious cargo."

Walter had grunted but agreed. And true to his word, he didn't crack open a single beer.

They stood in the lake, water up to their knees, jeans rolled up to the thigh, and waited. The water sparkled dark green, and he could see little fish darting here and there as if they were nibbling at his toes. They didn't talk, he and Walter, not for hours, but it didn't matter. The whole day was the closest to heaven Chase had ever been. He could almost forget the bruise on his left hip, from when Walter shoved him against the coffee table the night before.

At the end of the day, both their noses and the backs of their necks were sunburned, but it didn't matter. Chase didn't catch a darn thing, and Walter only got one scrawny pike and threw it back, but it didn't matter. Nothing mattered, except being with his dad.

Two days later, as Candy set Top Ramen and thawed chicken nuggets on the table, she broke the big news. "Walt, I got to tell you something I know you're not gonna like."

Walter tossed his tenth beer into the trash—and missed. It clattered onto the floor, and drops of Corona splattered the floor with the impact. "Well, spit it out. I'm not gonna be any happier if you fart around forever trying to tell me. What, did you overdraw the account again?"

Chase put down his fork and braced himself for a mad dash to his bedroom closet, where he could hide behind his Christmas sweater.

"No." Her voice sounded soft, like maybe if she spoke quietly, his reaction would be quiet too. "I'm pregnant. About four months."

After a beat or two of digestion, Walter let out a roar that could rival a bear and shoved the table over, sending hot Top Ramen flying against the wall. Chase scrambled out of the way and raced to his room. He threw himself to the floor and crawled under the bed. He pressed his hands so hard against his ears that he almost felt like he was underwater.

He could hardly hear the yelling, the crashing, the screaming. He could hardly feel the welt on his arm, where the scalding Top Ramen had splashed onto his skin. He could pretend he was a giant shark, swimming deep in the ocean, not afraid of anything. A shark could bite Walter's head right off his body.

Chase didn't venture out until after the final slam of the front door and the sound of Walter's truck revving up and taking off. He slid out on his belly, hearing whimpering.

Candy lay curled on the kitchen floor like a dying roly-poly, crying. Chase placed his hand on her shoulder, and she shoved him away with a yelp, like he was Walter rather than his five-year-old self. He flew back from her push and landed square on his tailbone. Chase felt his lower lip folding under like a baby's, and he cried. Cried so hard he couldn't hear Candy any more. Cried so many tears he blurred his vision of her. So he almost didn't see it when she eased herself up off the floor, her left arm hanging stiff.

He tried not to hear it when Candy told him to run next door and get Mrs. Sheridan to drive her to the ER. Said she needed an X-ray. And an ultrasound. And he definitely didn't want to hear it when she said she was going to lose the baby.

Mrs. Sheridan let Chase borrow some of her son's video game collection, and Chase stayed glued to the television screen for the next few days. He played until his eyes blurred over and then he played some more. People came in and out of the apartment, and although he didn't lift his eyes from the screen, he knew who they were. Mrs. Sheridan checked on Candy, who had been released from the hospital with a broken arm...but still pregnant.

Walter returned to the house with his shoulders hunched. He walked silently through the rooms, pouring every bit of alcohol down the sink. He found a new church and started going every day. He left the house only for confession and work. He sat next to Chase on the couch and stared at the video screen, but he didn't say a word.

Walter didn't drink a drop of alcohol from that moment until a few months after Daisy was born. Once everyone saw Daisy was okay—no dent in the forehead or misshapen body parts—things sort of slipped back. It started off small with little put-downs and irritations, but before Chase knew it, Walter was back to drinking like a fish and smashing windshields with baseball bats, never mind his kids who were still sitting inside the car.

Chase sat down on a bench a block away from school. He rested his head in his hands. Maybe thinking about all these things wasn't so good. The memories made him feel sick. But being with Rose, talking to Rose, made him feel safe in ways he'd never felt before. There was something in his chest that swelled when he was around her. Or when he thought of her. A bubbly, full feeling. He'd never felt it before in his life.

And she seemed to feel safe too. He'd been taking her lead on everything physical, because 1) it seemed like the right thing to do; 2) she was clearly more experienced in these things than he was; and 3) once things got physical, he didn't trust himself to think clearly. It was better to let her take the lead. Hopefully she had better control of her impulses than he did of his.

26
ROSE

ROSE REMEMBERED A TIME WHEN she thought sex would set off firecrackers in her brain, sparklers in her heart, and dynamite between her legs. Mostly it did nothing of the sort. Mostly, she didn't see what the big deal was. The biggest problem with it, in her book, was that if you had sex with a guy once, he was no longer satisfied with just rolling around and kissing. The guy just expected to have sex with you every time there was an available bed or a parked car. It was like once you passed through that door, there was no going back.

To be honest, "giving it up" so easily never really felt right to her. It was nothing like what her real mother had done, she told herself every time. Mostly she believed it. The thing was, she could have pissed off the Parsimmons even without having sex because they just assumed she was doing it long before she ever actually did. Despite their Christian upbringing, they'd put her on birth control pills when she'd barely turned twelve. Rose figured they'd have neutered her if it was legal.

But actually the birth control was what made her decide to go ahead and do it that first time. Why not? She already had to take a tiny pill every morning. She might as well get the fun out of it too, right? Only it wasn't fun. Her first time was horrible. Like some surgical procedure or medical experiment.

It felt like the guy was shoving his whole arm up inside her, over and over again until her insides felt raw. She bled a little, and it hurt to pee for three days. Not to mention that the guy was a total jerk about it. He told everyone else on the sophomore baseball team and then never talked to her again.

She felt dirty after too. She took about eight showers that night. She wondered if that was how her mom had felt every time after she turned a trick. Her mother must have found a way to turn it off in her head. In a weird way, "doing it" made Rose feel tougher, harder, and that felt good.

But when she decided to have sex with Chase, it was totally different. Tender. Slow. Considerate. He let her tell him exactly what to do so that it would feel good. He checked to see if she was okay. She wondered if it might have been his first time, but she didn't ask. He held her for a long time afterward, his body warm against hers. She leaned her head against his chest and could feel the beating of his heart. He ran his fingers through her hair. Over and over again. She matched her breathing to his and let her body melt. There they lay for a long time, until they both fell asleep.

As Rose drifted off, she realized something. For the first time since she left her mother, she felt two things. Safe and loved.

27

CHASE

NOW CHASE UNDERSTOOD VAMPIRES. THIRSTING after the forbidden once they'd had their first taste.

Because after he and Rose did it the first time, he craved her more than ever before. The worst was anytime he could see her but couldn't touch her. Like at work. Chase ached to brush past her, to get close enough to smell her hair, to see how neatly she could fit in his arms. Because Chase didn't trust his hands to behave themselves, he kept them in his pockets as much as possible. Wait until tonight, he reminded himself, wait until tonight.

Not that they had sex every night. Rose had made that very clear. She would decide when they did and did not have sex. He would not expect it or even ask for it. He didn't argue.

So far, they still mostly talked. And cuddled. Rose brought him a charcoal sketch or a piece of her poetry nearly every night. Before long, his left wall was covered with different artistic offerings from Rose, each tacked up side by side. And then every three or four days, she'd initiate something more.

After work, Chase watched Rose walk away, hanging back behind Mrs. Parsimmon, swaying her hips as she walked—runway style. "Come on, Rose. We don't have all day," Mrs. P. threw back toward her, barely turning. Rose stiffened up for a moment, like she was afraid to be caught. Then flipped her head around to glance at Chase. She winked and slowed her pace even more.

"You have it bad." Becca elbowed him as she passed by. "You're whipped."

"Shut up," Chase told her, grinning. "Hey, what are you guys having for dinner?"

Becca turned around long enough to roll her eyes. "Can't you at least pretend you want to come over to see my brother? Ever since this whole Rose-is-a-goddess phase of yours, it's like you forgot he exists."

Chase shook his head. "Guys are more mature than girls. We don't have to spend every waking hour together to convince each other we're friends." Chase followed her footsteps. "You think your mom'll make that sweet noodle thing?"

"It's called kugel."

"Yeah, kugel. The one with the brown sugar and butter melted on the bottom of the pan?"

"Doesn't your own mother feed you?"

"Not like yours." Becca was wrong. He couldn't wait to talk to Daniel. Okay...brag a little. He was having sex with Rose Parsimmon, after all. One of the hottest girls at school. But also, just to talk.

When Chase arrived at the Stein house, he found Daniel in the backyard under a big, leafy tree that made shade like an umbrella. The April sun shone strong, even this late in the day, revving itself up for summer. Daniel's hands were pressed together in front of his heart, prayer-like. Eyes closed. Daniel stood on one leg, the other leg wrapped around the first. Chase tried not to laugh. "What are you, a freaking stork?"

Daniel didn't move a muscle. He opened one eye. "This is tree pose."

Chase edged closer. "What would happen if I took my little finger and gave you a teeny, weeny push?"

Daniel jumped back, hopping from foot to foot like a little kid who had to pee. Then he leaped onto Chase's back, arms around his neck, Ultimate Wrestling-style. Chase flipped him around and pinned him to the ground. Daniel struggled for a minute and then laughed. "This is why we'd never be partners if we went out for the wrestling team. They'd never match the one-thirties with the two hundreds. No sport in that."

"Right on. Besides, I'd never go out for wrestling. Couldn't handle those tights." Chase let him up, knocking his head playfully. He could feel the beating of his own heart from the minor exertion, and it reminded him of the way his heart raced with Rose. So he told his best friend about what was, so far, the highlight of his life.

Daniel socked him in the arm, first thing. "All right, bro! You're a member of the club! What a birthday present!" Chase's seventeenth birthday was three weeks away. "I feel like I should buy you a cigar or something."

"That's okay." Chase tried not to smile too wide. "No cigar necessary. Even though I always like a little throat cancer to start off my day..."

And once it was out there, Chase felt all puffed up and proud, but he also felt something else he couldn't put his finger on. He looked around the yard to make sure no one else was listening. "So once again, I'm officially a sinner." He shrugged, kind of sheepish. It sounded pretty lame.

"Hey, bro." Daniel held up his hand. "Are you stressing about that?"

"I'm not stressing," Chase lied, scuffing his feet against the loose soil around the tree. "Just getting your religious take. You're the only Jewish Buddhist I know. Has anyone ever told you that you're a goddamn original?"

Daniel put his hand down. "Not really. Haven't you ever heard of Jubu?" Chase shook his head no. "That's a Jew who practices Buddhist meditation and spirituality." He paused. "I'm nowhere near as unique as I seem. Although, did I tell you I was thinking of gauging my ears?"

Chase looked at him straight in the eye, no hint of a smile. "If you gauge your ears, I will be forced to stop hanging out with you in public."

Daniel met his gaze. "You've pretty much already done that." He lasted a whole minute, unblinking, before the smile wriggled free. "Between your job and your girl, you're a busy guy. You've got to schedule me in."

"Sorry, bro. You're almost as cute as Rose, but not quite. Maybe if you highlighted your hair..." Chase teased. He shrugged and touched a pile of gardening tools with his foot. Half joking, he said, "So now I'm officially going to hell—if I wasn't already."

Daniel smiled. "Isn't that what confession's for?"

"I haven't been to confession in years. Maybe I should go."

"Listen, Chase." Daniel looked like he was preparing to channel Buddha himself. "Did it feel like a sin?"

Chase couldn't help but smile. "It felt like a goddamn miracle."

So why couldn't he just enjoy it and shake the guilt?

28
CHASE

CHASE HELD THE ENVELOPE FOR a long time. *Shocker.* Did Walter actually remember his birthday on time this year? He felt that familiar buildup and drop-off in his chest, as though his heart was veering around corners at a NASCAR event. He hadn't heard from his father since his Christmas card arrived late—in February.

He shifted the envelope in his hand, weighing it. It felt light—too light for a card. A greeting card would be out of character for his father anyway. "Damn waste of money," his father would say. "Three-fifty for a crappy piece of paper with some pansy-ass poetry!" Still, Hallmark had that ninety-nine-cent section. And it *was* Chase's seventeenth birthday.

Candy never forgot his birthday. April 30. "How could I forget fifteen hours of the worst freaking pain of my life?" she'd say, only half teasing. Chase had been nearly ten pounds at birth, and she never let him live that down. Today, Candy left a package of Little Debbie brownies, a small tub of Safeway Double-Dutch Chocolate frosting, and a candle on the kitchen table.

"Working late," she'd scrawled on a note. "You and Daisy celebrate for me. I'll be home by nine thirty or so." It sucked that Candy hadn't taken the evening off to help him celebrate. Figured.

Chase slid his finger into Walter's envelope and carefully edged it open. Chase knew what he wished it would say. "Dear Chase. Happy birthday, kid. I'm coming to town on the weekend. Let's hit Golf N' Stuff in Ventura and Texas Cattle Company in good old Camarillo when I roll through. Take care of the girls for me. Dad."

Walter loved Texas Cattle Company. Juicy, charbroiled hamburgers and free popcorn on the tables. Pictures of past Ventura County beauty pageant winners on the walls. "Not too hard on the eyes," Walter would point out. *Yeah, right. Like that would ever happen.*

Chase pretended he didn't see his own hands shake as he unfolded the letter. He steadied himself and brought the paper closer to his eyes. Words jumped out at him. Formal request. Custody reevaluation. Child support. His stomach sunk to his toes.

He skimmed it quickly. The letter was not for his birthday. In fact, it made no mention of his birthday. It wasn't even addressed to him. It was to Candy and to the Superior Court of California—County of Ventura, Family Law Division. Chase balled his fists, crumpling the letter. The room spun.

Chase squeezed his eyes closed. An image of Walter's face popped out at him, raging. Walter swinging a bat at Candy's car windows. Chase cowering, inside the car. Chase struggling with the seat belt, trying to unclick it, then giving up and covering his face and head. The bat swinging…*crack, Crack, CRACK* against the window. Waiting for the glass to splinter and shower down on him like searing rain. The window didn't shatter, just cracked like an earthquake fault. Chase opened his eyes before he could remember any more.

He wouldn't go. He'd refuse. Nobody could make him, right?

»»——→ ←——««

That evening, Candy held Walter's letter in her hand, her face all pinched up like she'd chowed down a lemon, whole. Chase shifted his weight a couple of times, wanting to ask her what she thought, but at the same time, not wanting to know.

Candy folded the letter back up, handed it to him, and retreated into her dark bedroom like it was some kind of cave. She hibernated in there for at least an hour. Chase paced the floor, listening for any kind of peep from inside the room that would show him Candy had a clue what to do. He heard nothing. Except for the occasional sniffle. Crap.

Finally he pressed open the door and peered inside. Candy lay on her bed, her covers pulled up to her chin.

"Mom?" Chase asked.

"We're screwed," she whispered.

"What?"

"We're goddamn screwed." She rolled over to face him, and even in the darkness of the room, he saw the glistening of her cheeks and knew she'd been crying. His heart twisted.

"We're not screwed." Chase insisted. "We just won't go. He can't make us go. Not if we don't want to."

Candy sighed and rolled back away. "I listen to bitter ex-wives complain about their custody battles in the salon all the time. The stories they tell would blow your mind. Ventura County courts are pro two-parent parenting, even if one parent is an abusive ass." Candy paused, her voice muffled. "No offense. I know he's your father."

"Yeah, but Mom, I don't *want* to go. I'll just say that in court."

"You're a minor."

"I just turned seventeen."

"You're a minor. And Daisy's a minor."

"Wait a second. You're telling me that Walter can throw me into a full-length mirror, hard enough to shatter it—and he'd still get custody? What about the time he cracked your windshield with a baseball bat when Daisy and I were inside? What about that?"

"Chase, baby. We have no proof. "

Chase could feel his heart beating all the way in his ears. "But he's been gone for years. We've been living here with you, going to Simi Valley schools and making Simi Valley friends. Where the hell has he been?"

"I listen to these stories every day. I'm telling you. All that matters is that Walter donated sperm, that he's cleaned up his act, and that he wants to be involved in his kids' lives. At least in the courts of Ventura County, the bias lies with parental rights for *both* parents, regardless of how incompetent, abusive, or scummy the parents happen to be."

"That can't be right. There has to be an age when the courts would listen to a kid. Maybe not for someone Daisy's age, but for me...I'm nearly an adult."

"Maybe," Candy muttered like a deflated balloon, "but you wouldn't want Daisy going there by herself, would you?" Her upper lip trembled.

Chase's heart climbed into his throat, picturing it. "No," he said softly. "If Daisy has to go, I'll go with her."

But then he'd have to leave Rose behind.

NOW

29
ROSE

SUDDENLY EVERYTHING IS HAPPENING QUICKER than it's supposed to. Rose wraps her winter coat around as far as it will go and curses her luck.

According to her original plan, she was supposed to leave a couple of days after Christmas. Due to circumstances outside her control, she moved everything up to early Christmas morning, and it's making the whole thing way too complicated.

The original plan called for sneaking out of the house at four in the morning and catching the eight-fifteen train on West L.A. Avenue. She knew that would be a little walk, but it seemed better than running the risk of someone recognizing her at the bus station two blocks down from her house.

The plan required money, so with kind of a Robin Hood philosophy, once and sometimes twice a week she'd strategically removed excess cash from Mrs. P.'s wallet. Not all of it, of course. She waited until her parents were asleep and went through her mother's purse, looking for bills she wouldn't miss. The woman only used cash. Rose didn't even know if she owned a credit card. It was so easy to make a twenty or two go missing without the Parsimmons so much as raising an eyebrow. They didn't count it, at least not when she was around.

All in all, Rose finds herself walking down Stearns Avenue with four hundred and sixty dollars to her name. Not to be stupid, she's spread it out. Two hundred in her backpack. One hundred in her bra. One hundred and twenty pinned to the inside of her sock, and forty in her jacket pocket. Somehow the money makes her feel safe, as if she has weapons or armor stashed all over instead of flimsy pieces of green paper. Enough money for a train ticket. Enough for a Motel 6 until she gets on her feet. Enough for food, water, and supplies for a long time if she spends it wisely. Not a lot, but enough.

So it's painful to think about wasting any of it on a taxi. Certainly, she can't take a taxi all the way to her final destination. That could deplete her money supply like a hole in a bucket of water. *This is where the timing thing just kicks me in the ass. It's no big surprise that neither the train nor the buses are running tonight, in the freaking middle of the night on Christmas.* It's not like she lives in the city, or even in Van Nuys. No. She lives in Simi Valley. Not a small town by any means, but still sleepy enough to have a backward public transportation system. Everyone and their mother have a car, pretty much.

Everyone has a car, and everyone has a cell phone. Everyone except her. So finding a pay phone in the middle of the night is no easy task. When she finds one by that Circle K across from the bus stop, she ducks her head in, flipping through the yellow pages and looking for a taxi service. Shit, she thinks. What a freaking waste of money.

Nala meows from inside her cotton tote bag. Rose almost left her behind at the Parsimmons', mostly because she knew what a pain it would be to carry her, but when the time came, she just *couldn't*. Nala looked at her with those big soulful eyes, and it reminded her too much of the day she'd lost her own mother, driving off in that cop car so many years ago. She couldn't leave Nala.

Rose rests the bag on the floor and Nala settles down inside, curling around herself. Rose holds her finger against the number in the yellow pages and dials it slowly. Oh well, she'll take a taxi just far enough to make herself invisible. Someplace where no one will know her signature Pocahontas face. She'll find a cheap hotel and wait it out. She tries not to think of what she has to do next. It makes her teeth chatter, and that panicky feeling stir up her heart. *Don't think about it. It has to be done. It's part of the plan.* She tries to breathe, but her chest feels heavy, like it's weighed down by a stack of encyclopedias. *Breathe. Think of something peaceful. Serene.*

She leans against the wall, waiting for the taxi with her eyes closed. She visualizes an ocean with rolling, crashing waves. That's what her crampy stomach feels like it's doing. These past months she's been practicing visualizing, escaping mentally. She's had to. Otherwise she really would have gone nuts, trapped in that house…in that room. The ocean always felt serene to her, and if she really focuses, she can almost hear the waves. Unfortunately Chase's voice rips her away from the sand between her toes, sort of ruining it for her.

"Rose?" Her name sounds like a question, an uncertainty, like he half expects her to turn around and be someone else, a girl who just looks like someone he once knew. She recognizes his voice before she even opens her eyes.

"What the hell do you want?" she asks, not in an unfriendly way, one eye open. Her voice sounds like sandpaper, but it's strange how easily words come to her after so long without talking.

He stands for a moment, like he isn't sure what to say. Or maybe he's just looking her over. She knows she looks different. She's braided her hair into two thick ropes, Native American style, for one. And she is wearing no makeup. Just cherry Chap Stick. No thick black eyeliner. No mascara. Just her naked face.

Uncomfortable with his eyes on her, Rose pulls the cuffs of her oversized coat over her hands. She's surprised he even noticed her in this coat. It's zipped up to her neck and so oversized that she practically disappears inside it.

Finally, Chase blows into his hands, then rubs them together. "I'm here to rescue you," he says, delivering the line with nowhere near enough gusto.

Rose can't help herself. "Oh, come on now, Prince Charming. If you're gonna say that, say it like you mean it." In the quiet darkness of the street, two headlights approach, slow slightly, then move past. The silence after the engine rumbles off seems thicker than it had before.

"She speaks," Chase teases tentatively. "Glad to see your sense of humor hasn't completely dried up."

"So shoot me."

He shifts uneasily. "That's only necessary if you're not already planning to shoot yourself. Wouldn't want to waste an extra bullet."

"What?"

"Or hang yourself. Or slice your wrists, or jump in front of a train, or any other gruesome thing Becca has dreamed up."

"Becca?" Rose tries to read Chase's face. It's been so long. She isn't sure whether the crinkles by his eyes mean he's joking or about to cry. "Oh, I vote for leaping in front of a train. It's so theatrical. Not to mention quick."

Chase grabs her by the shoulders. "I'm serious here."

Okay. Note to self. Eye crinkles mean serious. "You guys really thought I was going to kill myself?"

"So you're not?" Chase doesn't look sure.

"As much as my so-called parents think I'm a nutcase, I'm really not." The fluorescent light from the Circle K shines so brightly it's giving her a headache.

"People don't kill themselves because they're crazy. They kill themselves because they're desperate."

"Well, in that case—I am desperate. Maybe I should consider it." Rose reaches her hand behind her to touch the stucco wall, feeling the bumps beneath her skin. Nala rustles in the cotton tote by her feet.

"Rose, this isn't funny."

"Oh, come on, it's a little funny." Rose tries to keep the conversation light. It might distract him from figuring out her real plan. That is, if he hasn't figured it out already. "Are you wearing pajama bottoms? That's funny."

Chase looks down. "We haven't heard from you in eight months. You've disappeared from Simi Valley, holed up in that house, not returning emails or anything. And then in the middle of the night we get this email saying good-bye, that you hope we'll forgive you, and we can have your leftover shit? What were we supposed to think?"

"You weren't supposed to get the email until tomorrow. What the hell are you guys doing up in the middle of the night?"

"Man, you *have* been locked up for a long time. Don't you remember what it's like to be a teenager?"

Chase finding her has complicated things. She isn't sure she has the energy to keep this sarcastic banter going. She's a little out of practice. "How'd you find me?"

"I figured bus stops and train station."

"Yeah. Too bad nothing's running." Rose feels her stomach cramp again. *Shit.* She hopes she won't puke here in front of him. She turns her eyes to him, all serious. "Thanks for checking on me. I'm okay." Rose inches away from the fluorescent light of the store and back toward the darkness of the night.

"No, you're not okay. But you're welcome."

Rose manages to smile, maybe the first time in months. "Crap. You know me too well. I let you get too close, and that's nothing but trouble." She picks up the tote and slings it over her shoulder. Damn, it's heavy. Maybe she's been feeding Nala too much tuna.

"Come stay with me." Chase lifts her chin with one finger. "I bet I can get Candy to keep her mouth shut until we figure out what you should do. Especially if I tell her you're being abused and you have no place to go. She has a soft spot for that."

Wouldn't it be so easy? To just let Chase bring her home and take care of her. God, the idea of sharing the plan, lightening her load, almost makes her giddy. But no. No. She can't tell anyone. "Thanks, Chase," Rose whispers. She really means it. "But I have to do this on my own. I don't want to drag anyone else into it."

"Do what? And why? Why do you have to do anything alone? Just because you had two sets of parents who let you down doesn't mean everyone else will. Take a risk." His serious eyes pull her in like a lassoed bull. "Give me your *hand*, like that picture you drew. Let me help you."

"I'm all about taking risks," she tells him. "Don't you remember?"

"Yes and no. Sometimes the risk is trusting someone." Chase shakes his head, stepping back again to study her. "I don't get you, Rose. You're complicated."

A taxi pulls up. "You're just figuring that out?" Rose asks him, almost sadly. Her chest has that homesick don't-leave-me ache, which is silly, since she's the one leaving. "This is my ride." She tosses her backpack in, carefully sets the cotton tote on the seat, and heaves her tired self into the car. She breathes in. The air inside the car is stale but warm. She wraps her fingers around the forty dollars in her pocket. It makes her feel better, kind of.

"You can't go yet." Chase holds on to the door, but awkwardly, as if he doesn't know what he'll do when the taxi pulls away.

"I can and I am."

"But Rose, tell me this. What did you want us to forgive you for?"

She pulls the door shut, away from his grasp. "You're hung up on that, huh?" She rests her arm on the edge of the open window. "All right. I think I told you once that I can make anything okay in my head."

"So? What does that have to do with forgiveness?"

The driver shifts gears into drive. Rose leans her head out of the window, her thick braids hanging down. Her throat tightens up, but she still manages to say, "So maybe I was wrong. Maybe there are some things that won't ever be okay." And with that, the taxi pulls away, leaving Chase in a cloud of exhaust fumes.

BEFORE

30
ROSE

ROSE SAT ON THE GRASS, plucking piece after piece after piece so that she wouldn't have to think. Looking as tired as if he'd pulled two all-nighters in a row, Chase dropped the bomb. "Okay, so after almost three years of unpaid child support, my mom finally filed with the courts for back payment. That means the courts will deduct a part of each of my dad's paychecks and send it to Candy. Sounds good, right?"

Rose nodded.

"I thought so too. Only out of the blue my dad called Candy to tell her he'd sobered up and was a changed man. Said he wanted to share custody now that he had his shit together."

"Convenient timing," Daniel muttered.

"I know. Candy said, 'Gee thanks, but no thanks.' Then Walter countered with a legal request to reevaluate custody. He wants us to live with him part time."

When Rose learned that Walter lived in Bakersfield, she groaned out loud. Same state, but a good three-hour drive. What good did that do a sorry-ass, non-driving reject like herself? The Parsimmons had refused to let her take driver's ed, making her unlike every other sophomore in the free world. They claimed her lack of impulse control could make her a hazard to the road.

Rose lay on her back in the center of a dandelion patch. She could see the mountains from where she lay, and for a moment it seemed as though they were closing in on her, moving closer and closer, ready to flatten her. The warning bell rang in the distance, and she saw blurry shapes of students standing, moving, heading toward lockers and classrooms. They were blurry because of her tears. She rolled over onto her stomach and said hotly, "So what, Chase, he *forgot* he had kids for three years?" She swiped her arm across her eyes, hoping no one noticed. "You have to fight this."

"I want to fight this," Chase agreed quietly. "I researched it online, and they'll let anyone over fourteen address the court. But I don't want to take the chance of the court making Daisy go without me."

"Hire a lawyer!" Becca bounced from side to side like she was getting ready to box. "Get someone to fight for you both!"

"Yeah, and pay for him, how? We can barely make the rent."

Daniel balanced Becca's agitation with complete calm. Seriousness. "Our parents would help you. Hell—the synagogue would help you. They've always got one fundraiser or another going. They have a cash collection box in the office—for tzedakah—for good deeds. This would be a good deed. I have an in with the rabbi, you know."

Chase laid his hand on Daniel's shoulder and sighed. "My mom won't accept charity."

Rose felt like a piece of stale taffy, pulled so hard she just might break. She snapped to her feet. "It's time for her to step up to the plate and fight for her kids!"

Chase reached his hand up toward her. "Look, Rose, my mom means well, but she's never had the balls to stand up for me before. Why should she now?"

Rose looked around, searching for an answer. "I say let's run away."

"Are you out of your mind?"

"At least then we would be together." The second she said it, she realized it sounded much more dramatic than she'd intended. She could hardly breathe.

Chase stared at her and pushed himself to his feet. Becca and Daniel stared too.

"I can't leave Daisy."

"Bring her."

"Rose, neither you nor I have our shit together enough to take care of a kid. I don't mind playing uncle now and then, but I don't want to be Daisy's dad." Chase reached over Rose's hair, gathering it away from her face. He looked at her, almost like he was apologizing. "Besides, I want to go to college—Becca, don't you dare make a crack about my grades."

Daniel sighed, tilting his head back until he was looking at the clouds. "Would you ever consider just calling the guy? Saying, 'Hey look, Dad, I miss you and all but I have a job out here and my friends, and I just don't want to move'? You know, talk to him man to man?"

Chase stared at Daniel, unblinking, for a moment. "I guess it can't hurt to try."

31
CHASE

CANDY AGREED ALMOST IMMEDIATELY THAT Chase should call Walter. Her eyes brightened and she ran to find Walter's phone number. Daisy crouched at his feet, and Candy sank down next to her. Dialing the numbers, Chase didn't know whether he wanted Walter to pick up or not. Might be kind of nice to get the machine. The machine couldn't yell at him, couldn't make him feel the size of an insect, couldn't laugh.

No such luck. "Done Rite Roof Repair, this is Walter." His voice had that singsong customer service quality. It sounded nothing like the voice Chase remembered.

Chase seriously considered hanging up. But he figured Walter would call right back, pissed now that someone had crank-called him. So he waited for the words to come to him. They seemed to get stuck somewhere in his throat.

"Hello?"

"Hi," Chase barely whispered.

"You've reached Done Rite Roof Repair, what can we do you for?"

"Walter—Dad—it's me, Chase."

The pause circled around him, making him dizzy. He'd just about convinced himself that Walter didn't remember him when he heard a response. "Well, shit." That was a Walter hello if he'd ever heard one. "Haven't heard from you in going on three years."

Chase nodded, forgetting that Walter couldn't see him. Daisy edged closer, as if she was trying to protect him from an invisible enemy. "I...I...uh..." Chase stuttered stupidly. "Walter—I have a girlfriend out here now."

Again the long pause. "Well...all *right*." Walter said with forced enthusiasm, like Chase had just scored a touchdown. "How's *that* going?"

Now it was Chase's turn to give a labored pause. He felt torn. Brag to his dad and try to earn some respect, or honor the girl he loved? He might have gone for the bragging, but Daisy and his mother sat there listening to his every word. "It's just that...I don't want to leave Simi." Chase felt little bubbles of sweat gather at his brow. "I want to see you— Daisy does too—I just, I don't want to move away from my girlfriend."

Quiet. It struck Chase that he'd spent more of this conversation in silence than with words. If Walter had been standing in front of him, Chase would have been scared shitless, sure, but at least the silence wouldn't have felt so uncomfortable.

"You got my letter, then." Walter's voice sounded strained. "You're telling me you don't want to come live with me for the summer?" Chase searched for the words, all too aware that his pause told his father more than words ever could. "I'm not talking full time here, just summer and maybe a couple of months at the beginning of the school year."

"Next year is my senior year, Dad."

"I haven't seen you in three years."

Suddenly Chase felt brave. Walter wasn't about to reach his hand through the phone and strangle him. He could say what he wanted.

"Honestly, I haven't had any windshields shattered over me recently, and I haven't minded so much," he said, then waited. No response, so he went for it again. "Candy hasn't broken her arm in a while either."

Chase could almost hear Walter grinding his teeth through the phone. "Look, Chase." Walter spoke so softly that Chase actually leaned forward. "I'm different now. I stopped drinking. I'm hitting twelve-step meetings a couple times a week." Chase thought about pointing out the irony in the word "hitting" but decided against it.

Instead he held the phone away from his ear, trying to read Candy's expression. The silence worked in his favor. "Hey kid, I'm not gonna force you guys to come stay with me, but I just want you to know that I'm different now. And I miss you."

There were a thousand things Chase wanted to say. *Why contact us now, after all this time? Do you really want to see us, or do you just want to get out of paying child support? If you care about us so much, why don't you come visit?* Of course, he said none of that. He'd gotten what he wanted, an out. Chase sighed. "We'll stop by next time we pass through Bakersfield." He had never been to Bakersfield in his life.

"Hey, can I talk to Candy for a minute?" Candy and Daisy sat so close to the phone that they could hear his voice anyway. Candy shook her head back and forth, mouthing excuses.

"She's not here right now." Chase lied. "She's uh…"

It sounded like Walter held the phone away from him while he cursed. He obviously hadn't changed *that* much. "Just tell her to call me. Tell her we're two civilized adults. We should be able to have a conversation every once in a while." Candy raised her eyebrow at the word "civilized."

When Chase said good-bye, he felt his whole body lighten. Daisy grinned and Candy laughed nervously. "Damn. I never would have thought it would be that easy," she said.

"*Easy?*" Now that it was over, Chase's anger surged. "*I* was the one on the phone, not you." Candy tightened her ponytail, and suddenly she looked very young. "Why wouldn't you talk to him? He can't break your arm over the phone!"

Candy's eyes flashed. "Lay off it."

"No, come on," Chase insisted. "Why don't you ever have any balls?" His voice gathered strength, like all the things he didn't say to Walter had built up, gathering force like water behind a dam. "You *never* stood up for us. Sure, *he* hurt me. But you *let him* hurt me. Who's more to blame?"

Suddenly the sight of Candy in front of him, chickening out as always, sickened him. He couldn't stand to look at her one second longer. He squeezed his eyes shut and slammed his fist into the palm of his hand. It stung like a bitch, though, and that brought him back to reality. Wary, he opened his eyes, only to see Daisy inching backward, arms crossed like she was literally holding herself together. She looked scared. Of him.

He paced his breathing. *Relax*. He could feel his adrenaline shooting through his veins. "Don't worry, Daze. I'll stay cool." He looked back at Candy. Maybe he'd go for a run. That would help him chill. "I'll drop it, Candy, I promise. I just have to say one more thing." Now his voice steadied. "Pull it together and start acting like a mother."

Candy opened her mouth as if to say something, but she closed it again, her words unsaid.

32

CHASE

ROSE HAD ALWAYS THOUGHT "LOVESICK" was nothing more than an expression. But here she was, hunched over the toilet, praying to puke so that she'd feel better. Thoughts raced through her head over and over, like an iPod stuck on repeat. *Chase is gonna move away. He'll leave me, just like everyone else. I was a goddamn idiot to think this time would be different. That someone would actually step up for me.* Any flashes of hope fizzled. *I will be left with my jail keepers. I don't even have a best friend to vent to.* Ever since Becca got all up in Rose's face about the Parsimmons, things had been strained.

She went back to her room and lay on her twin bed, one arm flung over her eyes. It didn't help that heat had settled over the Valley early this year. Barely May, and already the house felt hot as a toaster oven. The porch wasn't much cooler, even with the Santa Anas blowing through.

She flung herself onto her comforter and buried her face, blaming Mrs. P. for the Pepto-Bismol pink that coated everything in the room. Too hot to lie facedown for long, she rolled over. The wardens came to check on her, as expected, before they went to bed. She pretended to be asleep. Eyes closed, one arm draped over them, lips slightly parted, and slow, deep breathing. She heard the creak of the footsteps approaching and then the slight brush of air as the door swung open. They stood and watched her.

She heard Mr. P. whisper, "She looks sort of sweet when she's asleep." And Hursula's quiet response, "I know. If only she stayed that way when she was awake." Then the brush of air again as the door closed, a gentle thud against the door frame, and the creaking of the steps moving away.

This was the time of night Rose normally psyched herself up for the evening escape. She usually waited another hour or so, of course, until there was no movement within the house, but tonight, there seemed to be no point in going to Chase's. Why? So she could love him more? So she could have sex with him? So he could go off to his father's and leave her alone? She'd trusted him, she'd opened up to him, and now he'd be leaving her.

She fell asleep there, her thoughts still tossing and turning while her body slept. She woke at midnight to hear a tiny cluster of taps against her window. It sounded like a tree branch rustling in the wind, but she knew there were no tree branches directly against the window. She leaped out of bed, her heart instantly bumping around in her chest. Again, light tapping. In one quick movement she threw back the pink flowered curtains. There, nose pressed against the glass, stood Chase, his hair tousled and wind blown.

After the initial wave of shock passed, Rose rushed forward and put her finger to her lips. *Shhh!* She eased the window up slowly, soundlessly. She carefully removed the screen from the window and gestured for him to climb in. "What the hell are you doing?" she hissed, not sure whether to be mad or glad for the company.

"I had to see you," he whispered back, so close she could feel his breath on her cheek, and she shivered. "I emailed you, but you didn't respond, and I didn't want you to worry."

Her throat caught for a second. She swallowed. "Well, tell me."

"I'm not going to my dad's."

"No shit?" Rose tried to sound casual, but she was pretty sure she didn't.

"My dad always had this image of what he wanted me to become. Tough, you know. Maybe even kind of a player."

"A player?"

"I'm not, of course. You're the only one I've ever really been with. But all he knows is I have a girlfriend. And I told him I won't leave you."

Suddenly, Rose's insides felt like she'd just sipped a mug of hot chocolate and could feel the warmth slipping down inside her. "*You won't leave me*," she repeated.

Chase pulled something from behind his back. A single stem. A rose. He kissed her forehead. "I know you think giving you a rose is corny. But I don't." He put the rose between his teeth and stepped closer. "I'd kiss you with this in my mouth, but I don't want to poke you with a thorn," he mumbled around the stem.

"You're a dumb ass," she breathed, loving him. "I might have the flu. I shouldn't kiss you anyway."

"Any flu you have, I want."

"You're an idiot. I'll have to beat you up." She gingerly took the stem from his lips. "You broke two rules. Rule number one: coming to my house. Rule number two: you're not supposed to be in charge, remember?"

Chase wrapped his arm around her. "We might have to renegotiate that." He pulled her toward her pink bed in her pink room. "And if you must beat me up—go ahead."

Rose leaned forward to pin him to her mattress. She wrapped her hands around his wrists and put weight on her arms. Without warning—no creaks, no thuds, no warning movement in the air—the bedroom door swung open. There stood Hursula, in a light flowered nightgown, staring at the two of them. Her eyes turned hard enough to cut glass.

33
ROSE

ROSE MIGHT AS WELL HAVE been Rapunzel from *Tangled* locked up in that tower, totally isolated. Except for school, she couldn't leave the house. After an hour on the phone with her shrink, Mr. and Mrs. P. decided she was a "danger to herself and others." Not in the traditional loaded-weapon kind of way, but more in the keep-that-girl-locked-up kind of way. And definitely keep her away from that no-good Chase kid.

The day after Hursula stormed in on them, she dragged Rose over to the synagogue office to force her resignation. At first Mrs. Rosenberg had greeted them with her wide horsey smile, setting aside the stack of tzedakah money she'd been counting. But once Hursula started explaining Rose's fragile mental state, Mrs. Rosenberg's smile melted, until finally she just stood there with her lips pressed into a thin line. Becca stepped into the office just then, but stopped short. She looked like she was trying to catch Rose's eye, but Rose kept her face down. With a sigh, Becca grabbed a couple rolls of paper towels and left.

Rose could feel the isolation taking its toll. Like an addict, she felt herself going through withdrawal. Chase withdrawal. Love withdrawal.

Attention withdrawal. She felt physically ill. She could hardly even eat. She caught him for moments at school, but it wasn't the same. No afternoons at the temple day care. No five-minute make-out sessions in the coat closet. No long, drawn-out talks. No being held in his warm arms for hours on end. No falling asleep to the rise and fall of his chest.

At first, Rose wanted to cut class just to be with him, but Hursula dropped in the front office to check her attendance every day, so it seemed too risky. And now when he saw her, all he seemed to want to do was fantasize about these fairy-tale solutions that would never materialize.

"The Steins could take you in." *Yeah, but the Parsimmons would never let them.* "Be extra good—and they'll back off this." *You don't know them. Once they make up their mind, it sticks. They think they're protecting me.* "I'll go talk to them. I'll explain." *That what, you were tutoring me in math? That you thought you'd save me the trip to your house? That you love me?*

Rose could barely keep her nose above water. Just shuffled along, home to school, school to home. Slept at home. Slept at school. Slept at home. Ignored Chase and Becca so that they would go away and let her crawl back into her turtle shell where she wouldn't have to feel anything ever again.

So when Becca barreled across the quad to confront her, the accusation caught her by surprise. "You self-centered bitch!" she hissed loud enough for Rose to hear, but no one else. Rose had been sitting against the eastern wall, knees drawn to her chest, trying to keep her mind blank.

Instantly, Rose's senses switched on hyper-alert. They'd been dulled for so many days that now the light seemed too bright and the sounds too loud. "What are you talking about?" She could hear the slamming of locker doors, the swooshing of shoes padding down the halls, and laughter, laughter everywhere, coming at her from all sides like she was the butt of some joke.

"You stole the tzedakah money!" Becca yelled down at her, louder this time, her hoop earrings large enough to bang against her chin when she moved.

"The *what* money?" Rose pushed herself to standing and faced Becca directly, realizing once again how short Becca was, even with two-inch platform shoes.

"All you ever think about is yourself. Poor Rose, stuck with rotten parents. Poor Rose has to quit her job." Becca stood close enough that Rose could smell the bubblegum she used to cover the cigarette stink. "You never get off your pity potty long enough to notice the rest of the world."

Rose felt like she'd woken up in class after being called on for an answer—not knowing the question or the topic or the page. "Becca, I—"

"I know it was you. I saw you watching Mrs. Rosenberg count the tzedakah cash box. The money went missing three days later."

"*What?*" Rose started to step backward, but bumped into the locker behind her. The air felt suddenly thick, and the room too crowded. "Becca, I can't set one foot out my front door without the parent police breathing down my neck."

"That hasn't stopped you before!" Becca snapped. "You have a one-track mind. You want to get your parents back at any cost. I know you." Becca's eyes narrowed. "You don't care who you hurt. In fact, I don't think you care about anyone but yourself." She turned on her heel and started to walk away. "If you cared about anyone else, you'd realize that they're going to blame Chase," she tossed over her shoulder. "Someone saw him in the office the day the money disappeared."

34
CHASE

IF CHASE HAD KNOWN ROSE'S mother would fling open that door at a quarter past one, he *never* would have knocked on her window. If he had known her parents would make her quit the job, he never would have so much as thought about breaking a single one of Rose's stupid rules. If he had known that money would go missing from the temple office, he never would have gone up there to look for extra green paint. The day-care kids could have painted blue grass or purple grass. Green grass was overrated.

But of course, he knew none of that.

Chase cornered Rose before Math Analysis. She walked with her head low, her long silky hair draped over her face. He grabbed her arm and pulled her into an empty computer lab. "Ouch." She wrapped her fingers around his, prying them loose.

"Relax, Rose," he said softly. He hadn't meant to scare her. "You've been avoiding me. I just wanted to talk for a minute."

She backed away from him. "Haven't you messed things up enough?"

"Hey, I'm sorry about that. Stupid, I know."

"Beyond stupid."

"I *said* I was sorry." An edge crept into his voice. "That doesn't mean you have to completely cut me off. It's not all or nothing, you know."

"It is to me." Rose looked through him, her eyes glassy.

"What is wrong with you?" He pulled her closer again. "You're not *on* anything, are you?"

"It's none of your business," she snapped. Then, softer, "No. I'm not on anything. I'm just not sleeping. I can't kick the flu. I shouldn't even be here right now—I'm probably contagious. But staying home in that hellhole is not an option," she said. "And I can't turn my mind off at night. Maybe I'm being punished for all the crap I've pulled. Maybe God is punishing me."

"Don't you dare buy that bullshit. Who's feeding you that crap? Your parents?" Chase asked, but Rose shrugged. "They may say that, but that doesn't mean it's true."

"It doesn't mean it's *not* true either."

Chase sighed, releasing her arm. "Rose." A dangerous thought caught in his mind. He tried to shake it free. "You didn't take that money, did you?"

As if he'd flipped a light switch, her face changed. Tightened. Withdrew. Hardened. "Are you *serious*? You're seriously going to ask me that?" The dullness faded from her eyes, and they scared him.

Chase sort of shrugged. He hadn't known she'd be so offended.

"You *bastard*." She grabbed on to his shirt now, with two fists. "*You* probably stole that money. You thought you'd get out of it by blaming me. Well, *screw you*." Each word burned through his skin and right into his soul.

"Let go of me." Chase felt his adrenaline pumping and that scared him too. He tried to breathe deeply, in and out, but the urge to shove her away built and built.

"You and your freaking 'I want to be a better man' crap. It's bullshit." She beat on his chest now with her fists. "You are who you are. And you are what you do. I know I'm shit. But maybe you're shit, too."

Chase clenched his jaw. He needed to run, to pound his feet against the pavement, to channel that adrenaline toward something other than her face. He stepped back toward the door, reaching for the knob.

"You can't handle it, Chase?" Rose had that counter-attack look. Where had he seen that before? "I thought you said your dad raised you not to be a wuss."

Chase felt the sting of that as sure as if she'd backhanded him across the face. "I don't want to hurt you," he managed through gritted teeth.

"Hurt *me*?" she cackled, following him, not letting him escape. "I think you've already done that."

That was when he pushed her. Not a hard push—just a get-out-of-my-way-and-leave-me-alone push. The adrenaline had kicked in, though, so it hit her harder than he'd intended. She stumbled back a little. He thought he caught a glimpse of shock in her eyes, and that look made him feel about as small and weak and insignificant as a dead flea. Then acceptance.

"*Screw* you," she said sadly. "You're just like all the rest." She pressed her fingers to her temples and mumbled to herself. "This is why I never love anybody." Then she brought her eyes back up to his. Now he saw hate, and that made him want to crawl into a locker and die. "Don't you ever freaking touch me. I don't care if you took that money or not. Just leave me alone. I never want to see you again."

Chase stumbled backward himself. Shoved open the door. Rose lunged for the trash can and puked. She brought her head up to look at him through steely eyes. "And I hope you get my freaking flu. Maybe God will punish you too."

35
CHASE

CANDY GOT WIND OF THE missing money before Chase even stepped foot off campus. Man, those women at Salon Joli could talk.

After the fight with Rose, Chase took off from school running. Running past the lockers. Past the C building. Past the campus security.

Chase barged through the front door just as Candy hung up the phone. "That was the attendance office, reporting you AWOL." She hadn't even set down her purse, just stood holding on to it with two hands, her knuckles turning white. Chase slammed the door behind him and went for his room. Candy blocked his path. "Hey."

"Leave me alone." He tried to step around her.

"You were right, Chase. I need to stand up and be your mother." She planted herself directly in front of him. With her that close, he could hardly see her face, she was so short. "I've let too many things slide. Your grades…when you're capable of so much more, the way you disrespect me when you get pissed, letting *that girl* come here at all hours of the night." Something about the way she said "that girl" got under his skin. "So you tell me. What did you do with the money?"

A roar ripped out of him that could've rivaled a caged lion. Candy stepped back. He could see her face now, showing surprise, if anything. "Why do you assume I took that money?" Chase howled.

Candy's eyes flicked from side to side, as if she was trying to decide what to do. Chase felt like a helium balloon, hovering over himself, watching himself get angrier and angrier. He wanted to yell down at himself to knock it off, to go take another run, to do something to calm down, but it was as if he was yelling from too far a distance. He couldn't quite hear himself. Or maybe he didn't really *want* to hear himself.

Chase moved away from her, pacing back and forth across the length of the kitchen/living room/dining room. Angry as he was, it only took him five strides to get from one end to the other. Rose's words rang in his ears. *Don't you ever freaking touch me!* Chase tried to remember. He hadn't hurt her, had he? He *wouldn't* hurt her, would he? He loved her. *Just leave me alone. I never want to see you again.* She couldn't mean that.

He'd opened himself up to her in a way he never had before. That was special. At least to *him*. Suddenly, everything came into focus. Maybe it hadn't been special for *her*. Maybe she'd snared him in her trap just like she had done to every other fool who'd written her name on the bathroom walls. She said he was different. But maybe that was part of her game. "Bitch," he muttered out loud.

Candy chose that unfortunate moment to decide her course of action. "What did you call me?" She hesitated for a moment, then barreled on ahead. "This is exactly what I mean. Your lack of respect." Chase continued his pacing. "Look, Chase. I know you've been trying hard to control this temper you've got. That's why I don't understand why you'd take that money—"

Chase hunched over and screamed into his stomach like he was in searing pain, his fists balled. "*Mom!*" he yelled through gritted teeth.

"Don't you know me at all? Don't you owe me the courtesy to get my side? *No!* You just assume I did it!"

Again the hesitation. Her voice grew quieter. "So tell me. Tell me what happened." Her hand reaching for his shoulder.

"Don't touch me!" He twisted away from her. "Nothing happened! Okay? All I know is that money got stolen."

"But they saw you there——"

"I *work* there!" He turned to her, pain and hurt welling up. "Have I ever stolen anything in my life?"

Silence.

"A stick of bubblegum? Candy from the drugstore? Any freaking thing?"

"I…"

"That's right. You don't know. Because you weren't there. And if you were there, you were talking to your friends with me tagging along like a little freaking puppy dog." His breaths came out in little puffs now. "But if you had been paying attention, you would know that I never in my whole pathetic life have ever stolen a damn thing! If you knew me, you wouldn't accuse me of this." He crouched over again, this time feeling tears rush in behind his eyes. "But maybe nobody knows me." *Not even Rose.*

"Maybe that girlfriend of yours took the money," Candy backpedaled. "People talk about her. Say she's no good."

Chase grabbed her then. By the shoulders. Grabbed his own mother and shook her. "*Shut up!*" he yelled. "*Don't say that!*" She looked like one of those bobblehead dolls, eyes wide open and goggling, her head moving back and forth.

She brought her hands to his, holding on like it might steady her, and she dug her nails in. "*Stop it!*" she screamed back. "You are out of control! *Stop it!*"

So he did. But not before he backhanded her. Across the face. He wanted her to stop yelling, which she did. He watched her, slow motion-like, twist in the direction of the blow, spiraling almost. Her hands immediately clutched her face, before she even hit the ground. Her cheek turned a stinging red. She lay there, breathing heavily but still, as if she was playing dead. He wondered if she'd tried that trick with Walter. But he wasn't Walter. He *wasn't*. Then why did he feel like him?

With a sudden jolt, he was back in his body, no longer watching from the helium safety above. And Jesus Christ, *it hurt*. He hurt. His chest ached. His soul ached. And oh-my-god—he had hit his own mother. *Oh. My. God.*

For the longest second in history, Chase stood staring at his hands. They did not look like his own. Large. Rough. Calloused, as if he'd spent his first sixteen years roofing houses with Walter instead of holding a No. 2 pencil. His hands were shaking now, as if they understood what they had done. They had betrayed him.

For all his striving-to-be-a-better-man crap, he'd just turned into the guy who beats on his own mom. Chase wasn't sure whether to run or to cry. But then he realized his cheeks were wet. He was already crying, the pain seeping out his eyes. Candy cried too, peeking up at him at first like a rabbit from a den, then relaxing visibly, like she knew the rage was over.

"I'm sorry, Chase," she started, holding out her hand. "You are out of control." She hesitated, and then went ahead and said it. "Just like your father."

Chase couldn't breathe. It was like an air bag had exploded into his chest in a 90-mile-an-hour collision. Head on. His brain buzzed from lack of oxygen. *Just like your father.*

Candy spoke almost to herself, pulling her bare knees inward. "I don't know what to do." Chase let himself fold and crumple to the floor so that he was sitting an arm's length away from her.

"I'm sorry for the things I let happen to you and for the things you had to see. I'm sorry for trying to be your friend instead of your mother." Candy gathered herself up so that she crouched, rocking back on her heels. Her cheek looked redder by the minute, like a boiling lobster. "But now I see you with this anger, this rage, that's bigger than you are. And it scares me." She wiped her eyes with one finger, trying to catch the mascara before it rolled down her crimson cheek in a black trail.

Chase whispered, "It scares me too."

"I'm gonna say something that might piss you off, Chase, but I don't care. I'm your mother and I need to say it." She didn't need to worry. Chase felt deflated, limp, like his bones had turned to mush. "I think you might be better off living with Walter."

The mention of his name was like scraping a match to the matchbox. Only today the match was wet. Chase expected a flicker, a flash, a fire, but got nothing. Rose didn't want him anymore. No reason to stay for her. He deserved to lose Rose. She did not need a guy as messed up as him in her life. They thought he took money from the synagogue. He'd probably be fired from the day care. No reason to stay for that. The only reason to stay was Daisy...and Daniel.

"He's sober now. He's got ten months sobriety. I called him. We talked." Candy paused for a moment, like she was waiting for a pat on the back. Chase just stared at her. "I mean, he's still Walter. He's no saint. He's got a short fuse. But now that he's pulled himself together a little, maybe he can help you figure yourself out."

"You'd send me there?" If he could feel anything, he would have felt worry. Dread. Fear. But he couldn't feel a damn thing.

"If he's the same, you can come right back. But if he's different...if he's grown up now, maybe it'd be good for you."

"I'm sorry, Candy—Mom." His voice sounded flat.

"I know. I'm not trying to hurt you. I'm trying to help you."

"What about Daisy? I watch her more than you do."

Candy looked embarrassed by that, or maybe it was just the ever-deepening red on her cheek. "Then I guess I'll have to grow up too, won't I?"

36
ROSE

ROSE CONFESSED TO TAKING THE tzedakah money three hours before they found it. Turned out the whole thing had been a misunderstanding. Keeping that amount of money in an unlocked cash box in the temple office had always been an area of concern, apparently. The rabbi deposited it in the bank every two weeks.

The word was that Mrs. Rosenberg, as assistant rabbi, had made an extra bank run the evening before her annual young adult camping trip. She explained that the box seemed full, and, well, why take the risk of waiting the extra week? Problem was, she forgot to tell the rabbi before she left. Or the office manager. Or leave a note for Mrs. Stein. As far as everyone knew, the money had gone missing.

Rose figured she had nothing to lose by taking the blame. Chase wouldn't call her anymore. She'd burned that bridge, and thank god. She decided to confess the moment the thought entered her mind. That would clear Chase's name. Sure, he'd hate her even more, but that was okay. It would make it easier to hate him back.

The Parsimmons accepted her confession with no more than a

raised eyebrow, but their heads practically spun in circles when Mrs. Stein called to clear things up, and they figured out her confession was a lie.

Mrs. P. slammed the phone into the charger, her eyes wild. "*What* is going on? Are you *crazy*? Are you on *drugs*?"

Purely for spite, Rose picked at the loose fabric on the underside of a couch cushion.

"Are you trying to make *me* crazy?" Hursula leaned against the couch arm for support, then switched tactics and spoke to Mr. P., who sat on the LazyBoy with his arms and legs crossed. "We need to watch this child twenty-four hours a day. Either that or send her to some kind of locked boarding school."

"We looked into those last time," Mr. P reminded her. "Their monthly payments are more than our mortgage."

Hello? I'm sitting right here. Rose glared at them and yanked harder on the loose part of the cushion. With any luck, she'd ruin it completely.

"There's only one thing left to do. It'll be tough on all of us, but I see no other choice." Hursula sank down onto a couch-chair, her voice grim. "Home school. Then we can watch her. All the time."

That snagged Rose's attention like a thorn. Her heart missed at least three beats. "No *way*!" she yelled, standing up, forgetting her mission to silently destroy their couch. "No way in *hell*!"

"Watch your language in this house," Mr. P. said, standing up too. "We'll do what we see fit."

"I *hate* you!" Rose screamed, pulling fistfuls of her own hair. "I *hate* you! You're *ruining* my *life*!"

"Well, that may be the case," Hursula said, her voice gathering strength as she went on, "but we're your parents and we have to do what we think is right to keep you safe."

"You are *not* my parents!" Rose screamed so loud she thought her brain might burst. They just stood there staring, mouths open. She slammed her way into her room, knocking over a lamp on the way in. The sound of ceramic shattering was music to her ears.

Mrs. P. came in to talk to her a few hours later. Rose spent the whole time lying on her bed with her face to the wall. Hating her. Trying not to cry any more. Her face ached, swollen from all the tears.

"Oh, Rose," Hursula sighed. "When are you going to grow out of this silent treatment thing? It's so *juvenile*."

And the light in Rose's brain clicked on.

The Silent Treatment. The only real way to make a statement. They'd taken everything that mattered to her. The only thing she had control over was herself. Her voice. And that's when Rose decided to stop talking again. Completely. No matter what.

Rose didn't have a clue that, at that very moment, Chase sat packing his bags for the move to Bakersfield.

37
CHASE

WITHIN TWO DAYS OF HIS arrival at Walter's pink stucco condo complex, after Chase had braved the new school, Walter gestured for him to pull up a folding chair for a man-to-man chat. Even though so much seemed different about Walter, Chase felt his palms grow moist and his heart race around in his chest like it was training for the Olympics.

Besides, Chase wasn't sure how much of the difference was Walter and how much of it was him. When Walter left three years ago, Chase had been almost fourteen, getting ready to start high school. And now Chase was one year shy of being a grown man, and side by side to Walter, he stood nearly as large.

Walter. The new Walter took up two-thirds of the doorway as he ducked through it, looking like a cross between a gorilla and an out-of-shape surfer. He spoke softer than Chase remembered. "Dude," he started. Since when did Walter call him 'dude'? "Once school gets out, you're with me for the summer. Understand? You need to learn a trade anyway."

A trade? Chase considered Walter's thick, sandpaper-rough

hands—lined with deep grooves and calluses. Chase turned his own hands over to look at them. "You want me to roof with you?"

"Yep. It's a good honest business."

"I'm sure it is," Chase stammered. "I just—I want to go to college."

"Last I heard, your grades were Cs and Ds."

Last you heard? Last you heard? Chase wanted to yell in his stubble-dotted face. *What do you know?* Chase balled his fists. "Whatever," he mumbled, mentally checking out. This was not going to work. He'd give it a week or two and then head back home.

"Listen here, Chase." Walter's voice lowered and toughened. Chase snapped back to focus like one of those rubber-band slingshots he made in elementary school. "I'm glad to have you here. I *wanted* to have you here. But I understand the reason your mother sent you was for a little attitude readjustment." He paused for a moment, and Chase met his eyes head on. Steady. Serious. "Don't worry. I won't readjust your attitude the way I have before."

"Uh-huh." Chase watched Walter the way he'd watch a poisonous rattlesnake. Walter's hair hung longer than Chase remembered—a little past his ears and scraggly, but in a cool kind of way.

"I'm different, Chase," Walter explained. "I know now that I'm an alcoholic. A raging, out-of-control alcoholic. My life has only begun to become manageable in the last ten months since I got into the Program."

Chase once again wanted to tune him out. Being drunk didn't excuse the things Walter had done. Being drunk didn't excuse being *mean*. Chase tilted back in his folding chair so that it leaned back onto its hind legs. "The Program?"

"Alcoholics Anonymous. I have a sponsor and a higher power, and I've finally found some serenity." Serenity. Again that word.

"And a hot girlfriend." The deep throatiness of the voice surprised Chase, and he turned around to find a waif-like girl padding in with bare feet. As she stepped, the wooden beads around her ankle jangled. Chase noticed a second string of wooden beads around her neck and a long earth-colored skirt.

Walter half turned, holding his arm out to her, curving it around her waist. "This is Lex, Chase. My girlfriend."

The possibility that Walter might have a girlfriend, that he might have moved on from his family in some way or another, had never crossed Chase's mind. This girl, seemingly closer to Chase's age than to Walter's, could not have been more different from Candy if she tried. Every day, Candy spent twenty minutes on makeup alone, while this girl's face looked as fresh and clean as if she'd just stepped out of the shower.

Candy dressed in short skirts and tight tops. This girl wore a long, flowing skirt and a loose top. Lex moved like a ballet dancer—light, each bare footstep carefully placed. Candy's hair was long—styled, colored, the whole bit. This girl's hair was cut short, just about the length of Walter's, but it had been sculpted with mousse to stand up at all angles.

"Hi," Chase said, trying not to stare. She was, after all, his father's girlfriend. He wasn't sure how he was supposed to feel about that.

Lex reached her hand out to Chase and shook it strongly. "Ahh, a new victim." She grinned widely, showing rows of slightly overlapping teeth. "Don't look so scared. I'm training to teach yoga." Chase immediately pictured Daniel in a contorted yoga pose. "I make it my mission to get everyone to try yoga at least once."

Chase turned his eyes to Walter. "Even my dad?"

"He *is* stubborn, isn't he?" Lex laughed like that was the funniest thing ever. "I'm still working on him, I have to admit. I can get him to meditate with me when we're inside and no one could possibly see him, but he won't take a damn class. He thinks everyone's looking at him. Talk about self-obsessed!"

Chase stared at her. Then he turned and stared at his father. Walter shrugged and chuckled. If that had been Candy teasing him three years ago, he'd have dragged her down the hall by her hair. Chase shrugged. "I don't think yoga is my thing."

"Yoga is an acquired taste. Like fine wine," she said, staring pointedly at Walter with a look of amusement. "Only I don't drink wine anymore, so now yoga is my new release." She ran her hands through her hair, and it clumped together. She looked sort of like a *Dragon Ball Z* character, but he couldn't remember which one.

"Or your new addiction," Walter teased softly, looking first at Lex and then back at Chase. "Don't let her fool you. She's obsessed."

Chase didn't think Walter really expected a response from him, so he just sat there picking at his fingernails and watching, strangely curious. Lex snorted, though, and messed up Walter's hair. "That's the thing about your dad, Chase. He's always calling me on my shit." She laughed. "I don't mind, though. Someone's got to do it." She picked up Walter's hand.

"Your dad was there at my first meeting, when I had less than twenty-four hours sober. All I could think about was how long it would take me to walk to the nearest liquor store. I would have ditched the meeting if your dad hadn't stopped me, and who knows if I would have ever found my way back to a program? He might have saved my life."

"Glad to be of service in *every* way I can." Walter winked at her, his fingers still intertwined with hers.

Corny as hell and awkward too, but there was something about the look they shared in that moment, that look of connectedness, that made Chase think of Rose. Suddenly he missed her. And Daisy, and his mom, if he was honest. And Daniel. He felt that ache in the center of his chest—like someone had his work boot on his heart and lungs, pressing down. He knew how that felt, because in middle school Walter had stood there for nearly five minutes, one foot digging into his chest. The bruise it left displayed the ridges of his boot sole. But no one was standing on him now. He wondered if this ache was what it felt like to be homesick.

School in Bakersfield was school, just like any other place, he figured. Only he didn't know anyone. With a month left of class, no one seemed interested in making new friends, or even being friendly. He couldn't hang with the stoners or the goths or the rejects because he looked like a jock. He couldn't hang with the jocks because he wasn't a jock. He didn't seem to fit in anywhere.

So he used lunch break to go to the library to email Daniel, if there was a computer available. He didn't email Rose, although he'd thought about it a bunch of times. But she'd made it pretty clear she wanted him to stay away. That hurt worse than the homesick ache, but he tried to push it away. He'd actually even done a little studying in the library too, just to see if that would make a difference in his grades. Sometimes he used lunch to run the track a couple of times when a breeze made the heat bearable.

He wasn't there to make friends, he reminded himself. He'd be home by July, before the fireworks. Maybe that'd be just enough time for Rose to have cooled off. Because no matter what Walter said about the serenity crap, Chase knew Walter was liable to make fireworks of his own. Maybe Lex hadn't seen his temper flare yet, but Chase wasn't about to stick around for that kind of a show.

38
ROSE

AFTER THREE WEEKS OF COMPLETE silence at home, the Parsimmons packed Rose into the car and dragged her to see that pill-pushing headshrinker. Rose immediately flopped down onto his black leather couch and covered her face with an arm. The air conditioning blasted through the vents. The top layer of skin on her bare legs began to feel numb.

The Parsimmons sank into separate chairs and spoke directly to the doctor, whose eyebrows looked bushier than ever. It was as if Rose wasn't even there. "We think she's depressed, doctor."

Well, duh! Of course I'm freaking depressed. What do you think? You stole my life! You took away everything I care about and everyone who ever cared about me.

"Hmm." Dr. Gutman was a "hmm-ing" doctor if she'd ever met one. "We've had her on an antidepressant for years."

"Maybe it's not enough?" Mrs. P. asked, with a layer of worry to her voice that grated on Rose's ears.

"Hmm. And it looks like we've got her on some hormones as well, which also help to regulate her mood. The birth control pill serves multiple purposes here, I'd think." He chuckled to himself.

Real funny. I love how everyone in this room thinks I'm a whore. And suddenly an image of Chase popped into her head. She hadn't anticipated how much she'd miss him. Besides Nala, he'd been the only reason she had to get up every morning. But now he was gone, just like everyone else she'd ever loved.

"Hmm. Let me run through a battery of depression-related questions. How about it?" Dr. Gutman asked, but didn't wait for an answer. "Diminished interest in activities?"

Mr. P. piped up then, like this was a chess game instead of her life. "Check."

I have no activities to be interested in. You took them all away from me!

"Hmm. Weight loss or weight gain?"

"Check. She's hardly been eating."

Nothing tastes good.

"Hmm. Sleeping too much or too little?"

"Check."

I spend 90 percent of the day in my bed. To punctuate this thought, Rose turned herself facedown on the couch and pressed her face into the couch cushion. She didn't want to hear any more. The words came through, though, just more muffled.

"Hmm. Fatigue or loss of energy?"

"Check. She mostly stays in her room with the door shut."

And what would you have me do? Jump rope in the living room? Kickboxing in the kitchen?

"Hmm. Feelings of worthlessness? I guess we have to address that one to Rose." Dr. Gutman raised his voice to a near shout. "Rose, dear! Are you feeling worthless?"

The absurdity of the question struck Rose as funny, and she would have laughed out loud but she really didn't want to. So she didn't. She didn't so much as stir from her catatonic posture on the couch. "Doctor?" Mrs. P. asked, after a suitable silence. "She's not talking again."

"Hmm. If I remember correctly, she never talks in here." Dr. Gutman shuffled through his notes. "I guess that makes it difficult for me to ask her if she's having thoughts of death."

Depends on whose death you're talking about.

"She's not talking to *us* at all." Slight sniffle from Mrs. P., revving up the tear works.

"Hmm. Regression back to previous behavior." Some scribbling noises as Dr. Gutman wrote on his prescription pad. "All right then, let's increase her Prozac an additional 10 milligrams. That should do the trick."

If Rose had been talking, laughing, or reacting to anything that was said with more than an eye twitch, she would have cackled. Her parents had no idea that she'd been cheeking every pill they handed her. They put five or six of them on a napkin by her cereal bowl in the morning. All different shapes and sizes.

First she would pick out the vitamin and swallow it. Then she would cup her hand around the rest of them and dump them in her mouth, then push them into her cheek with her tongue and pretend to swallow. When their backs were turned, she spit them out into her napkin. Anything they wanted her taking, she didn't want sliding down her throat into her body. Besides, it was a behind-your-back screw-you, and that brought a smile to her eyes any day of the week.

Rose pressed her face further into the couch cushion, feeling the imprint of the seams on her face. It hurt a little and that was good. It reminded her that she was alive. Because she was starting to forget.

NOW

39

CHASE

SOMETHING DOESN'T MAKE SENSE. CHASE presses his face against the cool glass, thinking.

Daniel's hand-me-down Ford pickup pulled up thirty seconds after Rose's taxi turned left on New L.A. Avenue. Chase hopped in, and they'd been trailing the taxi ever since, like some kind of wannabe detectives.

He recounts the conversation for Becca and Daniel, as close to word for word as he can remember. He knows he's missing something. Like she's dropped some major clue and he just hasn't seen it.

"If she's not going to kill herself, I bet she's hiring someone to kill her parents. If that's the case, I'm not sure whether or not we should try to stop her. I might even like to help her." Becca sits wedged between Chase and Daniel in the front seat of her brother's car. Her fingers hold an unlit cigarette, and she fiddles with it, reluctantly obeying Daniel's rule of no smoking in the car. "Next thing we know, we'll see her story on *Dateline NBC*, and then there'll be a *Law and Order* episode based on it. I wonder which actress they'll get to play Rose."

"She's heading the wrong direction if she's planning a double homicide."

"Unless she's setting up an alibi. Shit. I can't breathe in here." Becca leans over Chase and out his window, sucking in the night air. She sits back down. "How sad is it that we are her best friends, and not one of us has a clue what crazy thing she is going to do?"

Chase inches toward the window on his side. "No offense, Becca, but can you just be quiet for a little while? I need to think."

"I'd be plenty quiet if I could just light up this damn cigarette!"

"Dream on," Daniel says, rummaging in the space where the CD player should be. He pulls out a pack of gum. "Here. Chew five or six of these in a row. You can barrel through the whole pack if you want. Just stop talking."

"Nice. You'll give me TMJ."

"You're talking," Daniel reminds her, keeping his eyes on the road. "Besides, TMJ is better than throat cancer."

Chase presses his palms against his temples. His head aches. The jostling of the truck and being pressed up against Becca's side doesn't help. He thinks about Rose. What did she mean when she said there were things that wouldn't ever be okay? Was she talking about the Parsimmons and the way they treated her? Was she talking about what she planned to do? If it wasn't something she could make okay, then why would she do it in the first place? Unless she thought she *had* to. And what would she feel bad about...but have to do?

The truck speeds up as it nears the freeway on-ramp, still trailing the taxi. When Chase closes his eyes, he can almost see her, wrapped in that winter coat like she was, his old Nike sweatshirt peeking out from underneath. Rose Parsimmon is as beautiful as they come. She would have looked pretty wearing army fatigues and dreadlocks.

But today Rose had seemed puffy and pale, and the sparkle seemed to have dulled from her eyes. She looked like someone had soaked her in water for days, and she moved like she had a broomstick up her ass. Like she hurt. Maybe her old man had been beating her. Anger bursts in his blood, hot as fire, at the thought of Rose being used as a punching bag...or worse.

When he thinks about Rose silent and staring at the walls for eight months, it's amazing she looks as good as she does. No sunlight. No exercise. That girl has stubborn in her blood. She'll do anything in her power to defy her parents. Hide that cat in her room. Sneak out in the middle of the night. Sleep around. Stop talking. Rose had told him once about the cocktail of medications, vitamins, and whatnot they handed her every morning and how she pretended to take them. She told him how they'd put her on the pill long before she was ever having sex, that they'd probably have neutered her if it were legal.

With his eyes still closed, Chase feels the shifting of the truck as it changes lanes and decelerates slightly to exit the freeway. In a flash, Chase remembers the warmth of her skin against his. The subtle saltiness of her lips. The way she kissed him with her eyes open. The way she wanted him to hold her for hours afterward. Thinking of her that way makes him sort of hot and petrified all wrapped as one. He opens his eyes. Chase has figured something out, but he doesn't know what.

And then like a lightbulb has switched on in his gray matter, he *does* know what. And it scares the freaking shit out of him.

BEFORE

40
ROSE

MR. P. POKED HIS HEAD into Rose's bedroom. She'd heard his work-boot footsteps squeaking down the hall, so she'd had plenty of time to scoop Nala off her lap, shove her under the bed, and pull the Pepto-Bismol-pink bed ruffle down around it. She'd never been so thankful for that bed ruffle in her life. The Parsimmons had no freaking clue about Nala. Cats were easy to hide.

Mr. P. cleared his throat and edged his whole body around the corner of the room."I brought you something," he told her, holding a large and rectangular object behind his back.

Mr. P.'s eyebrows furrowed as he took in Rose's puffy eyes and tear-streaked face. Okay, so she'd been crying, and Nala had been meowing on her lap and chasing her tears with her rough, warm tongue. She'd been missing Chase and Becca and generally feeling sorry for herself. So what? Even tough girls cry.

"You're going to have a lot of time on your hands," he said cautiously, bringing the object in front of him. A laptop computer. "And homeschool assignments, I'm sure," he added, more business-like.

"You'll need your own computer."

Mr. P. went on to explain that he'd purchased it from a fellow Daily Drip regular, a guy in pharmaceutical sales who'd decided to upgrade, so he'd offered Mr. P. a good deal to take the old computer off his hands.

Rose nodded, wiping her eyes in a way she hoped looked casual. It was hard to stop crying on a dime.

Mr. P. waited a moment, his face softening. He looked like he wanted to say something, but he didn't. Instead he busied himself with setting it up on her desk, plugging it in, and sort of humming a tuneless nothing.

Nala chose just that moment to meow, scraping her claws against the rug underneath the bed. Maybe she had to pee. Rose shifted on the bed, trying to make the bedsprings squeak to cover up Nala's sounds below. Mr. P. turned slightly and met her gaze. His eyes darted down to the Pepto-Bismol bed ruffle for a moment, then back up to hers, and there they stayed for at least a minute, unblinking.

Rose kept her gaze steady. She'd won every staring contest she'd ever had in elementary, and she wasn't about to lose this one.

Finally, Mr. P. shifted his attention back to the computer. "It was a good deal," he explained again, almost apologetically, like he somehow had to justify this financial splurge. "Can't pass up a good deal." Nala meowed again, but this time Mr. P. didn't turn back, just pushed the on button and let the laptop hum to life.

41

CHASE

SUMMER AT WALTER'S WRAPPED AROUND Chase like a caterpillar's cocoon, although he sure as hell wasn't going to turn into a butterfly. Before he knew it, July came and went, and August brushed past in a hurry.

The day-to-day hard physical labor of the roofing had torn up his back and arm muscles over and over again. Sometimes, he ached so bad it felt like someone had put his entire body into a vise and squeezed. And yet, he liked this kind of pain. The soreness made him feel real. And the increased definition of the muscles beneath his newly tanned skin didn't hurt either. He came home so worn out that all he wanted to do was lie down on Walter's couch and watch reruns of *The Simpsons*.

At least every other night, Lex came over so that she and Walter could hit a meeting. She usually slipped in carrying a bag of takeout. Thai and Indian seemed to be her favorites. Both foods Chase had never even smelled, let alone tasted, before meeting Lex. If someone had ever told Chase that his father would wind up dating this serene little yoga-teaching, pad Thai–eating pixie, Chase would have laughed.

Chase kept waiting to see the old Walter, but all he got were pieces of the old mixed with the new. Like the time Walter was irritated with a roofing assistant who spoke no English. He started to cuss him out, to work himself up—veins sticking out in his neck. But then Walter stepped away, muttering to himself. Made a phone call to his sponsor and came back to try again.

Or the time Walter stormed around the house because someone used the last of the soap without telling him. Not pounding anyone or throwing anything. Just yelling and stomping around like a little kid. But those things were like single grains of sand on a beach—they were nothing. Before, Walter had been an out-of-control monster, terrorizing his wife and kids. And now he was just a roofer with a temper. Go figure.

Every other night when Walter and Lex traipsed off to seek their higher power, Chase lounged around, enjoying his privacy. Tonight Chase grabbed a soda from the fridge and set himself up on the computer. Walter's television and computer faced each other in the living room, so Chase could channel surf while he Internet surfed. The only thing that would have made the setup more perfect (besides a hot Rose Parsimmon on his lap) would have been a bag of Flamin' Hot Cheetos. Chase resolved to get himself some.

Daniel instant-messaged Chase every couple of days, and called about once a week. In typical Daniel Stein style, he sent gossip-filled updates, funny YouTube videos, random Buddhist sayings, and the occasional political cartoon. And inevitably, every once in a while the discussion turned to Rose. Chase had been trying so hard not to obsess about her, but she'd been popping into his dreams, uninvited, nearly every night.

Chase: Her parents probably have her locked up in that house. There should be a law against that. Isn't it child abuse or something?

Daniel: Yeah, well, so is beating your kid, and we all know how often parents get arrested for that.

Chase: Ouch. Point taken. Besides, I bet they'd just say they were keeping her in for her own good, or some crap like that. I wonder if I should contact her. I haven't since I left. I figured she wouldn't want to hear from me.

Daniel: Who knows? Who knows if she even gets her messages? Becca's been trying to get hold of her. I keep telling her to forget about it already, but you know my sister. She gets obsessed.

Chase: Walter keeps talking about letting go of the things you can't control. He'd say we can't control Rose, so we need to let it go.

Daniel: Yeah, right. Try telling that to Becca.

Chase IMed Daniel back and forth for another hour, but his heart wasn't in it. His heart stayed stuck on Rose. Missing her seemed like a deep, dark abyss of churning water. Once he allowed himself to think about her, he'd be pulled under by the current and unable to get back up. *You're just like all the rest...Don't you ever freaking touch me.* Her eyes flashed before him then, the hate burning through her pupils.

Chase set down his soda. It suddenly tasted sour. He leaned his head back against the swivel chair. He had pushed her. Why? What was wrong with him? Did he inherit a bad temper from Walter just like he'd inherited his height and his eyes?

Chase remembered the quote Daniel had emailed last week: "Anger will never disappear so long as thoughts of resentment are cherished in the mind." Had Walter magically rid himself of a big, old bag of resentments?

Chase tried to figure out who he resented, who he had to forgive. Walter—for hurting them, Candy—for not protecting them, Rose for being so damn self-destructive, and last year's English teacher for assigning books to read over the summer. Suddenly, like a blast of cold air, Chase realized who he resented the most. *Himself.*

Slowly Chase typed in Rose's email address with plunk-plunk fingers. I am thinking of you. He felt like his fingers were marching into battle. I'm sorry for the way we left things. I want a do-over. What do you say? As he pressed Send, he wondered if Rose even had access to the Internet. With her parents, he couldn't be sure.

42
ROSE

ROSE WOULD HAVE BET EVERY Prozac capsule in the bathroom cabinet that Nala understood her better than any human ever would. Too bad she didn't have any funky Alice in Wonderland pills to take her to a far-off land crazier than her own.

They think I'm nuts. Certifiable, in fact. Nala tilted her head just slightly to the left, watching Rose, then curled up in her lap. Rose could hear the Parsimmons talking in worried tones from the living room. They seemed to think that just because she'd stopped talking for the last three months, she somehow couldn't *hear* now either. They didn't even bother to lower their voices. *Hello, people. I still have ears.*

Mr. P. hemmed and hawed for a minute, revving up his vocal engine. "I wonder if it was a mistake to keep her out of school. I've never seen her this bad."

"I know it's hard to watch her this way," Mrs. P. said softly. "But you have to remember that it's for her own safety that we keep her here. And your health. She's liable to give you a heart attack with all the chaos she creates."

My own safety? What, I'm going to set fire to myself or walk in front of a train?

"I just worry about her all alone every day. She's been wearing that gray Nike sweatshirt for weeks. I think it's from that boy Chase or Chuck, or whatever his name was. But now it's August and a hundred degrees out there, and she doesn't even seem to care."

"Maybe we should call Dr. Gutman and have him up her meds again."

Bring it on! Rose wanted to taunt—that is, if she had been talking.

Nala pawed at her gently, her claws catching on Rose's Nike sweatshirt, like she was trying to tell her something.

What? I know what you're thinking. You're wondering why I don't just disappear. I could run away. I've done it before. Rose didn't say the words out loud to Nala on the off chance the Parsimmons might overhear. Didn't seem to matter, though. Nala seemed to get what she was thinking about even without words. *Well, maybe I will. And this time, if I leave, I'm never coming back.*

A flash of anger raced through her chest. It was time to take control of the situation and make some decisions herself. Stroking Nala's back, Rose repeated to herself, *I'll end things here one way or another.*

43
CHASE

IN BETWEEN WATCHING WALTER CHOP green peppers and grate mozzarella cheese, Chase threw out bits of conversation like seasoning. "Somehow, I never pictured you cooking a three-course vegetarian meal."

"Somehow, I never pictured you just standing there watching me cook a three-course vegetarian meal. Come on, get your hands dirty," Walter said, holding out an onion to Chase with a lopsided grin. Lex had informed Walter that all she wanted for her birthday was a home-cooked vegetarian meal.

"Oh, thanks. Give *me* the onion. You just don't want me to see you cry."

"Right as rain," Walter tossed out jovially, not bothering to look back. "Come on, now. Haven't we ever cooked together before?"

Chase heaved himself up from the kitchen stool. "Are you kidding me? First of all, the most I ever saw you cook was boiling macaroni or barbecuing hot dogs. And second of all, cooking *together* or doing anything *together* would mean we actually talked to each other. I don't think you and I had conversations longer than two minutes, max. And third of all, most of our conversations were you lecturing *to* me or yelling *at* me, not a back-and-forth kind of thing."

"That's how you remember it?"

"That's how it *was*." Chase took a breath, feeling braver by the minute. "I don't know what happened to you, but you're completely different."

Walter turned away from the counter and looked straight at Chase. "I guess I wasn't a very good father."

"You were mostly a shitty father." Never before would Chase have dared to say such a thing to his dad, let alone say it when there were knives anywhere within reach.

"*Mostly?*" Walter asked seriously. "That means I did something right?"

"It's all relative, no pun intended." Chase leaned back onto the stool for support, the onion still in his hand. Suddenly, he felt hot both inside and out. "You beat me like a dog. You scared me shitless. I watched you break my mother's arm more than once. There were times I thought you were going to kill one of us."

"I don't remember very much of that," Walter said, looking a little sad. "The drinking was so constant back then that I lost days at a time. I blacked out."

"I don't want to knock this recovery thing. But it's *bullshit* to put it all off on that. *You* did those things to us. *You* did. Maybe the alcohol helped, but *you* did it." Chase could feel his blood rushing to his face and angry tears building up behind his eyes.

"That's fair, I guess." Walter looked cornered, but resigned. "All I can say is that your childhood and my childhood were not that different. My pop drank like a fish and came after us as long as he could stand. I left home when I was about your age, and I never looked back." His eyelids seemed heavy.

"As much as I hated him, he was the only father I knew. I suppose I told myself I was teaching you to be a man. But a part of me knew I was out of control. When your mom was pregnant with Daisy, I got after her real bad one time…" His voice broke.

"I remember."

"And I–I guess I sort of woke up for a minute and realized I was turning into my father and I tried to pull it together, honest I did."

"I remember that too."

"My thinking was all backward and upside down, Chase. I guess I kind of got high off it, off the adrenaline, or something. I can't explain it. Shit. I don't even understand it myself." Walter ran his fingers through his hair, forgetting the bits of chopped green pepper on his hands, which now decorated his shaggy waves.

"I hated you for it." Chase wished he *was* cutting the onion, because his eyes were tearing up.

"I hated me for it too." Walter probably wished he'd held on to the onion himself, because his eyes were also full with tears. He waited for a moment, breathing heavily. "Do you still hate me for it?"

That Chase had to think about. "Yes and no." He sighed carefully. His chest felt tight. "I hate you for putting us all through that. I hate you for leaving us and for not helping us out with money. But I don't hate the person you are now. I don't really understand who you are now, but I don't hate you."

"I hear you." Walter brushed his hands together to clean them off. "I made so many mistakes I can't even count them. But I can't change them either. All I can do is try better from here on out. I beat myself up about them for a long time after I left you guys. But that only made me want to drink more. When I finally got involved with the twelve-step program, I met other people in my situation, and I felt like I got to start with a clean slate. Now, I'm just trying my best every day. It's not easy, because I think I'm a rage-aholic just like I'm an alcoholic. I have to constantly work to keep it in check."

Chase heard himself say, "I hit my mother." The words hung heavily in the air.

"I know."

"I don't ever want to be you—the old you."

"I don't want you to be me either. Half the time, I don't want to be me myself."

Chase turned around then, because it was too hard to look Walter in the face. He braced his upper body against the counter, leaning his head down toward it. "Why did you contact me? Why did you want to share custody after all that time?"

"I was ready. It was time. I wanted to try to repair things."

Chase whipped around, his face wet. "*Bullshit*. It was because of the child support."

Walter stepped suddenly closer and Chase instinctively shrank back. Walter stopped short. "It was time, is all. I wasn't ready before." Walter lifted his hands helplessly and dropped them down, like he didn't know what to do with them. "I had to be ready. Otherwise, what was the point? I'd just be right back where I started."

"But I wasn't going to come! I was going to stay with my girlfriend—and you were going to let me."

"I know. Just because *I* was ready to try to repair things with *you*, doesn't mean *you* were ready to repair things with *me*. I get that." Walter turned back toward the counter and picked up the chopping knife. He hunched his shoulders. "Where I come from, we don't say things like I love you. But that doesn't mean I don't feel those things. I just can't say them."

Walter worked in silence for a while, his back still facing Chase. The room seemed like it was spinning, for all the water in Chase's eyes. He stood there like a fool until Walter sniffled. "Cut that onion, already, why don't you? I can't have Lex walking in on us all weepy and shit."

So Chase did.

44
ROSE

ROSE HAD NEVER SEEN SO many cans of tuna fish in her life. Stacked one on top of another in the pantry, like the Parsimmons were preparing a tuna-fish survival kit for the next big earthquake. Rose stood there, mouth open for a moment, until she heard Mr. P. scrape his chair against the kitchen floor behind her.

He cleared his throat. "They were on sale," he explained. "And I, uh, noticed you've been eating a lot of tuna fish in your room." Rose whirled around and eyed him, trying to figure out what he meant. He couldn't possibly know about Nala, hidden in her room, could he?

Uncomfortable silence. "I like tuna fish myself," he added. "Good source of lean protein. Good for my cholesterol." He patted himself on the chest, and it was so corny that Rose almost groaned.

Rose grabbed a can and headed for the can opener, thankful she'd remembered to close her bedroom door. Nala had never ventured from her room, even the couple of times Rose had forgotten to close the door or shut her in the closet. It was almost as though Nala knew to be afraid.

Rose spun the can around the blade to open it, tipped it over the sink to pour out the tuna juice, and spooned out the wet tuna. As she carried the plastic plate to her room, aware of the concerned heat from Mr. P.'s eyes on her back, little bits of her plan peppered her thoughts.

1. She would not stay at the Parsimmons' forever.

2. She would not stay silent forever.

3. She would not stay depressed forever.

4. She would not allow them to keep her from her real mother forever.

5. She would do whatever it took to escape.

Whatever it took.

Granted, the plan was more like a wish list than an actual step-by-step strategy, but it made her feel like she was doing *something*. Even with the plan as inspiration, many days were lost to the darkness of sleep, so Rose knew she must still be depressed. There was one thing she knew for sure. An exit strategy was a necessity.

As strict as the Parsimmons were and had always been, they were stupidly naïve about the Internet. They had no idea how to set up parental blocks on the computer and were too proud to ask anyone for help. Not that Rose was visiting porn sites or anything like that. Just that she was researching for her plan, a plan she wanted the Parsimmons to know nothing about.

Logging on to the Internet made Rose feel more connected to the world. Even though she didn't respond to any emails or instant messages, she read them daily, often several times. Most were from Becca, with a smattering from Chase, and a bunch of spam.

At first it seemed like Becca was trying to apologize or connect in some way, but since Rose never responded, now Becca just sent jokes. And an e-card too, for her birthday mid-September. Sweet sixteen came and went with about as much excitement as a trip to the dentist.

How many shrinks does it take to change a lightbulb? Sent at 2:55 p.m. No response from Rose, although it was fun trying to figure it out.

Maybe…a hundred because they just sit there waiting for the lightbulb to talk about its feelings, and any idiot knows a lightbulb doesn't talk. Or have feelings.

Maybe…two. One to listen, and one to nickel-and-dime you for every second on the couch.

Maybe…zero. A shrink couldn't figure out how to change a lightbulb any better than he could figure out how to change a juvenile delinquent like Rose. The lightbulb would go unchanged.

Give up? Okay here's the answer: Only one, but the lightbulb has to want to change. Get it? Sent at 10:28 p.m. I miss you, Rose. I thought you'd like that one. Here's to all the Parsimmons' money you've wasted by sitting like a lump in a shrink's office. Ha! Some shrink probably bought his wife a pair of new boobs for all of that.

That image made Rose smile, as she thought of old, saggy Dr. Gutman, the psychiatrist, with an old, saggy Mrs. Gutman, sitting there with big, old perky boobs, kind of like a cross between a Barbie doll and the nanny from *101 Dalmatians*.

For the last month Chase had been emailing her as well, sometimes with sappy Buddhist crap he must have lifted either from Daniel Stein or from Hallmark cards. Just seeing his name on the screen tugged at her heart, but she pushed it away. Of course she didn't respond to either of their emails. If she let either Chase or Becca back into her world, she'd only hurt them worse when she did what she had to do.

Rose relaxed as her fingers fluttered across the keyboard, accessing the Google search page. Time to research her plan. Nala climbed onto her lap, smelling of tuna. *Watch out, fur ball,* Rose teased, *or I'll cut you off from your supply. I know you're addicted to Bumblebee tuna.*

The cat batted at her again, as if to ask, *Why, for the fifth time in one week, are you googling the word 'Chumash'?*

Rose raised one eyebrow at Nala, something she'd perfected in the mirror a week ago. *I know, I know, no one ever told me I have Chumash heritage. I just figured it out. I'm smart like that.* Rose knew she had to have some Native American in her because people always said she looked like Pocahontas or Tiger Lily. And she remembered her mother's face. Her strong nose. Her large eyes. The dark hair that hung to her waist, each strand fine, but so much of it that it looked thick and strong like an unbraided rope.

And Mrs. P. had that article on the Chumash hidden away in her secret Rose-info shoe box. The same box with the articles on prostitution. But it was the section on traditional Chumash jewelry that confirmed her beliefs. Because the photo of the abalone shell bracelet looked identical to the one she'd worn as a little girl.

Rose remembered how her mother had pulled the bracelet from the box she hid under her bed and wrapped it around Rose's small five-year-old wrist. "This was mine when I was a little girl, and now it belongs to you." Mrs. P. later called it a trinket. But it wasn't a trinket to Rose. It was a treasure.

With time, though, Rose's wrist grew, and the thin string holding the bracelet together didn't. It got so that the string and the shells cut into her skin. It was then that Mrs. P. finally snipped it off, using a pair of sewing scissors, and threw it away. Mr. P. had to hold Rose down while Mrs. P. did it. They didn't understand that they were cutting away her mother. Memories slipping like the shells off the string. Rose wondered what that bracelet would have looked like to her today with her grown-up eyes. Would it now look dinky, like it had been bought from one of those quarter prize machines? Or would it still look and feel like a treasure?

Rose shivered, even though the air inside her room was not cold. She reread to herself what she'd already seen the last five times she searched the Web. Somehow it was comforting. The Chumash had been a hunter-gatherer tribe, a matriarchal society. They never wasted any part of an animal or plant they killed, and lived life in balance with nature. "Chumash" sounded soft and sweet when she whispered it to herself. It sounded mushy, like chocolate pudding.

Today a small number of Chumash lived on the Santa Ynez Reservation, she read. Others lived in cities along the coast of Southern California. Rose felt her heart skip a beat or two.

She looked around at the flowered wallpaper and all the pink that she'd known for over a decade. She looked at the charcoal sketches she'd tacked on her walls, one after another, each perfecting the image of her mother's face. Always within the pupil of her mother's eyes sat a baby girl, as if her mother was watching over her.

Rose sighed. Was she really going to do this? She *had* to, didn't she? Things would not get better for her with the Parsimmons. In fact, they might get much, much worse.

45
CHASE

PASTOR TOM BOUNCED A BASKETBALL against the hot asphalt of the YMCA court, his palms a light gray because of the dirt, sweat pouring down the back of his neck, and his arms looking skinny and pale in contrast to his dark green Celtics shirt. Chase had never seen a pastor that looked less "pastorly" in his life. If anything, he looked like a skinny second-string basketball wannabe.

The YMCA wasn't exactly Chase's scene, and basketball wasn't his sport, but there were only so many video games a guy could play before his eyes started to cross. So he'd found himself shooting hoops on his own until Pastor Tom introduced himself and challenged him to a scrimmage.

"You don't look like a pastor," Chase told him, bouncing the ball away from him. The ball felt a little flat, like it needed to be pumped up, so he dribbled hard down the court. "You're not that much older than me."

Pastor Tom stole the ball back and squared up to shoot. He grinned, showing somewhat crooked but evenly spaced teeth, like he'd had braces once upon a time but never wore his retainer. The ball lifted off his fingers and arced toward the hoop. It circled and dropped through.

Pastor Tom grinned. "I'm twenty-eight, which is plenty older than you." He laughed from deep in his gut. "You look like you're twenty, but you're still in high school, so you can't be more than eighteen." Pastor Tom scooped up the ball and palmed it back and forth, breathing hard.

Chase moved for his water, the condensation-soaked canteen almost slipping out of his hands. He tipped it back and let the water rush down his throat, so cold it ached. "How do you know I'm still in high school?" Chase challenged. "Maybe I'm not."

Pastor Tom rummaged around in a black bag with "Got Jesus?" printed in white cursive letters. He pulled out a sports drink, some kind of cheap spin-off on Gatorade. "I have an 'in' with God. I know these things."

"Okay, now I know for sure you're not a pastor." Chase laughed.

"No, seriously." Pastor Tom twisted the top off the bottle and sat down on the asphalt. "I'm a youth pastor. That's a full-time job if I ever saw one, even though our congregation is small. But I also pick up ten hours a week as the assistant coach for the high-school track team. They give me a little stipend, but I don't do it for that." He took a little sip, and Chase could tell right away that it was the kind of sports drink that would turn his lips and teeth blue.

Pastor Tom went on. "I do it because I've always had that running bug myself, and being a pastor doesn't change it. Once you've got the running bug, you've got it forever." He smiled slowly, blue teeth and all. "And you, my friend, may just have been infected yourself. I saw you running the track last week. Your stride and your intensity are good. You ought to think about joining the high school team."

"Me?" Water almost spurted out through Chase's nose when he laughed. "On a high-school sports team? Not my thing." Chase eased himself down on the ground next to Pastor Tom, recognizing the aching of his quad and calf muscles. He'd run a good six miles the day before. "Besides, what about separation of church and state?"

"Don't worry, my friend. I leave my 'Got Jesus?' bag at home, and I don't say a word about God the whole time."

Chase shaded his eyes with his hands so he could see the man's face better. "Isn't that sacrilegious or some shi…or something?"

"Here's the thing, Chase. God can work through me, through you, through anyone, and touch our lives for the better. We don't have to force God's name down anyone's throat. We can just know this for ourselves and let everyone interpret it as they see fit. It doesn't matter what we call it, it just matters what it *is*. *Comprende, amigo?*"

Chase narrowed his eyes skeptically. "What kind of a Christian are you?"

"The flexible kind," Pastor Tom said, laughing like he thought he was a riot. Chase was glad this guy found himself funny, because Chase sure didn't. "No, really. I'm a youth pastor at a nondenominational church. We're pretty low key and casual in our approach, so we get a large following of young couples and families."

"Oh." Chase got the feeling he was about to get the religion recruitment pitch, and he wasn't in the mood. He considered getting up and shooting hoops again, only his calves were cramping up, so he stayed put.

"Are you religious?"

"Not really." Chase admitted.

Pastor Tom leaned forward, "Maybe you just need to find the right church."

"Yours, right?" Chase leaned back away from him. "Yeah, no thanks. I'm not into being *told* what to believe. I just want help figuring out what it is that I *do* believe. That's why I don't think organized religion is my thing."

"We're not that organized. You should see my car." Pastor Tom looked at Chase pointedly, then tilted his sports drink back and gulped the last bit down.

"Very funny. Just what I need." Chase pulled his knees to his chest, preparing to heave himself up. "A pastor who should have been a stand-up comedian."

"Oh, good, someone thinks I'm funny besides me," Pastor Tom joked. "How 'bout let's play a game of HORSE, and if I win, you come to youth group this week. If you win, you get to decide if you come."

"Is that a bet?" Chase asked, feeling a smirk come to his lips.

"It's not a bet. It's a negotiation." Pastor Tom popped up from the ground, looking rejuvenated by his sports drink and ready to take Chase on.

Chase stood up, realizing he stood at least three inches taller than the pastor. "Let's just get HORSE over with. You first." He headed over to the hoop, rolling his shoulders back and wishing he'd pumped up the ball more before he'd come. Maybe it was what he'd scarfed down for lunch, but he had a rotten feeling in his stomach that he was about to be creamed.

Five minutes later, sweat dripping down his back, it was clear Chase been right. And now he was stuck going to a freaking youth group in a town he didn't know with a basketball-playing wannabe pastor and a group of kids with actual morals. He wouldn't have anything in common with them.

For a moment, Chase wanted to call the whole thing off. But considering the list of sins he'd racked up so far this year, he didn't think it wise to tip the scale farther in that direction, just in case God was keeping track or something. Besides, he figured, maybe there'd be a roomful of hot girls. That could help him get his mind off of Rose. Clearly things were over with her. Forever. He'd screwed up and it was over. Time to move on.

He smiled, imagining it. A roomful of hot religious girls, dressed in short private-school uniformed skirts. Girls he could sit next to, smell their scented body lotion and shampoo, and look in their eyes, but who, for all intents and purposes, would be off limits. Question of the day: was that heaven or hell?

46
ROSE

ON THE THIRD SUNDAY IN October, when half the kids in town were buying Halloween costumes, Rose decided to take action. She'd wrap all the gifts she'd gotten for her mother over the years, the ones from the shoe box under her bed. She'd always kept them unwrapped in case she wanted to look at them or touch them. But now it seemed the right time to package them up. She tiptoed toward Mrs. P.'s gift-wrapping supplies, thinking she'd grab tape and different colors of tissue paper.

Mr. P. stood in the kitchen, barefoot, in a loose cotton undershirt and faded sweatpant shorts. She couldn't help but notice the thick, graying hair covering his arms and back as he reached into the cupboard for the gluten-free corn flakes. He'd gotten a four-pack at Costco, so everyone in the house had been eating gluten-free corn flakes for weeks.

Rose had been counting down the minutes, even the seconds, until he'd get dressed and leave for the Daily Drip so that she'd have the house to herself for a couple of hours. The man read the entire paper sitting there, start to finish. Mrs. P. had gone to a neighbor's house to help prepare for a Tupperware party.

Something about the way Mr. P. moved to the fridge made Rose stop. It took him forever to lift the milk from the bottom shelf of the refrigerator. He breathed heavily. Midway between the fridge and the counter, the muscles in his arm and hand seemed to give out. His wrist flopped forward like a piece of strung-out Silly Putty. The milk carton fell to the linoleum floor with a thick fist-in-the-gut sound. Milk pooled around the carton.

Mr. P. didn't grab his chest and drop to his knees like they did in the movies. He just turned to Rose, his eyes as wide as silver dollars, his face sweaty and red. His right arm held on to his left, and he stood there teetering and watching Rose. He looked like the giant at the top of Jack's beanstalk, swaying back and forth as if he were about to tumble.

His lips didn't move, but she could read in his eyes what she was supposed to do just as sure as if he'd written it down step by step. She needed to get help. The kitchen phone lay within arm's distance behind Mr. P., but he made no move to reach for it. Instead, Rose lunged for it and pressed 9-1-1 before she could even think. When the voice came on, brisk and urgent, Rose felt the words freeze on her lips. It had been so long since she'd spoken to anybody. She wouldn't forget how, would she?

She could hear the operator through the receiver, saying "Hello? Hello?" from what sounded like far away. And suddenly, she heard her own voice, also from far away, and very hoarse, say, "Heart attack! Send an ambulance!"

She dropped the phone then, and although she could still hear the operator asking questions, now she really sounded far away. Still, Mr. P. stood, little sweat bubbles popping up across his nose like tiny raindrops. Their eyes connected for a moment that felt as long as an hour. She wondered what he was thinking. *Pick up that damn phone and give our address!* Or, *Can't you do anything right?* Or, *I'm sorry I didn't get to know you better.* Or maybe he wasn't thinking about her at all. Maybe he was wondering if he was going to die.

47
CHASE

CHASE STRETCHED HIS CALVES AND warmed up his quads. The other runners did the same, and Chase smiled or held up his hand in greeting, but he didn't bother making conversation. He'd only had practice for a couple weeks, but he already looked forward to that burn. The burn of his muscles, the burn of his chest, that strange combination of exhaustion and exhilaration that stuck with him for hours.

As his feet pounded the grass, little bits of water sprayed up and dampened his socks. *Practice*. He'd never had practice before. The word felt funny in his mouth. It sounded like something some jock would say. And he was no jock. But to shut Pastor Tom up, he'd joined the Bakersfield High School cross-country team.

"It'll look good on college applications," Pastor Tom had promised. He didn't even mind that Chase planned to return home for second semester so that he could graduate with his class. A few of the kids from youth group were on the team, and even though Chase had only made it to a couple youth-group meetings, they seemed to accept him as one of their own.

Chase knew he was an unlikely runner, all big and bulky like a polar bear. In fact, when Becca found out he'd joined the team, she just about laughed her Rockstar energy drink right out her nose. Chase knew he didn't have speed on his side. Stamina, maybe, but not speed.

Still, there was something so cleansing about it. The pumping of his arms, wind in his ears, hearing nothing and everything all at once. His heart working hard like it was pumping steel. His thoughts just flowed while he ran. No right or wrong. No shoulds or shouldn'ts. Chase sifted through his thoughts, figuring out which ones to come back to and which ones to discard, getting rid of the ones that just cluttered his mind. And then he felt lighter somehow.

Chase never led the pack. Generally he wound up in the middle of the second half of the team. That meant he just picked someone who seemed to be plugging along at about the same speed, and he paced himself. Matched his footsteps, matched his stride. At first, he had to focus on it, and then the pacing happened mindlessly. That left his mind completely free to drift.

Drift to Rose. Transforming from hot and heavy to arctic cold in a matter of moments. And now she'd practically disappeared from the face of the earth.

Drift to Candy. Sending him off with a prepaid calling card, whispering hard and fast, her mouth moving all weird to keep from crying. "I'm doing this because I think it will be good for you. But if it's not, you come home, understand?"

Drift to Walter. Different but the same. Drunk, he had the strength of the Incredible Hulk, and sober, he was back to being Bruce Banner.

Drift to Daisy. Daisy called nearly every day with a whiny, hurt, why-did-you-leave-me-behind tone to her voice. "You'd better come back soon or I'll paint your walls pink and steal all your leftover T-shirts for nightgowns."

Drift to running. It hadn't ever formally been a part of his life before. Looking back, running did sort of come naturally to him—but usually after an emotional explosion. Putting it before the explosion, to ward off the volcanic eruption, seemed genius. He shook his head at how dense he'd been not to think of that before.

Drift to church. He could hardly believe he'd actually been attending. Youth group here and there mostly, although he had gone to a couple worship services. Pastor Tom's church seemed more like "religion lite." Sure, they talked about God and prayed and all that, but most of what they seemed to do was volunteer in the community. Soup kitchens, wrapping presents for Toys for Tots, cleaning up local parks, and once a year, building houses in Mexico. Maybe because the sermons felt more like classroom discussions than lectures, Pastor Tom's church didn't have that oppressive feel he remembered from when he was a kid. Go figure.

Chase hit his last few strides, then walked it off. His legs felt rubbery and weightless. This long, lean kid named Brian strode past him, looking like he'd already caught his breath. "Good job, Chase," he said as he passed.

Chase stopped moving, just hunched over with his hands on his knees. "You too." His words came out breathless. His social life had dwindled to exchanging a few words in the locker room during water breaks and attending the occasional youth group. Fine by him. There didn't seem to be a reason to spend a lot of time making friends he would just leave again in January. He'd been spending lunch in the library too, jamming out as much homework as forty-six minutes would allow. He couldn't bring himself to actually do any homework at home, but at least he wasn't totally blowing it off anymore.

For the first time in his high school career, Chase felt like he had it together. Like he had a plan. There were even a bunch of college applications open on his desktop. He hadn't started any of them, of course, but they sat there waiting for him. Maybe he could make something of himself after all.

48
ROSE

THE PARAMEDICS ARRIVED, TALKING TO Mr. P. slowly and loudly, as if he was hard of hearing or stupid. Helping him onto a stretcher. Sticking a thin needle into his vein and taping it there. An IV. One of the attendants speaking into a walkie-talkie. "Possible stroke victim. Nonresponsive to questions. Appears to be in his late fifties or early sixties."

Stroke? Rose started to shake her head. No. She wanted to say, "This is a heart attack. He has a weak heart and high cholesterol." But nobody was looking at her. She could barely form the words with her mouth, let alone make herself heard above the commotion in the crowded home. She'd never thought of the house as small, but now with two paramedics and a stretcher in the middle of the kitchen, she felt claustrophobic.

She looked down at Mr. P. then, only to find him staring back up at her. His mouth slightly open, like he was trying to tell her something. She started to reach her fingers toward his, realizing how foreign that felt. She hadn't touched him, nor he her, in years.

Her fingers didn't do more than flutter toward him, though, because they were interrupted by a strange combination of screaming and sobbing. Mrs. P. burst through the door, her flower-print dress swaying with the motion like it was in the middle of a giant tornado. Her eyes looked terrified, like she was about to lose her best friend, and maybe she was. Rose found herself wondering why Mrs. P. had come back so early, except maybe she'd heard the sirens or forgotten something.

One of the paramedics began explaining to Mrs. P. as they secured her husband onto the stretcher, strapping him down. Rose felt herself shrinking, shrinking, shrinking, until she was no bigger than a fingernail.

Even so, Mrs. P. swung her attention around like a whip. "*You*," she accused through sobs. "You knew he had a bad heart and still you gave us nothing but stress." Her eyes shone with tears. Even though Hursula had never so much as touched Rose's little pinky, Rose got the feeling that Hursula was grabbing at her like a drowning woman, desperate to latch on to something, but only pulling Rose down with her. "And now all that stress—*your stress*—has killed him!"

The words stung like a swarm of killer bees. Over and over again. Rose replayed the words in her mind long after Mrs. P. had turned and ushered the paramedics out the door. One of the paramedics turned to Rose, looking as though he wanted to say something, but the other barked an order at him, and he went on.

Standing next to the front windows, watching the ambulance drive away, sirens blaring, with Mrs. P.'s car following, Rose thought of comebacks. They popped into her head uninvited, when all she wanted to do was cry. *He's not dead, you imbecile! How could I kill him if he's not dead?* Or *If I was going to try to kill someone, it would have been you!*

Tears dripped down her face like water from the leaky faucet in the guest bathroom. She stood with her cheek pressed against the window, feeling the cool glass. Rose pulled the ends of Chase's old Nike sweatshirt over her hands. It was pretty much all she wore those days. She felt so hidden in it. Like no one could see her, let alone hurt her.

Suddenly, Rose felt tired, like she'd been awake for years, not just a few hours. She lay down in her bed, pulling the covers all the way up to her chin. She cried for a bit, then let the sleep wash over her and take her away.

49
CHASE

A SLIGHTLY IRRITABLE DANIEL AND A nicotine-deprived Becca sat with Chase in the living room of Walter's pink stucco condo, a blank college application open on the screen. When Daniel offered to drive up to Bakersfield and spend a long, focused weekend helping him edit and revise his essays, Chase hesitated only briefly. He agreed the way he would if someone offered him free braces. With both relief and dread.

"No offense, Chase, but you should've gone out for football or wrestling. Something that could've gotten you a scholarship," Becca informed him while breaking off her split ends. "Your grades aren't exactly stellar."

"You're a real ray of sunshine, you know that?" Daniel scolded her.

"I try."

As much as Chase hated to admit it, Becca had a point. Too bad he didn't have some kind of secret talent. *Like Rose.* Rose's grades blew chunks, even worse than his, for sure, but she probably had a good chance of getting an art scholarship someday. He'd never seen anyone so talented. He wondered if Rose would be applying to colleges at this time next year. Thinking of Rose left him with an unsettled feeling in his stomach. He wished she'd respond to his instant messages or emails.

"Chase might surprise you, queen of pessimism. His SAT scores rock. Plus people can do amazing things. Check this out." Daniel held up a yoga magazine as evidence. A woman stood on one leg, the other pulled behind her back in an arc. The sole of her foot was nearly touching her head. She held her foot with both arms, so that from a distance, her body almost made the image of a backward letter *P*.

"It's called Natarajasana." Daniel read from the article, stumbling over the pronunciation, but trying to sound like he wasn't.

"If you can't say it, I highly doubt you can do it," Becca said.

Daniel grinned. "Also known as dancer's pose."

"The human body is not meant to bend that way," Chase said, laughing. "You've got to meet my dad's new girlfriend. You guys could be soul mates."

Daniel slowly unrolled his middle finger for a friendly "f-you." Of course at that exact moment, Walter and Lex came home from their meeting, smelling like cigarettes and stale coffee. In unison, both Walter and Lex raised their eyebrows at Daniel's finger. Daniel pulled his finger back in real fast, like he thought he'd get in trouble. His cheeks turned sunburn red.

"Oh, you guys are so cute," Becca said to Walter and Lex, way louder than she had to. "You even make the same expressions!"

Walter and Lex both made "oh, gross" faces and then tried to check each other out without looking like they were checking each other out.

"Sorry," Becca apologized. "I'm way too hyper. I've been cooped up with these idiots for too long. Plus, I guzzled a couple energy drinks."

"Maybe we can remedy that," Lex said, floating over to introduce herself. Before Chase knew it, Lex had invited Daniel and Becca to come take a free yoga class Sunday morning. Then she and Walter whisked Becca out of the apartment to the movies.

Once they'd left, Chase eyeballed the topic question prompt. "Now I have no excuses."

"It's not as bad as it seems," Daniel said. "Even though each of the schools has their own personal-statement essay question, and they all word it slightly differently, all the schools basically ask the same thing. Once you finish one, all you have to do is cut and paste, add a little fluff, and 'voilà!'"

"Easy for you to say. You're not sitting at the computer." Chase sighed and leaned back in the computer chair. "Okay. Here is the topic sentence. 'Taking risks may lead to self-discovery. Discuss a risk you have taken in your life and how it has led to you understanding yourself better.'"

With Daniel cracking pistachios in his teeth and looking on for moral support, Chase started to write. At first, he had shied away from writing about the old Walter, the new Walter, and what he'd learned about his father and himself by coming to live in Bakersfield. Daniel insisted, however, that universities loved personal statements about overcoming adversity.

So Chase typed until his fingers felt stiff. Long after Daniel fell asleep on the couch, his legs hanging over the edge, Chase kept typing. His fingers slowed even more, but his brain ran in circles. The one thing, the biggest thing he'd begun to learn about himself was how to tame his own anger. But he couldn't write about that. He'd been too ashamed to even tell his best friend that he hit his mother. Putting it down on paper would make it real.

But then again, Chase realized, staring at the computer screen so hard the words blurred, it *was* real.

50
ROSE

IF MRS. P. HAD A tail it would have been between her legs as she slunk into Rose's bedroom in late November. Rose sat on her bed, wrapped in a quilt. She watched the leaves drift from the small oak tree planted in their back yard, the one she used to climb before she got too old for that kind of thing.

Rose didn't turn to look at Mrs. P., just stayed staring out the window. Maybe if Rose ignored her, she'd go away. But Mrs. P. didn't take the hint. She sat herself down heavily in Rose's desk chair, then stayed there sighing. Deep exasperated sighs. Rose thought of Nala, curled up asleep in her closet bed, and hoped she'd stay put. Another sigh. Finally, because she wanted to get this over with, Rose sighed herself and shifted her focus over to Mrs. P.

A flicker of relief crossed Mrs. P.'s face but disappeared as quickly as it came. Rose saw her scanning the walls of the room, now nearly covered with tacked-up charcoal and pastel sketches. Mrs. P. sighed again. Rose decided she would count how many more times Hursula sighed during this conversation. Sigh. *Okay, that's one.* "I want you to know that I am in here in part because your father asked me to come talk to you." Sigh. *Two*.

Mr. P. had arrived home three weeks ago. He'd stayed in the hospital for a week and then transferred over to a rehab hospital for another week and a half. It turned out he'd had a mild stroke, and there'd been something wrong with his heart, as well. It had a fancy name that Rose couldn't remember. But it meant he had to take everything easy. An occupational therapist came to the house twice a week, and he went back to the rehab center for speech and physical therapy.

Now Rose was no longer the only Parsimmon who needed therapy! The thought of it would have made her laugh, if Mr. P. didn't look so goddamn pathetic. Since he came home he looked like he'd aged ten years, like the hospital had sucked the life right out of him instead of pumping it back in.

It didn't surprise Rose that Mr. P. had asked his wife to talk to her. Maybe he'd just softened in the hospital, like ice cream left out too long. Or maybe he'd been softening for a long time. But ever since he came back, Rose had noticed him looking at her, *really looking*, not watching or guarding or supervising. Not looking through her. But looking *at* her, like he really saw her for the first time.

Mrs. P. placed a package of brand-new oil pastels on the comforter. "Peace offering," she said quietly. Rose's heartbeat couldn't help but quicken, as she stared at the fresh, soft tips, and she wanted to reach her hands out from inside the quilt and touch them. "You've always been such an amazing artist, and I'm glad to see you've been sketching. Dr. Gutman always said that art was a therapeutic outlet for you, that even if you didn't talk to us, at least you were expressing yourself in this way."

Rose felt her eyes harden, and she dropped her hands to her lap. Did everything have to be therapeutic? Mrs. P. sighed again—*three*. "You're not going to make this easy on me, are you?" Sigh—*four.* "Oh, lord in heaven, give me strength."

Rose considered flipping Mrs. P. the finger. But all her old sassiness seemed to have evaporated, along with her use of the English language. She just stared as blankly as she could, knowing silence was her strongest weapon.

"Your father wants me to make sure you know that it's not your fault he had a stroke." Mrs. P. looked unsure, like she didn't fully believe her own words. "He's had high cholesterol and heart problems for years. Runs in his family." Sigh—*five.* "I don't know what I ever did to you, Rose. All I did was take care of you."

Rose slid her eyes over to peek at Hursula's face. Crazy as it was, she looked like she meant it. "You always had clean clothes—and new clothes too, whatever the style was. Not that you care. All you ever wear these days is that filthy sweatshirt." Mrs. P. shook her head, her thin hair wafting back and forth, then settling around her face. "I ordered the Disney Channel the first week you came to us. I bought you toys. You never went hungry. What did I do wrong?" she demanded now, her voice angry.

So your definition of parenting is providing me with stuff? Sitting me in front of the television? Isn't there more to it than that?

Mrs. P. wilted, sitting there on the pink bedspread. "I'd have thought you'd be grateful, seeing as where you'd come from."

I'd rather sleep on an old mattress in a crack addict's apartment and eat saltines for every meal if I could have my mother's arms around me. My mother's hand to hold across the street, my mother's breath against my ear, my mother listening and touching and watching me as though I mattered. But you took that away from me, didn't you? You couldn't just be my guardian or my foster parent. No, you had to sever ties with my real mother, my flesh and blood, and you never bothered to ask me.

"We always got you the top medical care, even tests and doctors our insurance didn't cover." Mrs. P.'s voice grew stronger, as if now she was trying to convince herself as well as Rose. "And now you're really worrying us. We're back with the silent treatment, and I'm wondering if you've got some kind of eating disorder on top of everything else." Rose accidentally made eye contact after that one, but she quickly looked away.

"Oh, you think I haven't noticed? I notice a lot more than you think I do, but sometimes I pretend to be oblivious because it's clear you want your space from us. From me." Pause—no sigh this time. "*What* is going on?"

Rose tried not to react. She focused instead on the pastels, her fingers itching to try them out, to let them race across a sketchbook page as if they had a mind of their own.

Another sigh, but this one was long and drawn out, like a slow leak from a helium balloon. Long enough to count as three sighs—*six, seven, and eight.* Mrs. P. hunched her shoulders and placed her hands together like she was praying, looking up at the cracking plaster on the ceiling.

"Sometimes, I wonder if I was ever meant to have kids." Her skin bunched up near her eyes and it looked like she might cry. "I gave you everything we were too poor to have when I was a kid. But I've gotten nothing back from you. No respect. No love."

News flash. You can't buy a kid's love. You could have bought me the moon and all the stars in the sky and let me eat ice cream at every meal and still—you wouldn't have been my mother. Rose took another peek at Mrs. P. and saw that her eyes were full. Rose didn't feel sorry for her, though, not one bit. Okay, so if she was honest, maybe a little bit.

Didn't you think I might miss my mom? Didn't you think I might like a phone call or a card every once in a while? But every time I've ever brought it up, you cut me off and changed the subject.

"I wanted a child—a little girl—so badly that I could think of nothing else. I knew I would do for you what no one ever did for me. I made sure you never had to go to school in hand-me-down clothes. I remember being so happy—things seemed to be going so well at first.

"But then, you changed and I didn't know what to do with you." Sigh—*nine*. "You know, no one ever shows you how to parent. You just have to figure it out as you go." Sigh—*ten*. "I'm not apologizing, mind you. I know I did my best. You were so damaged by your early experiences, and I did my best to help you." Mrs. P. sounded like she was trying to sell Rose something, and Rose wasn't buying.

Rose stared straight at Mrs. P.'s nose. "Okay, last thing, Oh Silent One. Because we're so worried about you, your father and I are re-evaluating our decision to keep you out of school. I know it's the middle of the first semester, but if you want to go back, you can." Rose looked at Mrs. P. carefully. That offer seemed a whole lot like a piece of sharp cheddar cheese wedged inside a mouse trap.

For a moment, Rose considered it. She thought about sitting with Becca in the quad while she snapped bubblegum, walking from class to class, working her locker combination. But then she remembered her plan. No—going back to school would only complicate things. So slowly, Rose shook her head back and forth.

51

ROSE

AS THE LAUNCH DATE OF her plan approached, Rose started to wonder if maybe she should leave something behind for the Parsimmons to remember her by. Rose flipped through a dark brown photo album, one of four or five thick matching albums chronicling her childhood and, after an hour or so, found the perfect picture.

She must've been seven or eight, and there she sat, smack in the middle of rows and rows of strawberries at Underwood Family Farms, her lips and cheeks stained red, and wisps of hair splaying around her face. Mr. and Mrs. P. held baskets of their own, but they posed for the picture by leaning in and smiling at the person behind the camera. Rose seemed to be focused on the strawberries piled high in her basket, and her face literally glowed with pleasure and anticipation.

Rose slid the picture out of its protective plastic sleeve and propped it up against her computer so that she could get a good look at it. As she smoothed out a large piece of sketch paper and moved the charcoal lightly across the page, she relaxed.

She would sketch this picture, this memory of them all together and relatively happy, and as a gift, she would draw her own face tilted upward toward the Parsimmons, rather than downward at the strawberries, so that it would appear her pleasure came from being with *them* rather than from the anticipation of sinking her teeth into another juicy strawberry.

Nala swished her tail around Rose's legs, purring in that deep throaty way of hers, then leaped up onto Rose's lap to take a look at the evolving picture. *See? I'm not a complete monster—I'll leave this behind when I go. It's way better than a letter. What would I say in a good-bye note anyway? "Yeah, gee. Thanks for feeding me for the past eleven years. Sorry for the trouble." No—a sketch was the way to go, definitely easier than struggling to find the right words.*

Rose paused to listen for the Parsimmons, but heard nothing. They'd gone out grocery shopping forty minutes ago. A couple weeks ago, when the Parsimmons were at speech therapy for Mr. P, she'd beelined for their home office. Time to delve back into the Rose file. The same file in the third drawer that she'd found at age eleven. Back then it meant nothing to her. Thick—with all kinds of info from shrinks, psychological reports, articles on reactive attachment disorder, and school report cards.

She searched for any kind of documentation related to why or how the Parsimmons had been able to keep her mother from visiting, but she came up dry. Finally she found something worth looking at. Adoption paperwork and a copy of her birth certificate. The birth certificate had been altered, of course, to protect the identity of her birth parents. Didn't she even have a right to find out her original last name?

On a whim, Rose did a Google search and found that in order to have the county share information about her birth mother (including her name or Rose's real last name, or both), she'd have to be eighteen. At age eighteen she could file paperwork requesting to find out about her biological mother. If, and only if, her biological mother was also willing to fill out paperwork allowing that information to be shared, she could find out her true identity. But there were a lot of what-ifs in that, and Rose was only sixteen. Eighteen felt a lifetime away. So clearly she couldn't go about this the legal way. She'd have to be more creative.

This whole process of finding her mom reminded her of those thousand-piece puzzles she used to attempt in middle school. Every time she got stuck, she'd turn the piece round and round in her hand, getting the feel of the smoothness and just generally stalling. Just when she was about to give up completely, she got it. Turned the piece thirty degrees to the left, and suddenly she could see the shape of its partner nearly leap out of the puzzle to meet it. Perfect fit.

Rose turned to a fresh page and began to sketch an outline of a woman, all in black charcoal. She'd give it to her mother, if she ever found her again. Rose shaded the sketch carefully, darkening the woman's face. She pressed the charcoal hard against the paper, curling lines across the woman's body until she was made of puzzle pieces herself. Her mother's friends and the pastor from the Lutheran church—where she sometimes went to pray—he called her Jewels. The pastor always brought out paper and crayons for Rose while he pulled Jewels aside to talk.

Rose set the charcoal down and scratched underneath Nala's chin, the cat making a sound from deep within her throat that could only be described as pleasure. *First name Jewels, last name Taylor?* Rose thought she remembered her mother calling her "Rose Taylor" that time she got in trouble, when she hid her mother's mascara so she wouldn't be able to get ready for work. Jewels had been irritated, and that was a punishment worse than anything the Parsimmons could ever try to do to her. All Rose wanted was for her mother to look at her with regular eyes again, not those hard, tired old eyes.

Rose had handed the mascara back over as quickly as she could, but Jewel's eyes didn't soften for a long time. When they finally did soften, her mother pulled her onto her lap, her makeup all done for the night out.

"I don't like leaving you," her mother told her, so close their noses nearly touched. "But don't worry, this won't be forever. I'm putting aside a little every day. Pastor Isaiah is setting up a bank account for us. When we have enough, we'll find ourselves an apartment in some sweet hick town and I'll waitress or bartend. Maybe I'll even go to school. Be a nurse or something."

When Rose remembered that conversation and the fleeting hope she'd felt, her blood turned hot in her veins. *What about our plan?* She ripped the paper out of the art tablet and held it, ready to crumple it up into a hard little ball. *Why didn't you come back for me? How did the Parsimmons keep you away?* She stomped her foot so hard that even through the carpet of her room, it startled Nala, and she darted into the open closet.

Then came that immediate pang of remorse, not so much for scaring Nala as for having those thoughts about her mother. *Sorry, Mom. Sorry. I'm not mad at you. I'm not. Don't be mad at me. Come back! Don't leave me!* She set the sketch back on her desk and smoothed it with her hands, not caring that the charcoal smudged as she did so.

Rose shook her head roughly, the way you'd shake a cereal box to get the colored marshmallows to float to the top. She had to focus. The clock was ticking, and the plan required a strict timeline. Just the facts.

- The name Jewels Taylor.
- Pastor Isaiah from some Lutheran church in Hollywood.

It gave her a place to start. She sat at her computer and Googled the name "Jewels Taylor." Then "Jewel Taylor." Then "prostitution arrests in the County of Los Angeles." Nothing of interest surfaced.

But suddenly, that's when she saw the puzzle piece differently. What if it was Jules rather than Jewels—short for Julie. Julie Taylor? She Googled Julie Taylor. She came up with an actress, an author, pornographic pictures of a blond woman in a nurse's uniform, and a type of wine. Nothing that seemed related to her mother. She remembered the article she'd seen in Mrs. P.'s shoe box, something like "Prostitution Still a Problem on Hollywood Boulevard—Outreach Programs in Development." So with a lump in her throat the size of a baseball, she Googled the title of that article, adding the year it was written.

That was when she came upon the link to an *LA Times* article from eleven years ago, shortly after she'd come to live with the Parsimmons. Brief, but long enough to make Rose's heart twist itself all up like a sopping wet handkerchief trying to wring itself out. "Found off Hollywood Blvd: Body of an unidentified twenty-one-year-old female prostitute, believed to be of Mexican American or Native American descent. Please direct any information surrounding her death to the Los Angeles Police Department, attention Detective Cutter."

Rose's hands shook. She held them together tightly, trying to stop the shaking. The dead prostitute could have been any of at least ten hookers she remembered. It wasn't necessarily her mother. Still, her whole stomach tightened, and a dull ache turned sharp, making her wrap her arms around herself and rock. Her eyes brimmed, but she pushed the tears away with her balled-up, shaking fists.

She stood up from the computer, not wanting to touch the mouse again, as if it were a real mouse—or a rat, even. But she didn't want the Parsimmons to stumble (or snoop) onto the article either, so despite the hundred times she'd been told not to turn the computer off without properly shutting it down, she did anyway. Just pushed the power button and the computer died. *Died*.

Her thoughts felt unclear, murky, shaky like her hands, and she wished she'd written her plan down. She wished she hadn't logged it all in her mind. It was almost time to put the plan into action, though. She was sure of that—she could feel it in her body.

It doesn't matter if I'm scared. I can be scared shitless, but I still have to do this. Because what's the alternative? Rose promised herself one thing. She would be with her mother one way or another. No matter what. She had to pull herself together so she could do this right. She couldn't get caught. That would ruin everything.

52
CHASE

MAYBE IT WAS THE PAINT fumes or the numbing exhaustion of his right arm, but standing there doing community service, Chase felt somehow closer to God. Weird.

He held a paint roller in his hand and ran it up and down the wall. Slow. Even. Just enough pressure. He could feel little droplets of paint splatter from the roller onto his hair, face, and arms, but he didn't mind. Pastor Tom propped open the side door of the Boys and Girls Club, and Chase breathed in the crisp lightness of early December.

Roll up. Roll down. Dip in paint. Roll up. Roll down. Dip in paint. The rhythm of it calmed him. Just what he needed, now that submitted all his college applications. He'd worked up the courage to email Rose a few more times, mostly just updating her on his college application process and suggesting that she start keeping a portfolio of art pieces she could submit for college scholarships when she was a senior. That girl needed a plan. She couldn't just sulk, trapped in her room, for the rest in her life. No response from her, of course, which alternated between making him sad, worried, and royally pissed off.

Daniel had driven up again this weekend, Becca in tow, this time just to hang out. It hadn't been hard to convince Daniel to come help the youth group remodel the local Boys and Girls Club. Graffiti had taken over the teen room, some of it gang related, racial, and anti-Semitic. Becca griped and complained at first, but when it came down to it, she ran her roller against the wall like a pro. She and Daniel were working on repainting the bathrooms, and Chase could hear them arguing from where he stood. It made him smile.

Pastor Tom came up behind him. "You need a break here?"

"Nah," Chase said, even though he was losing feeling in his hands. The tips of his fingers tingled.

"You've been at it a long time."

Chase chuckled. "Isn't that the point?"

Pastor Tom dipped his own roller in the paint, pushing it back and forth to get the entire roller covered evenly. "You're on the cross-country team. You've been to six youth-group meetings, two sermons, and a handful of community service events, but I'm still trying to figure you out."

"Am I that hard to read?" Chase switched arms for a moment, trying to paint with his left. It didn't go on as smoothly, but it gave him an excuse to keep working and avoid meeting Pastor Tom's eyes.

"Okay. Here's what I know. You're a hard worker. Focused. Disciplined. You don't seem to mind pain. Maybe you even like it." Pastor Tom slapped Chase on the shoulder in a way that felt more coach-like than pastorly. "These are qualities that make a good runner, so I'm not knocking them. But the pastor in me wants to know why you're so hard on yourself."

Chase considered Pastor Tom. His calves ached from the cross-country meet on Thursday. Finally Chase turned to him and asked, "Have you ever made a mistake? A big mistake that you just couldn't go back and redo?"

"Hasn't everyone? Isn't that just a part of life?" Pastor Tom had paint splattered across his nose like freckles.

"I'm talking about something you knew was wrong but you did anyway. How do you make yourself okay again?" Chase asked.

"Ask for forgiveness." Pastor Tom gave the cookie-cutter answer, and it pissed Chase off.

He sighed. "I apologized, if that's what you mean." What else did he expect, talking to a pastor?

First Pastor Tom asked, "Have you been forgiven?"

Then Chase said, "I think I've been forgiven by the person I hurt." His mom had forgiven him, he was pretty sure. Rose maybe not so much.

"Yeah, but the bigger issue is, have you forgiven yourself?" Pastor Tom set down his roller.

"No. I guess not." Chase set down his roller as well, stretching his arms and fingers. Everything ached. "I suppose you think I should go confess it to God and ask for forgiveness."

"You think if God forgives you, it just goes away?"

"I don't know." Chase *had* kind of thought of it that way.

"Let me put it this way," Pastor Tom started, "If God lives in all of us, doesn't it follow that first you have to forgive yourself?"

"Easier said than done. How am I supposed to do that?" Chase sighed. Weren't pastors supposed to give him answers instead of just asking more questions?

"Forgiveness is different for every person. But you can start by realizing you're human. By doing kind acts for others, like you are right now. By trying to be a good person. The Bible talks about restitution and reconciliation—all ways of giving back."

Chase picked up the roller again. He dipped it, coating it in paint. "So if I'm doing all those things, why is it still hanging over my head?"

"Forgiveness is a process. Maybe you're still in it. Maybe you have to shift the way you look at things. Don't forget that human beings make mistakes. You can't change what happened, right? All you can do is try to move past it and learn from it so it doesn't happen again," Pastor Tom explained.

Chase considered this for a good minute or so. Although he'd made this promise to himself before, this time it somehow felt more secure. *I'll never let it happen again.* These last months had changed him. He could feel it.

Pastor Tom went on. "You're a work in progress. Just like every person in this room." He turned back toward the smattering of people painting the walls and chatting throughout the large auditorium. "Just like every person in this world. Just like me."

Chase set the roller down and cracked his knuckles. Maybe he *would* take a little break. Pastor Tom picked up the roller Chase had just set down. "Go grab a soda or something. It's an early Christmas gift from me, since I won't see you over the holiday."

Chase grinned. "You talked me into it." He'd be going back home to Candy's for the holidays and returning to Simi High second semester. Maybe there'd be a way to reach out to Rose. Throw pebbles against her window or something like that. He'd miss Pastor Tom a little. The guy had kind of grown on him. He'd miss Walter a lot. But, Chase figured, it didn't have to be three whole years before he saw his father again. Now they actually had a relationship.

"I'm not letting you off too easy," Pastor Tom reassured him. "I promise you there'll be work left even if you give yourself a five-minute breather."

Chase laughed and said, "If you're telling me not to push myself so hard, you better watch out, because you just might talk me out of a good race time."

"I doubt it." Then it was almost as though Pastor Tom jumped into coach mode. "Work hard. Play hard"—and then he cracked a smile—"and pray hard. Just cut yourself a little emotional slack while you do it. Got it?"

53
CHASE

CHASE WANDERED DOWN THE JEWELRY aisle of the Simi Valley Target, his sneakers squeaking against the shiny floor. He'd put off his holiday shopping until the last possible day, Christmas Eve. Trying to pick gifts for Daisy and Candy totally stressed him out. Candy liked big earrings. Hoops. Dangly ones. Chase touched a pair of silver ones, long and thin until the bottom, which looped around. He held them up to his ears and looked in a mirror.

"Just your type," someone teased from behind.

Chase whirled around, feeling his cheeks redden before he even came face to face with Mrs. Rosenberg, the assistant rabbi at Becca's synagogue. "Just looking, uh, for my mom," Chase stammered.

"I figured." She smiled, showing her horsey teeth. "I haven't seen you in so long, Chase. I didn't even know you were back in town."

Chase put the dangly earrings back. "Yeah, I came back to spend the holidays with my mom and sister. And I'll stay here for this last semester so I can graduate with my friends."

"That makes sense. Welcome back. Hey, if you need a job while you're here, let me know. The day-care kids loved you."

"Thanks." Chase pushed the hair out of his eyes. He felt awkward or shy or something, but he didn't know why. "Well, nice to see you. Merry Christmas. Oh—oops, I mean Happy Hanukkah."

She chuckled. "No worries. I *will* enjoy Christmas. We always eat Chinese food and do a movie marathon." She paused, like she was trying to decide whether to add something. Then she went on, "Hanukkah has actually been over for a couple weeks."

Damn. "So I guess that means Daniel's present is late."

"I think he'll forgive you."

"Yeah," Chase agreed. He waved her off and turned back to the earrings. His eyes caught on a pair of small, round earrings with layers of folds. He picked them up and brought them closer. They were roses. Small roses. Immediately he thought of Rose and remembered the heart-shaped necklace he'd gotten her last year. But she hadn't returned any of his emails. She didn't want anything to do with him. Still, his fingers lingered. He could buy them and leave them hidden in that planter on her porch. Tape a note on her bedroom window to let her know they were there.

He turned them over to look at the price tag. Shit. If he bought those, he wouldn't have enough money to get something nice for Candy and Daisy. Slowly, he set the rose earrings back on the rotating display.

He shook off a nagging feeling. It made no sense to buy them, he told himself. He'd probably never talk to Rose again, anyway. She'd made it crystal clear that she was not interested.

NOW

54
ROSE

ROSE BREATHES IN THE UNIQUE odor of stale cigarettes, sweat, and Lysol. There's something about a cheap motel that makes her feel at home. She must have stayed in a few as a little girl. No little wrapped soaps by the sink, and no tiny bottles of shampoo or hand lotion. It seems clean enough, but she sure wouldn't eat a cookie that fell on the rug—three-second rule or not. Between the taxi and the one-night motel stay, Rose has dropped over a hundred dollars in an hour and a half flat.

It could have been more, though, she reminds herself. If she'd taken the taxi all the way to the Lutheran church off Hollywood Boulevard, she'd have spent most of what she'd stashed in the backpack. *Besides, even if I'd shown up on the steps of the church, I might not have been able to find anyone who remembered my mother, who knew whether she might have been the unidentified twenty-one-year-old prostitute murdered and dumped eleven-odd years ago.* Rose's stomach aches. She isn't sure what hurts more—thinking her mother is dead, or thinking she *isn't* but still hasn't come to rescue Rose from the Parsimmons.

Shit, her stomach hurts. Her stomach hurts so bad she almost can't think. The world weighs heavily on her, like a two-ton weight dragging her down by the middle. Never mind, she thinks. I don't want to do this anymore. I changed my mind. She feels Nala rub against her ankles and wind her way around her feet, trying to comfort her, but it doesn't work. For a split second, Rose wishes she hadn't turned Chase away.

Her stomach muscles tighten, and a wave of ache washes over her. The aching started out dull. But now the ache takes her breath away. Like it really is an ocean wave washing over her, and she can't breathe until it passes.

When it does pass, Rose sinks onto the bed. Nala leaps up next to her, licking Rose's hand with her rough tongue. Rose feels the pressure of tears backing up in her throat and her eyes.

Rose wishes for the thousandth time that she had a picture of her mother. She could squeeze out a few tears if she could just see her mother's face. She wants to remember the things that have started to fade from her memory. The way her mother's nose has a slight crease at the tip, hardly noticeable unless you really look for it, as if someone had taken a cookie cutter and pressed it into her soft skin ever so gently at birth. She remembers the way her mother's eyes catch the light in the sunshine, the way they sparkle when she isn't working, when she wears no makeup at all. She wonders how much she resembles her mother now.

Two sounds make Rose jerk up her head. They happen at the exact same second, so that afterward she isn't sure whether they were two distinct sounds or one and the same. A soft but determined knock of knuckles on the motel door. A muted *pop* that Rose feels almost more than she hears. She stands up and freezes, unable to move or even to think. Then the gushing of water. Like a bathtub faucet.

She looks down at a growing puddle on the floor. She hadn't realized there would be so *much*. The gushing slows and then her stomach settles, like dirt adjusting after an earthquake, and out comes another mini flood. "Well, shit," she says out loud. "My freaking water broke."

55
CHASE

IN THE SPLIT SECOND BEFORE Daniel's Ford misses the traffic light, the full reality of what's happening slams into Chase. He feels like an idiot for not seeing it before. Chase grips the door handle the way a panicked thought grips his heart. *She isn't getting rid of it, is she? But if she isn't getting rid of it, why is she hiding it from me?*

"Why didn't you go for the yellow? You could have made it!" Becca squirms in her seat like she wants to climb right out of her skin. "We're going to lose her now!"

"Relax. I didn't want to kill us."

Chase turns his whole body on the truck seat to face them. "We *can't* lose her." He steadies himself. "I just figured out what's happening... and *we can't lose her.*"

Becca's voice takes on an irritatingly high pitch, reminding Chase of a wayward garden hose filled with water and flipping around—until Daniel punches her in the arm. Chase's eyes scan the road while he brings them up to date. They sit quiet, thinking. Digesting.

The red light lasts nearly a minute. Daniel floors the gas through the intersection, but the taxi has long since disappeared. Chase's heart accelerates like he's just chugged a keg of Red Bull.

After what seems like hours but is probably only minutes, Chase spies a taxi exiting the driveway of a Sleepy Nite Inn. Or is it a Motel 6? Or a Comfort Inn? All three are right next to each other. Who knows why some idiot would decide to build three motels right in a row like that. Probably the same logic that makes gas stations pop up on opposite corners, so that their customers can stare at each other while they pump gas and wonder whether they got the best deal.

"Turn here!" Chase demands. "We're splitting up. We each take a different one. Go to the front desk and try to find out if Rose has checked in."

"Van Nuys Hospital is right down the street. Shouldn't we check there?"

"I'm just following my gut. If I'm wrong, we'll hit the local hospitals next." Chase nudges Becca out of the truck as soon as it slides into a parking space. He points her in the direction of the Motel 6 and heads for the Sleepy Nite. Standing in front of the registration desk, he realizes no hotel employee will tell him where Rose is staying. He could be a stalker for all they know. Besides, Rose wouldn't have been stupid enough to register with her real name.

As a birdlike woman with a raspy voice greets him, Chase's mind calculates and recalculates options. "Can I help you?" she asks. If there ever was an antismoking poster child, it is this woman. She reeks of tobacco. Her teeth are yellowed in the front but blackened on the inside, and her voice sounds like throat cancer is knocking at the door. He should drag Becca in here for pure shock value.

"Yes. I just dropped a young lady off about five minutes ago, and I realized she left an earring in my cab." Chase stands in front of the desk so the woman can't see his pajama-bottom pants. "The earring looks expensive, so I thought I should bring it back."

"Young girl?" The woman's eyes keep flicking back to a television screen in the background. *It's a Wonderful Life.*

"Yeah. Hair in braids like an Indian princess."

"Oh, her. Room 22."

"Thanks. Merry Christmas," Chase calls over his shoulder.

"Don't celebrate it. But I get time-and-a-half for working on a holiday, so you don't hear me complaining."

Chase makes a noise he hopes sounds like agreement and heads back out to the cold early morning air. The cold seeps into his flannel pants, and he shoves his hands into the pockets. Room 22. He knocks softly the first time, not wanting to have the wrong room—not wanting to come face to face with some hick in a wifebeater tank top, irritated at being woken up in the middle of the night. He hears a female voice curse inside, though, and it sounds like Rose.

The second time he knocks, he puts a little wrist action in it. Still no answer. He makes his next move before he fully thinks it through, which is good because if he had, he never would have had the balls to do it. He simply leans into the door and turns the handle. It must not have been fully closed, because the door opens.

Rose sits in the middle of the cheap motel rug, halfway in between the plaster-chipped wall and the bed, right smack in a puddle of water. Her cat is perched on the bed, watching him, poised and ready to flee. Rose lifts her chin toward him, like she's looking at him, but her eyes are far away. "Leave me alone," she mumbles.

His heart climbs into his throat and makes it tighten up like a corkscrew. "Is it mine?" He barely squeaks, standing in the doorway, halfway in, halfway out.

"Leave. Me. Alone."

"No." He steps in fully, pushing the door closed behind him. He kneels down to her level, and it's all he can do to keep his eyes from tearing up. "Rose, you owe me this. Are you having my baby?"

"Leave me the hell alone." She stares at him now, her eyes hard.

"Why didn't you tell me?"

"You would've wanted me to get rid of it."

Oh my god. It's mine. Chase tries to steady his voice. "No—I would have *wanted* to consider some options. I sure as hell wouldn't have moved to Bakersfield and left you alone to figure it out." Chase takes a deep breath and grabs a couple towels from the bathroom. He tosses one to her.

"Oh, come on. You're no better than any other teenaged accidental sperm donor. You would have pulled together money for a clinic. Guaranteed."

"Maybe you don't know me very well." Chase sits down in front of her so she can't avoid his eyes. "I'm all for pro-choice and that shit, but I can't imagine being okay with *erasing* my *own* child." She looks away. Chase shifts his position once again so he can see into her eyes. They still seem distant. "And I'm here now. What's your plan?"

"My plan?" She laughs almost, but it isn't an oh-that's-funny laugh, it's a life-is-shitty laugh. "Well, I wasn't supposed to go into labor today, that's for sure." She hesitates. "It sounds stupid now, saying it out loud."

"Tell me you weren't planning to have this baby in a dingy motel room."

She looks at him for a long time. "If I go to a hospital, my parents will find out."

"Okay, so I'm new at this whole childbirth thing. But back in the day when women used to birth their children at home—and, by the way, they had mothers and sisters and aunts all there to help them, and sterile sheets and boiled water—back in the day, women *died* giving birth. Babies *died* being born." Chase feels a new rush of adrenaline, and he straightens up. "No offense, Rose, but this isn't all up to you. This is half my decision."

Rose clenches her teeth. "There is no *freaking* way I am letting my parents get their hands on this baby. I'd rather die."

"So you want to keep it?"

"Well, I'm certainly not going to dump it somewhere, if that's what you think." She stares at him, but his gaze doesn't falter. "And you know how I feel about being adopted. How could I do that to someone else? What else can I—" Rose breaks off, doubling over, groaning so loud that Nala leaps from the bed and darts into the bathroom. Chase can see now, as she hunches, a distinct roundness in her middle. Amazing how much big, baggy clothes can hide.

"I'm getting you to a hospital." Chase stands.

Rose glares at him from the floor. "Screw you. I'll refuse to go."

"Then I'll call the cops. You'll be endangering the life of a child if you try to do this on your own."

Rose looks like she is about to come back with something caustic, but instead she grabs for his hand and holds on tight. She looks up at him. Her eyes are no longer distant. They are right there with him and wider than he's ever seen them. Terrified. The dark centers looks like a black holes. "I don't know what to do. I thought I did, but now I don't. I just…I promised myself I'd give this child a better start than I had."

"You don't have to give your real name at the hospital. Just say you have no insurance. They have to help you anyway if it's an emergency."

"Yeah?" Rose whispers.

"First we'll make sure you're both safe, and then we'll worry about what to do, okay?" Chase boosts her to a standing position. Rose doesn't answer. He finds her eyes again. "You're not alone with this anymore. We'll figure something out. Okay?"

"Okay." She mouths the word, but no sound comes out.

56
ROSE

WHEN BECCA ARRIVES, SHE LOOKS all sheepish. "Glad you're all right," Becca mumbles to Rose under her breath and then she adds, "Sorry for being so hard on you." Daniel scoops Nala up into his arms.

Rose does her best to smile, even though her belly starts to tighten again. She's in no mood for a heart-to-heart. It feels like someone has stuck her middle in a vise and squeezed. "Hey, if you dish it out, you got to take it, right? I just don't take it very well."

Becca seems to take that as an invitation to try to reconnect. "You're my best friend, Rose. I have to tell it to you how it is. Who else will?"

"Who says I want to hear it like it is?" Rose asks, shuffling past her. She's only half kidding. "Just agree with everything I say and we'll get along fine."

"When have you ever known me to keep my mouth shut?"

Rose grips her belly with two hands. "Only when you're eating or smoking a cigarette, and even then…not so much."

Chase steps in front of Becca, putting his arm around her shoulders.

"Right now would be a good time to start practicing the art of silence. I'm sort of on a time schedule. We've got to get to the hospital."

"*You're* on a time schedule?" Rose interrupts. "*I'm* on a time schedule."

"Ahhh. It's good to have you back." Daniel sighs, all sappy and sarcastic.

"Screw you." Rose almost smiles again, and this time it's genuine.

"You know what else?" Becca says, and she sounds tentative. "You need to work on your comebacks. A little variety here, please?"

"Yeah. Next time you're in this much pain, I'd like to see how creative your comebacks are. I can hardly see straight, let alone think of a comeback."

Chase pulls the motel bed apart, using the middle fuzzy blanket to wrap around Rose's shoulders as they walk outside. He boosts her into the truck and then buckles her seat belt for her. It's been so long since someone has taken care of her. It feels strange, almost painful. Or maybe she's confusing that with the contractions. Damn, those hurt. Each one more than the last.

It gets so that her vision actually narrows when one hits, the edges turning to blackness, leaving her only able to see what's directly in front of her. So it's Chase that leads her into the emergency room and helps her fill out paperwork. He eases her into a wheelchair and then a hospital bed. She uses "Julie Taylor" for her name and a fake address. Lies about her age.

The actual birth of the baby passes in a pain-filled haze, except the way Chase stays by her head the whole time, smoothing her sweaty hair and telling her she can do it. Except for the way the baby's wailing brings Rose goose bumps and tears. Except for the way Rose's heart turns to mush when the doctor holds the baby out to her—tiny, wriggling, and looking royally pissed off.

But the baby stops crying the minute the doctor lays her on Rose's chest—all gross and gooey and looking like something from a science fiction flick—and yet she's beautiful. The baby opens her eyes for a second and looks at Rose. Studies her. Then with her ear against Rose's beating chest, the baby closes her eyes again. Like she knows she's home. That part Rose knows she'll remember every day for the rest of her life.

57
CHASE

FOR A TOP-SECRET BABY in a hospital with a two-visitor-limit, there sure are a lot of people squashed into Room 227.

Hours earlier, Chase had broken down and called Candy when Rose kicked him out of the room for her cervix dilation check. Relieved to miss that, Chase's excuse for calling his mom was that he didn't want her to worry. He had, after all, left the house in the middle of the night—no note, wearing pajama bottoms.

In reality, though, he called because he wanted her to *know*. And because he wanted her to *come*. And come she did, with "Auntie Daisy" in tow. Slightly shocked, of course, but who except Rose wasn't? To her credit, Candy didn't criticize at all. Maybe she realized how hypocritical that would be.

Daniel had called his parents too, giving them some but not all of the information about where he was and what he was doing. His explanation wound up being both splotchy and guarded, causing some degree of alarm. The Steins hopped right in their car as well, and since Mr. Stein drove and his sense of direction was light years better than his wife's, they wound up arriving only minutes after Candy.

Chase thought Rose would've been pissed with a capital P about all the uninvited guests, but she seemed surprisingly mellow. Maybe it was whatever meds she'd taken for the pain. Of course, everyone there had a few words of wisdom to impart to Chase and Rose—something Chase found more than a little irritating, but it didn't matter. It was *their* decision. Legally adults or not, they'd created a baby, and the decision was theirs to make...and theirs to regret.

Daisy sits perched at the foot of Rose's bed, her hair sticking up every which way and looking more uncombed than ever. She peeks over at the bundle in Rose's arms. "Man, this is way better than the cat. I'll babysit any time you want!"

Rose just stares at the baby, like she's trying to memorize her tiny face. Chase doesn't think he's ever seen a human being that small, although obviously he'd been around when Daisy had been born. This baby—*his* baby—weighed in at a tiny five pounds, two ounces, but the hospital staff assured them she was healthy. She didn't need to spend any time in an incubator.

Her whole chest rises and falls as she breathes, sleeping in Rose's arms. The nurse dressed her in a baby-doll-sized shirt that buttons between her legs and a thin little beanie on her head. She's wrapped in a blanket like a burrito with one miniature foot sticking out. The foot doesn't even look real. It looks like it belongs to a doll. Tiny, pink, and softer than anything he's ever touched.

Mr. and Mrs. Stein hang back by the door, out of the way. Becca pulls a chair up next to Rose. "The cat's in the car with the windows cracked and a dish of water. She should be fine, and we'll go out and check on her every hour." Becca pauses, and her face looks uncertain.

Rose doesn't even glance up. "Watch out, Rose," Becca adds. "You look like you're falling in love."

Rose murmurs, "Nothing wrong with that." She strokes the baby's head with her hand, the IV moving along with her.

Now Becca really looks uncomfortable, like she's buttoned her jeans too tight or something. "Not if you're gonna keep this baby. But Rose, *think* for a minute. How in the *world* can you keep this baby?"

Now Rose looks up, her eyes full of tears and hate and fear all mixed together. Daniel puts his arm on Becca's shoulder. "Maybe now isn't the right time…"

"Look at her! She's practically got stars in her eyes," Becca interrupts. "If she's thinking of giving up the baby, she can't let herself get so attached."

Chase surprises himself by saying, "We're not giving up the baby." All eyes turn his way. "Well, we're *not*. How could we?"

No one says anything for a long moment. Becca seems like she wants to say more, but instead she looks down at her feet. A surge of adrenaline pulses through Chase's veins. *Who asked you?* he thinks. "I need to take a walk," he hears himself saying. "When I get back, I think Rose and I need some time alone. Why doesn't everybody go get something to eat?"

He elbows through the crowded room, fists balled, telling himself to breathe. *Breathe.* He wants to run hard, to get the pent-up adrenaline pumped out of his body, but somehow he doesn't think the hospital looks kindly on new fathers sprinting through the corridors. So he just walks. Fast. And hard. Past a nurse's station, past a crash cart in the hall, and past a crowded waiting room.

The buildup of the night, the lack of sleep, the pressure of the biggest decision in his life—they all weigh on him, like he's carrying the world around in a giant red Santa Claus bag slung over his shoulders.

He thinks about it every which way, and nothing seems right. He makes a mental list of his thoughts.

> 1. No way I'm giving my baby up for adoption. I'd feel like I failed her somehow. She'd never know me. I'd never know her.
> 2. No way am I ready to be a dad. I can't even get my shit together to finish my college applications without Daniel's help.
> 3. No way I'm giving up college—if I get in.
> 4. No way I'm letting Rose keep the baby without my help. She'd refuse to go back to the Parsimmons, so she'd have no one to help her. No money. No home.
> 5. Maybe I could do it. My mom did it. Had me as a teenager. Sure she missed out on prom and college and all that, but at least I grew up with my own mother. Now that Daisy and I are getting older, she can have her own life again. Candy just flip-flopped the order of things. Kids first, life second.
> 6. Shit. This list-making crap is getting me more worked up, not less.

Chase wanders the halls with glassy eyes, thinking and rethinking. Somehow he finds himself in the hospital chapel. He kneels and bows his head, something he hasn't done in a long time, not even during Pastor Tom's sermons. If there ever was a time to truly reconnect with God, this is it. But he's out of practice and he doesn't know what to pray for. So he kneels there in silence, his brain buzzing with thoughts, until his knees hurt.

Dear God…Chase starts, then freezes. He can only think of questions. He's sure that's not the right way to pray, but it's all that comes to his mind.

Why is this happening to me? Why are you putting me in a situation like this? It's lose-lose. Neither decision is good. I'm not ready to be a dad, and I'm not willing to walk away from my own kid. What am I supposed to do? What lesson are you trying to teach me…and can't I learn it some other way? Chase straightens up. This is pointless. *Jesus Christ*, he swears to himself, then looks up at Jesus on the cross above him. *No offense*, he adds.

Nothing makes sense. Will it ever? Has it ever really before? Should he call Pastor Tom? Where the hell are spiritual guides when you need them?

He tilts his face toward a stained-glass window. Christmas sunshine streams through, splaying into a pattern of light on one of the pews. Chase watches it for a moment, remembering the stained-glass windows he stared at in church as a child. He thinks of the small one in Pastor Tom's church, and even the synagogue stained-glass at the Steins' temple. It's funny, no matter what church or temple he attends, those stained-glass windows always bring a feeling of peace. He reaches his hand out and lets the colored light spill over his fingers.

And then, quite suddenly, he knows what to pray for. *Serenity.* His own. Rose's. The baby's. He bends his head and prays that they will all leave the hospital at peace with whatever decision has been made.

>>——→ ←——«

When Chase returns to Room 227, Rose sits alone, her knees pulled up to her chest, under the sterile white hospital sheets. "Where's the baby?" Chase asks.

Rose turns her face toward him, her eyes puffy and her face tear stained. "Nurse took her."

"Why?" Chase tries to keep the panic out of his voice.

"Just tests, I guess." Rose shrugs her shoulders like she doesn't care, but it just makes her look more deflated. "Shit, it still hurts, Chase. I thought it was over already, but I keep getting stomach pains. They're like aftershocks or something. The nurse said it's normal, but it sucks."

"Is that why you're crying?"

For a moment, he sees a flicker of the old Rose, ready to retort, but it fades away. "No," she says quietly. "I'm crying because Becca is right. I can't take care of a baby."

"Not by yourself. But maybe *we* could. Together." Chase puts his hand on her knee. He looks around the room. The second bed sits unoccupied, ultra-white sheets neatly pulled tight. Rose's clothes are wrapped in a plastic bag and sit on the counter by a small sink. Aside from a television hanging from the ceiling and some ominous-looking machines behind Rose's bed, the room seems almost empty.

"You're in no better shape than me."

"You're not thinking of giving her up, are you?"

"I'm a mess." Rose sniffles. "I had this grand plan of running away nine months pregnant and finding my birth mother or this random pastor who knew her eleven years ago. Like that was somehow going to solve everything. Like she'd take me in and we'd raise this kid together or some fairy-tale Disney crap like that." Rose plays with the IV stuck into her hand. "Shit. I've screwed up everything I've ever done. I'd screw up this baby too."

"No, you wouldn't. I saw the way you held her, Rose. You love her. Have you ever loved anything that way before?"

"No," she admits, her eyes going to that faraway place. "Maybe my own mother. But how much you want to bet that's how she felt about me when she held me the first time? And where did that get me?"

Chase shakes his head. "I thought I'd be coming in here trying to convince you to consider other options. Now that you have, I'm not so sure I like the options you're considering." He sighs, lifting his hand to touch her hair, then letting it fall again, her hair untouched. "This is half my decision, you know. I could keep her even if you decided to take off."

"I know." She leans her head back and closes her eyes. "I will hate myself for the rest of my life if I leave her here. She's so fresh. So pure. So good." Chase nods. He knows. Life hasn't tainted her yet. She seems so peaceful and serene. Isn't that what Walter and Lex are always looking for? What he himself is looking for? Serenity? Well, it's right there in that baby. You could bottle it and make millions. But how long before life sucks that precious peacefulness right out of her?

"Well, we don't have to make the decision right this minute, do we?" The room feels stuffy and the air thick. Chase wishes he could open a window or something. He hears something beeping from down the hall, loud, making his heartbeat quicken, but then it stops. "How many days will you be in the hospital?"

"I think two. Unless I hemorrhage or something." Rose says, and Chase senses some semblance of humor. "Then I get to stay a little longer."

"Very funny." He tries to breathe. "I have to think some more before we decide this thing."

"I'll do you one better. I'm gonna pray."

"You? Pray? Where's my phone—I'd better record this." Chase almost smiles, thinking he could wheel her down to the chapel, now that he knows where it is. "You don't strike me as the praying type."

"No shit," Rose almost sounds like herself for a moment. Then her lower lip turns under, like she's trying not to cry. She whispers, "Maybe it's time for me to start."

58
CHASE

CANDY MEETS CHASE OUTSIDE THE door to Room 227 as he exits. She's probably been waiting there, pacing back and forth. Today, anxiety seems as contagious as the flu, just traveling through the air, infecting everyone. Her smile too forced, Candy greets him so full of anxiety he can see it throbbing in her neck. "I had you when *I* was sixteen."

"I know that."

"Sometimes I think having you saved my life."

Chase raises an eyebrow.

"You gave me a purpose, a reason to wake up every day." Candy shakes her head at the memory. "But it was hard, Chase. *Shit,* it was hard. I gave up the dreams I had for *me.* All of a sudden they didn't exist anymore. *I* didn't exist anymore. I tried to hold on to my social life as best I could, but everything was different. I got trapped in a relationship with Walter that we both know wasn't healthy, and I couldn't see a way out." She hesitates and then goes on. "It's just that having a baby doesn't have to be so hard."

Chase bristles, irritated. Great speech if he hadn't already knocked someone up. He turns away, but Candy grabs his shoulder. "I'm not telling you to give up the baby, Chase. Shit. I'm not saying this very well." She stops and presses her shaking fingers to her lips. Chase can't help but notice her green-and-red Christmas-themed fingernails.

"What I'm trying to say is that I'm older now. I'm in a stable relationship with Bob. He's a solid, reliable man. He has a good job. Let me take the baby. You can see her every day, do as much or as little as you want. Same for Rose. It'll give you a chance to have a life, and me a chance to do it better."

Chase stares at his mother. Takes in her faded skinny jeans and the "Kiss Me, Santa!" long-sleeved T-shirt that hugs her breasts a little too tight. She hadn't bothered with mascara or lipstick, so her face seems washed out. His mother. Candy. Some women are just having their first child at her age. "Thanks, Cand—I mean, thanks, Mom. I'll think about it, okay?"

Candy seems so vulnerable, standing there, looking her age for the first time in forever. She's let her teenage years bleed into her twenties and now into her thirties. She's sacrificed her youth to take care of him. Is it even fair to ask her to do it again?

Chase has barely taken three steps down the hospital corridor before Becca loops her arm through his. "I have an idea." She leans in toward his ear.

"Becca," he sighs. "I can't hardly hear myself think for all the thoughts I've got banging around in my head."

"Just listen to one word. It's genius." Becca waits, holding on tight. "Rosenberg."

"What?" Chase pries her fingers from his arm. What's she trying to do, cut off his circulation?

"Matthew's mother. Mrs. Rosenberg. She's been trying to adopt another child."

Suddenly, Chase's mouth is so dry he could have downed a gallon of water like a tequila shot and still been thirsty. "You're saying we should give up the baby...to her?" The fluorescent hospital lights seem too bright and make his head ache.

Becca pulls him around to face her. "It's perfect. Think about it. Why doesn't Rose want to give up the baby? Because she's petrified the baby would wind up mismatched with some awful family—and have the same kind of experience she's had." Becca's face practically glows with excitement, or maybe it's the reflection of the overhead lights against her skin. "I haven't totally figured out Rose's parents yet, whether they're as horrible as Rose says. But Mrs. Rosenberg was born to be a mother. Any kid would be lucky to have her."

Chase extends his arms, moving Becca away. "Rose might go for that, but I'm not sure I will. Maybe I want to keep the baby. Maybe I don't want to give her up at all." He looks around for a water fountain.

Becca's eyes search the crevices of his face like she's looking for something written there. "You'd have to give up college, wouldn't you?"

"I don't know." He starts to walk past her. His feet make scuffing noises against the hospital floor. "I have to think. I just need some quiet to think."

"You might hate me," Becca starts, her voice half its regular volume. Chase cocks his head so he can hear. "I called Mrs. Rosenberg and asked her to come."

"You did what?" Chase's mouth is drier by the minute.

"You heard me. I figured Rose would need some convincing, so I called her and asked her to come."

"Rebecca Stein, you have balls of steel. Too bad you don't use your head."

"Oh, but I do." Becca grins.

"And by the way, you reek of cigarette smoke. Better not stand near your parents. How many did you have today?"

"Eight. But I quit an hour ago."

"I'll believe that when I see it."

"It's true. Daniel took me on a field trip to see the cancer unit... which honestly didn't do much for me because I can't think twenty minutes down the line, much less twenty years." Becca chews at a hangnail. "But then he bribed me and that did it."

"With what, bubblegum and Blow Pops?"

"No. He'll take me to practice driving every day I go without a cigarette. But he's gonna do a sniff test. You know, breath, hair, clothes. So unless I plan on taking five showers a day, I gotta quit."

"May the force be with you. You're gonna need it." Chase waves his hand behind him and pushes through the double doors that separate the maternity wing from the rest of the hospital. "And may the force be with me. I'm gonna need it too." He heads toward a soda machine, hoping it carries bottled water.

Daniel stands in front of another vending machine, his face pressed against the glass. "What's wrong?" Chase asks. "You trying to smell the snacks?"

"As of twelve hours ago, I've become a vegan, which means the only thing I can buy from this machine are the peanuts. I hate peanuts." Daniel punctuates his words by tapping against the glass. He sighs and sits down on a green bench.

"Hmmm. You might have to give up the vegan thing if you don't want to starve." Chase rummages through his pockets and comes up with five quarters for a bottle of Dasani.

"Guess so. It was nice while it lasted." Daniel pulls his legs up onto the bench and crosses them. "I felt so...enlightened." His hair sticks up in the back, and Chase figures it's been a while since he's seen a mirror.

Daniel is the one person Chase actually wants advice from, maybe because he doesn't give it lightly. "I'm dying here, man. Don't you have any Buddhist words of wisdom for me?"

"Nah."

"Jewish wisdom?" Chase asks, staring at a cluster of people hurrying by, carrying presents and a hideous Big Bird balloon.

"Nah. All I got is what I would do." Daniel waits a moment while Chase guzzles his water and then goes on. "I'd try to figure out what would let me sleep at night."

"You mean like could I sleep at night if I knew she was in someone else's home?" Chase asks. Daniel nods. "Only if I knew that person." An intercom pages a doctor to the ER, pauses, then pages the doctor again.

"Could you sleep at night if you knew you gave up a chance to go to college?" Daniel unfolds his legs and sets them back on the ground.

"Yeah, but I'd always wonder what-if, you know?" Chase looks up at the fluorescent hospital lights, as if the answer is written up there. "I mean, sometimes I wonder what got Walter so angry all the time. And I wonder if he felt stuck. Stuck with some girl he got pregnant and this whiny-ass kid. I just don't want to feel stuck."

Daniel scuffs his tennis shoes against the scraped-up hospital floor. "You know Becca's got it in her head to fix you up with Mrs. Rosenberg?"

"She told me." Chase groans. "And Candy's got some idea about taking the baby herself. Crazy. But then maybe I could still go to school..."

"No offense, but somehow I don't think Candy will be up for Mother of the Year any time soon."

"Tell me about it. I'm living proof of that. I know my parents made a lot of mistakes. Here's what I want to know. Did they screw up because they were young, or did they screw up because they were *them*?" Chase asks, but Daniel just shrugs.

"I don't know," he says softly.

Chase feels the pressure of something behind his eyes, the way a dam must feel before it breaks. He hopes he won't cry. "This whole thing is a freaking trip. One day I'm filling out college applications and trying to figure out who I am, getting to know my dad…and the next I'm a *father*? No way. I think my head might explode."

"Not much time to get used to the idea, I know." Daniel stands up and reaches to sling his arm around Chase's shoulder. He can barely reach.

"I thought she was on the pill…" Carrying sodas with straws, four doctors in hospital greens amble down the corridor, laughing at something one of them said.

Daniel shakes his head and pats Chase on the back. "What about doubling up on the protection? Didn't I teach you anything?" He waits a beat, and when Chase doesn't say anything, he adds, "Just kidding. I'll shut up now."

"An accident. Happens all the time, right?" Chase thinks out loud. "But how can I be upset about something as perfect as that baby girl?"

If Daniel answers, Chase can't hear him. He moves past his friend and toward the elevator. He needs to get out of the hospital for a little while. He needs to run. He needs that burn. That adrenaline. That release.

So he does. He pumps his arms and pounds his feet against the sidewalk, hard and fast. The chill of a December day numbs the tip of his nose and the tops of his ears, and that feels good. Chase runs through mid-afternoon streets of Van Nuys until he can feel his heart all the way through his chest.

As usual, the running loosens his thoughts and helps him get himself unstuck. Suddenly he knows who to call. Panting, he leans over and pulls out his cell phone to dial the number. "Hey, Walt—hey, Dad?"

59
ROSE

BREASTFEEDING IS HARDER THAN IT looks. First of all, Rose's breasts are swollen like overfilled water balloons, the kind that burst when you barely pick them up because they're so full. Second, the baby's mouth can only open so big.

The perky swing-shift nurse keeps telling Rose how good breast milk is for the baby, how it's so much healthier than formula, how her own antibodies will be passed to the baby through breast milk. Rose doesn't even have a chance to tell the nurse she's thinking of giving up the baby. Perky Nurse reaches right over to Rose, grabs her boob, and helps her position it toward the baby's mouth, lightly brushing the tip against the baby's lips so her rooting reflex will kick in.

Rose isn't sure whether she should slap the nurse or thank her. And it's impossible not to stare at the baby's tiny pumping cheeks. Impossible not to love her. But Becca *is* right. With every pump of her cheeks, Rose is getting more and more attached. And it's dangerous to bond if she has any thought of giving her up.

That's why Mrs. Rosenberg's proposal tempts her.

At first when the assistant rabbi walks through the hospital door, looking strangely different without Matthew attached to her hip, Rose has no idea why she's there or even how she'd known to come. It doesn't take long to figure it out, though. Becca Stein, the matchmaker, who can't mind her own damn business.

She'll be happy to take both Rose and the baby if the Parsimmons agree, Mrs. Rosenberg explains, her wide lips curiously smile free. Rose can stay past the age of eighteen, as long as she follows the house rules. "And we're strict," she adds.

There's one sticking point Mrs. Rosenberg insists is non-negotiable. "If we go with this, you'll have to understand that the baby would be *mine*. Legally, physically, emotionally." Rose watches her smile-free lips quiver while she says it, like she's nervous or something. "Would that be hard for you?"

Rose cringes inside. It would definitely be hard for her. But everything about this situation is hard. She meets Mrs. Rosenberg's serious gaze head-on. "Why would you want a package deal? Why would you want *me*?"

"Why *wouldn't* I want you?" Mrs. Rosenberg asks, her face softening.

"Ask the Parsimmons. I'm trouble. A disappointment."

"Well, I don't tolerate trouble, so if you wanted to stay with me, you'd have to make some changes." Mrs. Rosenberg leans back against the wall like she needs the support. "I know you could do it. You'd have to rise to the challenge, because I only allow positive influences around my kids."

"And she'd be...*your* kid." Rose brushes her fingertips against the soft fluff that is the baby's hair. "And I'd be what?"

"We'd be open with her, of course. We'd explain that she's adopted, and that you gave birth to her." Mrs. Rosenberg says. "But I'd be her mother. Just like I'm Matthew's mother."

"I don't know…" Rose looks around the room, feeling like the walls are too close together. She wishes Chase would come back already. "Why do you want this?"

"Do you know how hard it is to adopt a healthy newborn?" Mrs. Rosenberg half laughs…to herself mostly. "I'm close to forty and my husband is forty-five. He's got diabetes. We're not ideal candidates." She shakes her head, dangling silver earrings bouncing off the side of her face.

"But I want Matthew to have a sister. I want it so bad I can taste it." She stops for a moment, runs a hand through her hair, then moves over to examine the contents of the IV bag, now half empty. She turns back to look at Rose directly. "And I'm a good mother. Yes, I work. But my work is flexible, and there is a quality day care right on site. But I guess you know that."

"Why don't you just adopt from China or something?"

"I might, if this doesn't work out. Although with a foreign adoption, I wouldn't be able to take the baby until she was almost a year. I'd hate to miss out on that first year." She sits herself on the edge of Rose's bed, uninvited, but somehow it seems more loving than rude. "This plan might be your best option, Rose. It allows you and Chase to stay peripherally involved. You get to enjoy her and watch her grow without having to give up your own lives. You can rest assured that she'll be in good hands."

Rose aches in the center of her chest. Her throat feels like it's been burned, it hurts so bad. "Maybe you could be her foster mother, and I could stay with you until I get on my feet?"

"No," Mrs. Rosenberg says quietly. "I have a lot of admiration for foster mothers, but it is not for me. I love too deeply. Once I let myself love that child, I won't let anyone take her away. Not even you. So know that going in."

"The Parsimmons won't let me live with you," Rose tosses out, feeling helpless and ripped in half.

"I think they might," Mrs. Rosenberg volleys back. "Look, Rose, you have to take ownership of your problems with the Parsimmons. It's not all them. Nothing ever is. You have a part to play too."

Rose swallows. She knows that's true. Sort of. But it's so much easier to blame the Parsimmons for everything.

Mrs. Rosenberg goes on. "Personally, I think if you handle this like an adult, you might be able to present an alternative living situation to them. They seem pretty burned out to me. They might be ready to hand over the torch to someone else." A sliver of a smile touches her lips for a moment. "Of course, that means you have to stop running away from your problems and face them. You'd have to call your parents."

Rose studies her fingers and holds in her tears as best she can. "I have to th-think about this." Rats. Her voice breaks. And now a tear slides down her face. Others follow, more than she can count.

"I know this is a hard decision. Please do think about it." Mrs. Rosenberg stands up, smoothing her slacks. She moves toward the door.

But that means giving up on the fantasy of finding her mother, at least temporarily. Moving back to Simi Valley. As much as she hates to admit it, the whole reunite-with-bio-Mom fantasy is just that, a fantasy. Even if she does find her mother—even if she's still alive—chances are slim that her lifestyle has changed all that much.

But Rose doesn't ever want to go back and live with the Parsimmons. Deep down she knows they don't hate her, not really. They just don't have a clue what to do with her. And deep down she knows she doesn't really hate them either. She just hates that she was taken from her real mother and dumped at their house. Rose wipes her face with her arm. She sits quietly except for those little crying breaths that feel like hiccups.

As Mrs. Rosenberg starts to slip out of the room, she asks, "If I gave her to you, would you still let me name her?"

Mrs. Rosenberg pokes her head back in. "Depends. You're not thinking of naming her something strange or hideous, are you? I am strongly opposed to naming children after pieces of fruit, months of the year, or states."

"You don't like Georgia?" Rose throws out halfheartedly before she catches herself. "No," she adds more seriously. "And I'm not making any promises here. But if I did give her up, I want to be able to give her something that can stay with her forever. Like my mom did for me."

Mrs. Rosenberg nods slowly. "Well, in that case, yes."

60
CHASE

TIME IS FUNNY. SOMETIMES A single minute drags out for a lifetime, and sometimes a month goes so fast it feels like it never even happened. Too bad Chase can't fast forward, rewind, delete, and pause what's happening in real life, just like a movie. If he could, Chase would have wanted to fast forward through much of his childhood. But right now, at this moment, the time spent making this decision is so important that he wishes he could press Pause and make it all stand still until he can sort things out. Because he knows once the decision is made and papers signed, there's no rewind.

But in the end, the decision seems clear. Sad, but clear. Like oil in salad dressing left out overnight, the answer just rises to the top. Chase and Rose talk about it long into the evening, long after their room empties and the hospital ward quiets down. With the lights dimmed, they take turns holding the baby, rocking her, and patting her back. Mostly she sleeps, her eyes gently closed, and her chest rising and falling with little breaths.

"This might be the only good thing I've ever done," Rose says softly, squeezed over on one half of the bed. Chase sits on the other side, his feet bare. The baby lies across their two laps, swaddled in a thin blanket with her arms pulled in toward her body. "Unless you count sharing my lunch in elementary school. Or letting someone bum a cigarette."

"Well, this is definitely the best thing I've ever done," Chase agrees. "We made her and she's perfect. Nameless, but perfect. Only she can't go without a name for too much longer." The heat of Rose's body against his and the baby across his lap warm him, despite the cool hospital air.

"I wonder how my mother picked mine. Did she figure out the symbolism of a rose? Did she give me my thorns for protection?"

"Man, you and symbolism. Just promise me you won't name her something from a Disney movie."

"Oh, come on. Don't you like Jasmine? Or Ariel? Cinderella?" Rose swats the back of his head. "I almost *want* to name her something out there just to be a rebel."

"Imagine, you a rebel."

Rose ignores this. "And she was born on Christmas. That gives us something to work with."

"How about Jingle?"

"Bells?" The baby stirs as if to protest. "Or Belle like from *Beauty and the Beast*?"

"Disney, that's Disney! I reserve the right to veto all Disney-related names."

"How about Nicholas for a girl?" Rose shifts to face him more, although it makes their butts press against the hospital-bed railing.

"Uh...no." Chase checks out Rose's face to see if she's serious. "Remember, she has to survive elementary school."

"What are your ideas, oh wise one?"

"I have one. But don't laugh." Chase clears his throat. "How about Serenity?"

"Serenity?"

"That's what I said." Chase leans over to touch the baby's hair. It looks and feels like duck fluff. "Because that's what I want for her. To hold on to all that is peaceful and serene about herself."

"Serenity, huh? Maybe." Rose puts her finger in the baby's palm. Tiny fingers wrap around her own. "Isn't there a famous tennis player named Serena?"

"Yeah, but I like Serenity better. I know it's unusual. I just think it fits her."

Rose brings the baby's hand to her mouth, pressing her lips into the delicate skin. "I can't imagine being without her. She was inside of me for so long. She was all mine. My little secret. I could feel her move, feel her turning around in there, feel her kicking."

Rose's eyes fill up with tears. She turns her head away, so that strands of hair fall down and cover her face. Her braids had come undone hours ago. "Being without her will feel like I'm missing a part of myself, like I'm walking around without my right arm. How do you manage without your right arm?"

"Are we sure we want to do this? We don't have to." Chase cuts in a little too quickly, saying what he's said twenty times before.

"You're not making this any easier by waffling so damn much."

"Okay, okay. It just sucks because what I *want* and what I know to be *right* are two separate things. I guess I don't feel that different from you. I'll feel like something is missing. Or I'll feel homesick... or guilty." Chase feels nauseous just thinking about it. "But at least we can still be involved in her life without sacrificing our own. And at least we'll know she's loved. And safe." The baby turns her head to the right and works her mouth like she's sucking on something, only she's not.

Rose wipes her eyes with the back of her hand. "Serenity." She rolls the name around in her mouth. "I could get used to that."

"For short, we could call her 'T.'"

Rose brushes the tip of her finger against the baby's nose. "Hey, little T, get ready. Because the world is coming at you. Fast." The baby's lips turn upward for a moment while she sleeps.

"Hey! Did you see that? She smiled! I didn't think babies smiled this young."

"They don't. It must have been gas."

"Or maybe she likes her name."

Chase listens to the baby's puffs of breath in and out, and tries to match his breaths to hers. He tries not to think of all the tomorrows and to just be there with her breathing. If Chase could take this moment in isolation, it might've been perfect.

"I think Serenity *is* the name for you," he tells her, kissing her soft cheek, his lips sinking in deeper than he'd have thought, like into a down pillow.

"Me too. I want one," Rose whispers. "Pucker up, little T." She leans forward to kiss the baby's mouth, loose hair spilling around her.

Chase gathers Rose's hair in his hands, holding it away from Serenity. "No. You pucker up," he says to Rose, kissing her for the first time in eight months, sending goose bumps racing down his arms.

"Well, aren't we a sappy bunch. We ought to be on a freaking Hallmark commercial."

"I missed you," Chase says, tucking her hair behind her shoulder. "Welcome back, Rose."

Chase knows that this moment is the closest to serenity he's ever been. He looks at the baby's little hands, dimples indenting the skin in front of each finger. You can tell a lot about a person by her hands. Soft. Delicate. Sweet. Serene. But strong. Her hand grips his finger in her palm like a clamp, like she doesn't want him to escape. Like she wants to hold on to him, to hold him there for that moment in time. That perfect, peaceful moment.

And then, for just the briefest slice of a second, Serenity opens her eyes and looks right at him. Kind of like she wants to say something. Kind of like she wants to tell him it's okay.

ACKNOWLEDGMENTS

Behind every good story is a good support team.

Thank you to Team Home Front: my husband, Rob, and my children, Ben, Noah, Jacob, and the little one on the way—my synonyms for *love*. Thank you for believing in me and for being the amazing people you are.

Thank you to my sweet son Alex, who was with us for such a short time, but still managed to teach me so much about life and about who I am. Alex, we miss you and will love you forever.

Thank you to Team Family Support: to Mom and Dad, Peggy and Bob, thank you for all the *love* and encouragement. To Jessie and Dale, Adam and J.A., Daniel and Jamie, Lois and Brian, Marjie and Jeff, and Michael, thank you for being the coolest siblings and siblings-in-law on earth. To Holly— my honorary sister—thank you for always being on my team.

Thank you to Team Moral Support: to Holly, Dorothy, Jill, Janet, Tina, Dream, Kristi, Jodie, Stephanie, Omario, Sanjay, Valerie, Darlene, Jennifer, Ophra, Steve, Pete, Jodi, Tara, Yvette, Michelle, Maria, Tom, Kelly, and Tim.

Thank you to Team Tech Support: Sherry, Hillary, Stacy, Marilyn, Stephanie, Lisa, Ian, Chad, Platte, Mindy, Hannah, Julie, Alexis, and Terry. Thank you for your keen eyes, pruning tendencies, and patient support.

Thank you to the Fabulous Team at Whitman: Wendy for your brilliant guidance, your balance of fleshing out and tightening up, and your supportive nature; Kelly for your wise oversight; Diane and Kristin for your careful eyes; and Jenna for your vision.

Thank you to Team Cheerleader: Deborah for being my tireless advocate, an amazing party thrower, and networker extraordinaire.

Thank you to Team Literature: Connie at Mrs. Fig's Bookworm and Mary at the Camarillo Library. Thank you for bringing amazing books to our community.

Thank you to Team Inspiration: This is a completely fictional work. But I am inspired on a daily basis by the teens in tough situations who not only survive, but thrive. To all the teens I've ever worked with... teenage-hood is temporary. Don't forget that *it gets better*.